AVOCADO BLISS

CANDACE ROBINSON
GERARDO DELGADILLO

"For Ethan, Nolan, and Nate, you three are champions." – Candace Robinson

"For Gio, Pau, and Marianna, my never-ending source of teen spirit." – Gerardo Delgadillo

1

Dacre

The security guard going through my bag waggles his finger at me and my smile drops.

I walk around to the side of the counter where the could-be criminals go. My blood pumps with irritation because with the constant traveling over the years between my parents, I've had more stops than not with the security.

"There are needles in your bag," he says. His ring-a-ding-ding mustache that curls on the sides wiggles as he talks.

Biting the inside of my cheek, I contort my facial expression into a serious position. "I don't know, I thought I'd go into the airplane bathroom and shoot up some diabetic insulin before I eat. Ah, the life of a Type 1 diabetic."

The security guard just gives me a dirty look and

hands me my backpack. I've learned in situations like these it's better to have fun with it because the truth behind the disease isn't something to always laugh about.

Beep! Beep! I spot my sixteen-year-old brother, Lachlan, who'd fallen behind when he'd made a pitstop in the restroom. He's just set off the metal detector at the airport—of course, he has.

I roll my eyes and tap the end of my nose, signaling that his septum ring is the problem. He shakes his head and reaches to remove the chain necklace wrapped tightly around his throat. I'd already told him to make sure he had all his metal off, but my brother failed to listen … again.

Ever so slowly, he takes off his necklace and flashes a wide smile my way. Since I know Lach better than anyone, I know he wanted to make the detector go off to draw attention his way. He loves the attention—I just want to leave.

Lach coasts through the metal detector one more time without a beep firing. Finally, we're ready to go.

I tug my brother to the side, tossing him his leather jacket—covered in an endless amount of band patches— from the bucket on the conveyor belt.

"My septum ring is quality metal, no beep necessary. And don't give me that look, Dacre." He bats his eyelashes and shoves on his jacket over his punk band shirt while we move forward. "It's not my fault I forgot to remove everything. What do they want me to do? Strip down completely naked?"

"God, you can be such a moron." I chuckle.

"That's only what I want you to believe." Lach grins, getting lost somewhere in his phone. Most likely texting his online boyfriend who lives right where we're headed.

Before I get distracted any more from baby brother number one, I search around for Ezra while sliding on my backpack. "Where's the baby at?"

"I'm not a baby. I just turned eleven." Baby brother number two pokes out from behind a large pillar, head in a comic book. He pushes his glasses up with his index finger.

"You're right," I say. "The other one's holding us up." I point at Lach. "If we miss the flight, you're going to have to explain to Mom that it was your fault."

"Whatever." Lach bites his lip and puts his phone away. "Let's go with your needle-weapons in tow."

"Seriously, shut up." I shove the idiot. "If you say shit like that loud enough, we definitely will miss the flight while we're getting patted down."

"I like that idea."

"You would." I like the idea of getting patted down myself, depending on who would be doing it.

I grab Ezra by the sleeve and drag him in the direction to board the plane back to Mexico. We've been going back and forth between our mom's and dad's homes for the past nine years. Our time seems to have gotten shorter and shorter with Dad, especially after he got a new wife and two new kids. I tell myself I don't care, but I have to admit it stings a little.

When I was younger, my mom picked up a job in Mexico that paid really well. Dad didn't want to move away, so at first, she went to and fro. Eventually, the rift between them began to spread even farther until they were ripped apart. Not before they thought it was a brilliant idea to have another baby to save their already failing marriage. Enter Ezra—along with no saving the broken shards.

We hurriedly follow the signs leading to where our plane is already boarding. Somehow, Ezra manages to still be able to read his Batman comic book at the speed we're traveling.

Up ahead, there's a small line of people beside rows and rows of pleather black seats—the majority of the chairs are empty. In the line, one person after another flips up their boarding pass to a clerk with long and wavy blonde hair.

Suddenly, I remember my fists are empty, and I shake my hand in front of Lach's face. "You have the boarding passes."

He pats down his jean pockets and holds up his hands. "Sorry, I don't."

"Not the time," I growl. "Where did you put them?"

"You're seventeen, not seventy. Take a joke, dude. I put them in your bag."

"If you hadn't slowed us down the whole time, I'd be able to take a joke, *dude*."

A new town in Mexico. I was fine with the other one—I was fine with being near the coast in Texas. I'm fine, always *fine*.

What I'm going to miss about both places are the waves—that was my escape. Other times it was a girl. I dropped my last girlfriend when Mom said we were moving—I wasn't willing to do the long-distance thing, even though she was. I'm similar to my parents in that aspect, I suppose. But she was also constantly worrying about my diabetes.

When we make it to the front of the line, I show the

lady our passes and she waves us through.

Our feet thud down the terminal gate to the airplane. Once on board, we shuffle our way down the too-narrow aisle. A small, middle-aged woman is struggling to put her backpack into the compartment. I give the bag a hard push, shove it in for her, and head straight to our economy seats without looking back.

Reaching up, I place my backpack in the compartment above our seats and Lach hands me his. Overfilled with who knows what. Actually, I don't want to know.

After beating the death out of his pack, I find Lach already in the seat near the aisle while Ezra is nestled against the window, nose still buried deep in the comic. "Seriously move over one," I huff to Lach.

Adjusting his septum ring, he says, "I don't want to feel caged in."

Whoever says the middle kid is never the favorite or babied is full of shit. Lach would probably ask someone to wipe his ass if he could, even though he's sixteen. "Look," I say, "I already feel a headache coming on and when my sugar is too high, I have to keep pissing."

"I don't mind getting up to let you by."

I stare at him unblinking, lips pursed in a tight line. "*Lach.*" Even though his name is one syllable, I draw it out as long as humanly possible.

"Fine, fine." He gets up and moves to the middle seat as if he had planned to do that the whole time. "*But*"— he holds up a finger—"we're prepared for this. We've seen *Con Air.*"

A deep chuckle rumbles up from my throat, my first of the day—my first for a while now. "Don't even get me started on movies about diabetes. '*When I was a kid, I wish*

I wouldn't have eaten so much candy.' Hansel and Gretel was the worst with their diabetes portrayal." Hollywood loves to make illnesses overly dramatic.

Lach laughs, and I smile. But part of me hates the fact that he doesn't really know what it's like to have this shit. And that part … I constantly try to push it down because I would never want him or Ezra to have to deal with the ongoing battle I have to put up with for the rest of my life.

I relax in my seat and do the only thing I can, pull out a book to read.

"You're reading *that?*" Lach sings softly into my ear.

"Got a problem?" I ask, flipping the book open to the page where I last stopped.

"Besides it being a hit ages ago, it's terrible."

"Well, I like it."

"Let me show you a real book." Lach holds up his Stephen King novel.

"Have fun with the King."

"I will."

Midflight, I feel my sugar spiking—the veins on the side of my head pulsate harder. Eventually unable to take it, I stand up and pull my bag from the compartment to find my insulin. An older flight attendant is passing out snacks and halts in front of me while I'm digging out my kit with the meter.

"You need something?" she asks, staring at me like I'm about to produce a switchblade from the pouch.

"My sugar is high." I already feel frustrated that I have to stop what I need to do and deal with her.

The sides of her mouth pull down, and she reaches into the basket of snacks. "Here, let me give you something." She hands me a packaged chocolate chip cookie. Instead of being a dick about it, because that little wrapped dessert would only make the situation worse since my sugar isn't low, I say, "Thanks," and toss it on my seat.

After I give myself a shot inside the claustrophobic restroom, I head back to my spot, finding the cookie missing in action. "Where's my lifesaver?" I ask Lach, who is wiping the crumbs from his mouth.

"Well, you weren't eating it." He tucks the Stephen King book into the pocket behind the seat in front of him, already done after not getting past page one.

"Could have offered it to Ez."

"I wasn't hungry," Ezra starts, eyes never leaving his comic, "and he snatched my pretzels, too."

"Of course he did." I take my seat and get back to reading.

The remainder of the flight is bumpy, and I chuckle to myself as I spot Lach clenching the armrests as we land. I don't think that would save him if we were to crash, but whatever gives him comfort.

Passport check is a breeze and after we pick up our bags, I search the area for Mom's dyed-blonde hair, which I can't find.

"I don't see Mom," Ezra says, pushing up his glasses and surveying the area.

She's never late to meet us. In fact, she's usually at the airport hours early. But then a loud male voice catches my attention. "Boys!" a young guy shouts in Spanish. He's maybe a couple of years older than me with jet-black hair pulled into a low ponytail. When none of us respond, he jogs up with a sign in his hand. He's wearing a striped tank top, highlighting his muscular build, and holds the paper up higher. Our names are printed on it as if he had it specially made.

Time to switch back from English to Spanish now that we've entered our second home, but Ezra speaks up first. "Sorry, we don't talk to strangers."

I can tell by Lach sucking on his lower lip that he's eye-screwing the young guy.

"I'm Francisco." The guy snakes out a hand for us to shake, and none of us do. He pulls his open palm away and holds up the sign again as if we couldn't read it the first time. "I've seen your pictures, so I know what you three look like."

"That seems a little creepy, actually. Let me shoot my mom a text," Lach states, taking out his phone, but he still sounds a bit too hormonal over this guy. I tug Ezra a little closer to my side.

"Your mom was waiting to tell you, but she got held up at work." Francisco smiles, showing off a large gap between his front teeth. "I'm her boyfriend."

"*Boyfriend?*" I ask, incredulous. Mom hasn't had a relationship since she was with Dad. Even then, she only went out on a few dates. And this guy is nowhere near Dad's age, nowhere near five years younger than Mom, either. I'd have to try twenty less.

Francisco scratches the back of his head. "Yeah, we met after you three left, right when she came to town. I was one of the guys who helped move her stuff in. And well, one thing led to another, if you know what I mean."

"No, I don't know what you mean, and I don't want to know either," I say, clenching my jaw. "How old are you, anyway?" The first thought that pops in my head is that this guy is screwing my mom because she makes serious bank. Then I want to knock myself out for thinking about my mom and this jerk like that.

He straightens and tilts his head to the side. "Twenty-one. Something wrong with that?"

"No." Hell yes, there's a whole lot wrong with that. I'll just talk to Mom when we get home because she's out of her mind.

"It's confirmed by Mom," Lach says when his phone beeps. "We are to ride home with Francisco."

Both my baby brothers shrug their shoulders—not a big deal for them, I guess. *Well*, it is for me.

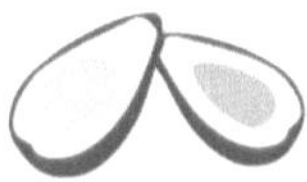

On the way back to our new home, I hop in the back of the car next to Ezra, who already has a new comic book in his hand. I think that's all he brought with him in his backpack.

During the ride, I try to sit in silence, tuning out Lach's overly happy conversation with Francisco. My thoughts race with eagerness to find Mom.

We finally pull up to the new house which matches the photos Mom sent to us. It's larger than our last home, with a red metal fence surrounding its border. The front is painted a canary-yellow with chestnut-colored bricks centered between two large rectangular windows and going upward to create the chimney coming out from the roof. Home sweet home. But is it? We're constantly moving, Mom always finding a better job.

She said this will be our last move, but I only have one

year left of school and then I'll be done, not having to be dragged around everywhere.

Could I have stayed with Dad? Of course, but feeling like an extra person in a house filled with an already tight family doesn't do it for me.

Mom's white car and my moped are parked in the driveway as I step out and grab my suitcase from the trunk. I skip any more pleasantries with anyone and walk inside the already unlocked house, finding Mom descending the stairs.

"Hey, Dacre, sorry I couldn't pick you and the boys up, I just got home and changed. Rough day at work." She wraps me in a long hug, and I give her one back, smelling a new fruit scent from her skin.

She pulls back, and I notice the long sundress she's wearing with a very lowcut center—I quickly avert my eyes to the gray-painted walls. It's like she dropped the last ten years of her age since we've been gone.

The door swings open behind me and Francisco and my brothers stroll in.

"I love it, Mom," Lach says, eyes wide as he stares up at the vaulted ceiling, the large living room filled with leather furniture, and a cow fur rug on the floor. Not sure about that rug and weird animal fur draped all over the couches, though.

"Let me show you boys around," Francisco says, already heading up the steps.

I tug on Mom's wrist before she follows them up and turns into a Stepford wife, without technically being a wife.

"What is this?" I wave a hand in her face, wanting to go ballistic in this television show environment where everything new is just supposed to be okay.

"What?" Her mouth stays slightly open, and she looks at me like I'm insane.

"This guy who appeared out of nowhere … who could be my new brother…"

She lets out a loud huff of air. "Are you going to be ridiculous about this? Cisco is a perfect gentleman."

"Cisco? *Cisco?* You know I don't have a problem with you dating anyone. Never did. But seriously? The guy is half your age."

She places her hand on the stair railing, lightly tapping her fingers against the reddish wood. "And?"

"And … does he even make as much money as you do? Or is he just using you for your stuff?"

"I don't give him *money.*"

"So you're just bangin' some young guy to make you feel younger?" I immediately regret what I say, but why else would she need to have some guy half her age around? At least Dad's wife is only three years younger than him.

"Watch your mouth." She grits her teeth, taking a step toward me. I'm about two seconds from her threatening to ground me, but I don't care.

"*Cisco* needs to leave."

"How can I leave if I live here?" Francisco asks as he saunters down the stairs, sliding an arm around my mom's waist.

"What!" I shout.

2

Sal

I'm a robot.

I can't sleep thinking about my pa's words. Before going to bed, he said, "Salbatora," and paused. Using my first full name meant one thing—lecture time. I stood and waited until he made a list. According to him, I'm:

1) Too efficient.

2) Work with Swiss-watch precision.

3) Every single thing I do is planned to the last tiny detail.

4) Too robotic.

First of all, no, no, no, and *no*. Besides, what's that thing about Swiss watches? I've heard that before, but to me, it doesn't make sense—wristwatches are so last millennium. And, I don't plan *that* much ahead.

In conclusion, according to his silly list, I'm made of moving metallic parts, my heart ticks with Europeanwatch precision, and a computer resides in my skull. By the tone of his voice, I know he wasn't complaining or anything. I guess it's his way of complimenting me, but he made me feel like an infertile avocado seed.

Not that I'm infertile or anything—that I know of. Besides, lately, I haven't had time for boys. Let's face it, working on the farm leaves little time to date. In my long seventeen years of existence, all here in this little Mexican town, I've only had one boyfriend. Before hiring our current cashier, there was a boy who worked the counter. I started to find him on the cute side, because I *thought* he loved avocados as much as I did. For some reason, I knew it would be meant to be because hearts and avocados go perfectly well together. What comes after supposed love? Sex. But hearts are fickle things, because afterward, he talked about avocado pie and I just knew it was *not* meant to be once that statement took place. Pie and avocados just don't mix. While that experimentation went awry, I learned a lesson—don't trust boys who think they love avocados.

It's past midnight now, and I can't stand being in bed. Stepping to the window, I brush the lacy curtains aside and let moonlight shine in. I don't know why, but watching the avocado trees out there, standing like little soldiers, brings this sense of pride and something else I can't quite describe. I feel it here. In my heart. Like when you work extremely hard on a project, and after a long time you see the fruit of your labor.

Fruit.

Ha. Ninety-nine-point-ninety-nine percent of the customers think avocados are vegetables. No, no, no. It's a fruit, because it has a seed, a gigantic one. So, yeah, these trees out the window, the lines of them, are indeed the fruit of my robotic work.

Pa saying I'm a robot also relates to technology. He's old-fashioned, or just plain old. I mean, he thinks big tech companies invented smartphones to dominate the world. He even has a big "conspiracy theory" about it. In his savvy words: "*Ay, mija, esas chingaderas lavan cerebros.*" Which translates to, "My daughter, those damn things wash brains." Yeah, yeah, that's what he says, and when I ask him why he thinks that, he just shrugs and says, "I have years of experience," and all those cliché things parents babble about.

It's the generation gap, I guess.

Unable to sleep, I pull on a pair of jean shorts, a t-shirt, dirt-caked sneakers, and a bandana with printed avocados on it. Once outside the house, I walk toward the farm in the back. My feet dip into the earth, passing rows and rows of avocado trees until I get to the far end where the newest additions stand. They're almost ready to "fruit" which makes me feel like a proud mama. I remember when they were just seeds, years ago.

"What are you doing out here, Sal?"

I jump in place. "You gave me a heart sizzle, Flor."

Flor steps from behind a tree and smiles wide, showing her crooked teeth. "Sizzle? What's that?"

"It's when something scary fries your heart." I press a hand to my chest. "Can you hear it hissing?"

"Hissing," she repeats, bobbing her head, her long, dyed-red hair cascading down her shoulder. "Everything scares you, Sal." She shakes her head. "You didn't answer my question."

"I came to check on my little babies." I motion toward

the trees then narrow my eyes at Flor. "What are *you* doing here?"

She produces a toy telescope from a side pocket on her short red dress and puts it under my nose. "Stargazing."

I put a hand to my hip. "You're stargazing with a full moon on the farm, after midnight, and using a telescope with a zoom worse than my phone's. *And* it will be a pure achievement to do it all without showing the tip of your panties." I narrow my eyes. "I think I already see a flash of white…"

"They're fuchsia." Flor wrinkles her nose. "Stop teasing me. Are you here for a boy, too?"

"What do you think?" I frown.

Flor scans me from my dirty shoes, shorts, and all the way to the bandana wrapped around my black pixie haircut. She motions at me. "Some guys find farm girls attractive, you know?"

I glare at her. "Not funny. Who's the guy?"

"Just a guy." She averts her eyes to the left.

As I glance in that direction, my chest tightens. "Are you heading toward the shack?"

She bites her lower lip.

Since what happened last year, I haven't been to the shack—I just can't. And I don't want anyone else roaming nearby either. "Have you been going there?"

She glances down. "Maybe?"

Her words make me want to shout at her because the shack doesn't belong to her. "You can't go there, Flor. You know that!"

"I have nowhere else to go." She looks at me and blinks, almost crying.

I sigh, still feeling the tinge of frustration. "You know it's wrong."

She nods and gazes at me, like waiting for my permission to leave.

I wave her off. "Just stay away from the shack."

"I'll try." She spins and steps in its direction, then stops and looks over her shoulder. "Sal?"

"Yes, Flor?"

She gestures around. "Who are you waiting for?"

Rolling my eyes, I walk away. Flor, Flor, Flor. She works at the farm's adjoining restaurant, and she loves to flirt with the male customers. She lives for the attention, a thing that baffles me. Her big honey eyes and her curves make her attractive in a short-package kind of way. She barely reaches the curve of my shoulder, and my height is below average.

As I pad ahead, I feel the desire to look back and find out who Flor is waiting for. No. I won't look back. I won't. Not in a million harvests.

A cracking sound behind me makes me stop, someone stepping on a dry tree branch. More steps follow, getting away from me. It has to be Flor's date.

Okay, *now* I have an excuse to check them out. I whirl around and peer at the silhouette rushing toward the shack. A guy. The door opens, and he enters in a rush.

Flor—she didn't listen to me.

Shaking my head with annoyance, I head back to my house. I wish Flor's parents weren't that strict, so she could go on a regular date during the day. My pa is cool when it comes to boys. I guess it's because I prefer to keep to myself. Besides, most Mexican boys like curvy girls. Not that I don't have any curves. I'm just not as developed as the other girls my age.

When I open the front door to the house, I find Pa standing inside with his arms crossed over his chest. "Couldn't sleep again?" he asks, knowing all too well about my little night walks.

I drop my shoulders. "You couldn't sleep either." Not a question.

"*Sí, mija.*" He blinks several times, then stretches his arms toward me. "Come here, Sal."

Moving to him, I wrap my arms around his ample stomach, bend a little, and press my ear on his chest, right where the heart is. And listen. *Thump, thu-thump, thump, thu-thump*—the sound of an old, broken heart. "I miss her, too," I say.

Thump, thu-thump, thu-thump.

I lift my head to look at him. "Pa?"

He blinks again, shakes his head, and gives me a little sob.

"She was—" A lump forms in my throat. "She," I start, sounding like a frog with a sore throat. I press my cheek against his chest again, and I inhale and exhale, his cologne entering my nose, trying to recover from this sad moment. I have this sorrow under control. I do. Not. I cry—not super loud.

After a long moment, when we finally stop tearing up, I incline my head.

He peers down.

We gaze at each other, a father-daughter wordless conversation.

"Pa?" I ask again.

"Yes, Sal?"

I wipe hot tears from my cheeks and show him my

hand. "See?"

Pa caresses my hair, grabs my shoulders, and pushes me away, just a bit. He concentrates on my face, I guess trying to read my mind, then takes my hand and examines it. "See what, Sal?"

"I'm not a robot," I say in a robotic voice.

He chuckles.

"Robots don't tear up or smile." I laugh.

Pa hugs me and kisses the top of my head. "Go to sleep, Sal."

"Long day tomorrow," I say in a deep voice, mimicking him.

He chuckles again. "Try and get some rest, *mija*."

Every time he calls me *mija*, it feels like home.

In my bed, I close my eyes and try not to think of *her*. Of course, her image pops in my head as soon as I close my eyes—dyed, shoulder-length, dark hair, weathered face, and an all-business expression. I can't believe it's been less than a year since she died. So unfair. So, so unfair.

Tía Matilda—Pa's sister.

She worked at the avocado farm since before I was born. Pa told me she even helped deliver me at the house because he and Ma didn't have the time to go to the hospital, as if they were in the year 1857. Natural birth. When Ma died a couple of years later after a long battle with Lupus, Tía Matilda became my second Ma. I used to call her, "*Mi tía favorita*," and she'd give me a yellow-teethed smile in return. But then ... months ago...

She became ill, her sugar levels shooting to dangerous levels.

And boom, a week later her life was over. Just like that.

Fifty-four years of life erased by a glucose decompensation. All because of complications from Type 2 diabetes. When we asked the doctor why she couldn't do more, she said, "It happens," as if it were nothing, waving it off. Which made Pa and me angry. But, really, there was nothing to be done.

Nothing.

Since then, I've taken over her chores while Pa finds a replacement. "It's so hard to find good help, Sal," he says. But I know it isn't that hard. He's just been too picky, thinking none of the potentials would be as good as his sister.

So, the workload has been pretty crazy since Tía Matilda died. I miss her—everything in the house, the adjoining restaurant, and the farm reminds me of her.

Tía Matilda used to drive all around town and nearby cities, making deliveries. I'm now in charge of them, and although I do miss her a lot, I feel free driving the old van with crates full of avocados in the back and meeting the customers.

Exhaustion invades my body, and I finally become sleepy.

After a dreamless night, a loud rooster singing *cock-a-doodle-doo* snaps me awake. Why do people call that singing? It's more like early-morning torture. I stretch and yawn, then sleepwalk to the bathroom for a shower. I slide into my usual work uniform—washed-out jean shorts, comfy white t-shirt, and a crimson bandana. Feeling better than last night, I head out of the house and take the five steps to enter the adjoining restaurant.

Inside, Flor slaps a fabric cloth onto one of the tables, getting ready for the morning crowd. When she spots me, she smooths her polka dot blouse and trudges to where I stand, avoiding the tables.

"Morning," she says, standing on her tiptoes and kissing me "hi" on the cheek, acting as if nothing happened last night.

"You didn't listen to me," I say, still mad at her for going to the shack.

"We'd already agree to go there. I couldn't stop him."

"You…" I pause to avoid saying something harsh. *One, two, three.* "How was your 'stargazing.'"

"I saw stars." Flor blushes. "That came out wrong! I … he…" She shakes her head. "We didn't do anything. No, we did something, but it wasn't like that, you know? Like, you know…"

I'm not sure what to make of her words—she's been ranting about going all the way for a long time, saying she's so ready, and blah, blah. But the truth is, as flirty as she is, she's kind of shy when it comes to actually getting with a guy.

"I'm going to turn eighteen soon," she blurts.

"What?" I ask.

Flor gets closer and whispers, "Eighteen-year-old virgins suck." She opens her eyes wide. "That sounds totally wrong! Virgins don't suck. Well, some do, but no." She takes a deep breath. "You know what I mean."

I put my brain to work and imagine what happened last night. "Let me guess. He tried to go all the way and you freaked out."

She bites her lip and nods.

I'd give her advice, but my one time wasn't anything special. Besides, I'm still upset at her—time to change the subject. "Let's get the restaurant ready," I say, getting into organizer mode, gossip time out of the way.

Every day's the same, like a puzzle you have to solve—do this, do that, and voilà, everything falls into place with perfection.

Wait.

Pa's right.

Maybe, just maybe, I'm becoming a bit of a robot?

No, I'm not. There's so much to do, I have to follow a strict schedule to get everything done. At least, before school starts in August. Which makes me realize Pa needs to find Tía Matilda's replacement before I start my senior year. He'll figure it out. Maybe?

Right now, I need to focus on my robot-tasks.

Later, when I step out of the restaurant to work on the farm, I find Pa standing in front of the house, staring at the mountains ahead, as if lost in thought.

"What is it?" I ask, joining him.

"Good and bad news," he replies, still looking ahead.

I grab his arm with both of my hands. "Bad news first."

He taps my fingers. "Chiapas."

I lift a brow. "Chiapas as in the state?"

"*Sí*," he replies.

"How can that be bad news?" I squeeze his bicep.

He inhales slowly and exhales even slower. "It's too far."

I don't get it. "And the good news?"

He moves his arm, making me let go of it, then wraps it around my shoulders and kisses the top of my head. "We made our biggest sale ever—a full van's worth."

I imagine the back of the van with avocado crates stacked on top of each other, and, yeah, that's a lot of avocados. "That's great."

"*Sí.*" Pa clears his throat. "Chiapas is too far."

I gasp, finally realizing why he keeps saying that. "You sold it to a customer in Chiapas state?" I have to ask.

"In Palenque."

"Palenque," I repeat. This Chiapas's city is by the *Selva Lacandona*, a wild jungle. "That *is* far."

"I know." Pa rubs his forehead, something worrying him. "The buyer needs organic avocados desperately, and he offered to pay a premium fee. Which sounds too good to be true, but we do need the money, so I accepted it."

"Is the farm in trouble?" I have to ask, even though I know it's been growing busier.

"No, but the organic avocado demand is big." He moves a hand in the air, as if trying to swipe the mountains away. "Matilda always dreamed about expanding the farm, you know?"

I nod. I heard them discuss this repeatedly, but Pa refused to expand, saying it would create more workload, and that he was too old for that. He isn't old. Besides, he has me—I can help.

"And now that she's gone," he adds. "I think she was right and we should have expanded the land and planted more trees."

"We own more land, Pa," I say, thinking of the now-abandoned cabin and its surrounding area. It's pained me to go near it, and the place isn't a home anymore. The shack's falling apart and is more of a ghost of what was anyway.

"We do?" He locks eyes with mine.

"Yes, the shack."

He frowns for a brief moment. "I guess we do."

"We have enough land to plant several new tree rows."

I stand on my tiptoes and kiss his cheek. "Do it for Tía Matilda—to honor her."

He spreads his gaze across the mountain range in front of us. "I'll think about it."

We stay silent, lost in thought and admiring the view.

"The delivery." Pa breaks the silence. "I can't drive. I've thought about it for a long time, and there's no other way. I *must* stay here and watch the farm's business." He looks at me intently. "I don't trust anyone else for this delivery."

"Wait, what?" I poke a finger at my chest, unable to believe his words. "You want me to…? Me?"

"Yes, I want you to drive."

I stare at him.

"You're almost eighteen years old, and…" He glances up at the sky, then sighs. "It wasn't an easy decision to make, *mija*, and we need the money if we want to plant more trees. Do you understand?"

I can do this but not by myself—the trip is too long. "I can't drive alone."

"You won't. Delivery will be once the crop is ready— in several weeks. He looks at me intently. "We need the extra help to get the avocados ready and make the trip. We *have* to hire someone, *mija*."

We. Not we—he does all the hiring. But it's already been too long since Tía Matilda died, and he hasn't moved a finger to hire her replacement.

No. I can't rely on him.

I'll look for a new employee myself.

3

Dacre

I don't say one single word after Francisco announces he's living in our new home—sharing a bed with my mom. Instead, I just shake my head and go up the stairs and look for my new bedroom.

"Dacre!" Mom shouts. But I ignore her and shut the door once I spot all the boxes with *Dacre* scrawled across in black Sharpie. Who would have thought that at seventeen, I would be acting like a spoiled brat? But I'm not. Because this is ridiculous. I've always kept quiet about her choices, about our constant moving. Maybe I should just keep pretending we are all part of an old sixties family sitcom.

Nah.

I drop my heavy backpack in front of my old bed, sheets already washed and ready for me to crash on. Which I do. My back hits the mattress, and my body barely vibrates when I bounce. All my other things are sitting in cardboard boxes beside the closet except for my curling weights in the corner. The dresser and stand with the TV resting on top are the only other pieces that make my room feel alive.

The bright yellow walls practically shout out at me to be happy and know that everything in life is sunshine. But it isn't. Hasn't been. Won't ever be. My door swings open to a happy face full of sunshine.

"Dacre, my man." Lach's huge smile wants me to punch it off his face. "I see the news about our possible future stepdaddy is a no-go for you."

With a heavy sigh and a death glare, I prop my pillow up and lean my back against the headboard. "The only reason you're fine with it is so you can stare at Francisco's body."

"Hey, that's not the *only* reason—he's nice." He plops down beside me and runs a hand through his blond hair. "Plus, I have a boyfriend, remember? Juan."

I know he's been talking to this guy online for the past six months, and Lach's only shown me his picture enough times that the image is embedded in my head. Shaved head, green eyes, perfect teeth.

"Right, the one you keep miraculously forgetting about," I point out.

"Nah, just because I look doesn't mean I'll touch. And, I'm meeting Juan tonight." He nudges my arm. "You wanna join us?"

"Um, no thanks. I prefer not to see the things you do when no one is watching."

"Oh, people can watch."

"Dude." I shove him off my bed, and he hits the floor

with a deep rumble of laughter.

"Watch us dancing," he says, still laughing. "What kind of sick shit is going on in your mind, bro?"

"So you're meeting at some kind of club?"

"Yeah, it's not too far from here."

"Fine." I'm mainly going because I don't trust this Juan dude, and I don't trust the places Lach chooses to venture to, either. It will also give me a good reason to not be around Mom and *Francisco.*

"Now cheer up, buttercup, all will be well."

"It always is, isn't it?" The lie rolls right off my tongue, as it has ever since I was eleven.

Lach nods and closes the door behind him.

Right after my eleventh birthday, I'd stayed home from school and I was just so thirsty. For the previous day and a half, I had been feeling awful and vomiting. I had gone to the refrigerator and grabbed the pitcher of lemonade and poured it into a glass. My throat still felt dry after finishing the entire cup, so I poured more and more. All I could feel was the pounding in my head, and that's the last thing I remember until I woke up in the hospital.

When I woke, my mom told me I'd been in a diabetic coma for a little over a day. Apparently, the lemonade had just been adding fuel to the fire. That's when I got the rest of my diagnosis.

And here I am now. Alive and not feeling very much so.

Right now, I miss the waves by our old home and the surfing I did at Dad's over the summer. The water has a way of pulling me out of my funk for a temporary amount of time. I'm not missing Texas or my old home in Mexico really—I'm missing a place that I've never had—somewhere I want to call my own.

I grab one of the silver curling weights and start working on my repetitions. Another thing I'm *lucky* with is having to work harder to maintain my muscle mass because of the diabetes. I've bulked up over the past few years, but it hasn't been easy. It's also a distraction—a damn good one.

Right as I start another repetition, the room starts to feel bright, and I already know my blood sugar is low by how shaky my body is becoming.

"Shit," I mutter to myself, setting the barbell down. I plummet to the bed and lean over to unzip my backpack to pull out the glucose tablet bottle. It feels lighter than I had hoped and when I shake it, I hear the sound of one lone tablet rattling against the plastic walls.

That means I can't stay in the room. That means I have to go to the kitchen. That means I have to encounter the happy voices radiating from downstairs and through the crack beneath my door.

I peel myself off from the bed and head down the stairs into the open foyer of the large kitchen. Ezra is bent over the table, skinning potatoes with Mom, a Wonder Woman comic book at his side waiting to be finished. There's a plate of chocolate chip cookies sitting between them—my energizer.

Lach is chopping up carrots on the granite island next to Francisco.

One big happy family.

Mom looks up, smiling, as if I wasn't in a bad mood earlier. As if I'm not in a foul one *still*. "Hey, Dacre. You want to help us?"

I swallow the anger still boiling inside my chest. "Sure." I snatch a couple of cookies, eating huge bites as I take a seat beside Ezra and tap his comic book. "Any good?"

"Of course it is." He pushes his glasses up and hands me a potato.

After minutes of silence except for the sounds of chopping and peeling, Francisco groans, "Oh no." We all stare at him. "I forgot to pick up the avocados on the way home after picking up the boys."

The boys. Like we're his boys. Fuck. That.

I stand up from the chair, biting my lower lip. "Where's the store at? I'll go and pick some up right now." I've got to get out of here.

"That's thoughtful," Mom says, blind to her oldest son's growing struggle. She's always been like that—with my feelings about the divorce, with my feelings about moving, with my feelings with the diabetes—especially the diabetes. I shrug it all off.

"You want me to drive you?" Francisco asks, rubbing his palms down the sides of his jeans.

Mom had my means of transportation already delivered. "I have a moped," I say as politely as I can muster. Which comes off pretty well, if I do say so myself—I could be an actor if I wanted to.

He nods. "Once you go back up the road, take the first right and keep driving straight for a few miles. Eventually, you'll see a large sign that says *Granja de Aguacates*"—He waves a hand across the air, arching it like a rainbow—"then take a right. They have the best damn avocados you can eat."

"Mmm. Okay." An avocado is an avocado, but all right.

"You want me to ride with you, bro?" Lach asks.

"I've got it," I say, a little too harsh.

Lach backs down, understanding I'm using the excuse for some alone time. And I'm going out with him tonight anyway.

I grab my keys and wallet from upstairs and fly out the door, finally able to breathe. My sugar feels good now—I tell myself it's all fine as I hop on my moped. I've had this magenta vixen since my birthday last year.

The road to the avocado farm is narrow and there's a row of adobe buildings to my left. The top portion of the structures is painted a dark red and the lower half white—wooden doors with small twin windows at the top are placed in the middle of each home.

It's sort of calming.

A dilapidated wooden sign catches my attention and in large green block letters it reads, *Granja de Aguacates*, and an arrow points right.

"Green paint for avocados, right?" I chuckle to myself and turn down the street.

Not even a mile down, a similar wooden sign slides into view, in better condition besides a gravel parking lot. I pull in and park while checking out the place. In my mind, I had pictured a dump. But it's actually quite quaint.

There's a large, pale-yellow building that seems to be a restaurant and grocery store in one—or so the sign says in bright-orange paint. To the side of the structure leading to the back, I'm able to see rows and rows of tall avocado trees. They go so far that I wonder how many damn trees there are. On the other side of the building is a small one-story house attached, painted a lime-green.

Once inside the store, the scent of chicken being grilled hits my nostrils, and the sizzling even makes my ears hungry. Nestled near the wall are two long picnic tables and a set of benches on each side, where people are busily eating a late lunch.

"You need any help?" a young girl asks from behind the counter. Her skin is the color of copper and she looks like she might be a little young, but her curves tell me otherwise. I'd say she seriously might reach under my nipples. A work badge pinned to her polka dot blouse reads *Flor*.

"Um, well, you guys sell avocados?" I ask.

She waggles her finger for me to pull up to the counter, her red ponytail swinging over her shoulder. I scoot closer and she curls her finger again until I'm leaning over the edge of the linoleum, her mouth practically touching my ear.

"You know, the sign does say Avocado Farm," she whispers, "and there just so happens to be that particular type of tree outside. But the question is, do we sell them? I would have to say yes."

"Smartass." I move back and roll my eyes.

"I'm just messing with you. There are avocados in the grocery section you can pick from, as well as other food items." She points around the corner where the fruit must be. "But, I actually suggest you go out back and pick the ones you want straight from the tree."

"Why's that?" I whisper, as if we're about to tell each other a secret.

"Because they're cute like you." She pats the tip of my nose and scoots back. "But sorry, I have a boyfriend. You might find something extra special outside, though." She shrugs, grinning. I roll my eyes again but smirk at her as I walk out the back door. She's obviously trouble, and not my type anyway. Nothing wrong with small girls, but I don't want to crane my neck down all the time.

Outside, there's tree after tree with ripe avocados ready for the picking. I walk out from the covered patio until I'm about four trees in. Something crushes under my foot, and I spot a squished avocado. *Shit.* I move away from the tree, as if it never happened. Standing below a branch, I look up and stare at it for a moment and think I should have just grabbed some from inside. Or possibly the one from the ground before I crushed it.

Curling up my shirt to gather the avocados, I expose my stomach as I reach up and pluck a green fruit from the branch. I stack four more into my t-shirt before I hear a voice behind me.

"Hey, are you trying to steal those?" a small girl wearing jean shorts and a loose t-shirt says, marching up in front of me. Not as tiny as the one inside, though. She rips one of the avocados out of my shirt and shoves it in my face.

"Oh, you speak English," I say in English, not sure why that's the first thing that comes out of my mouth when there's a piece of fruit pushed at my left eye.

"And Spanish," she replies in Spanish. Her short black hair has a bandana wrapped around her forehead to the back, kind of reminding me of the young guy from *The Karate Kid.*

"As do I," I say in Spanish, mostly to the avocado still moving back and forth in my face. With the tip of my index finger, I casually move her arm away. "Sorry, I wasn't stealing. I was just picking some avocados to buy."

"Oh?" Her scowl turns into a somewhat smile. "You actually buy them inside." The girl places her arm back by her side, still gripping the avocado in territorial mode.

"Hmm, that's funny. The girl inside—Flor—told me I should come out here and find something extra special. Yet I stumbled upon you." I automatically realize that came out wrong. "I mean special avocados."

The girl closes her eyes and lets out a loud sigh, gritting her teeth. "*Flor.*"

"What?"

Back to casual mode, she waves me off. "Nothing." She hands me back the fruit. "Just take these inside and you can pay for them up front."

"All right, thanks." Without another word, I start for the building.

"Wait," she rushes out. "Do you have a job?"

I turn back around and face the girl. "What?"

"I said do you have a job, as in do you want one?"

"No."

She ignores my answer. "Do you like avocados?"

"I'm buying them, aren't I?" What is this girl even doing?

"Look, we're down a person." She sighs like she's gathering up the courage to continue. If the shade wasn't blocking half her face making her look like Two-Face, I'd say she might even be tearing up. "We need another worker. There's going to be a big delivery coming up soon that will take two days to travel and we need someone to go. And we also need someone here in between travels."

A chance to be away from home for hours? Then a getaway for two days? I've barely been back for any time, but there's no way I can spend all summer at the house with Mom's new boyfriend. I already *need* the escape.

"Um, okay, I'll take it."

"Yeah? Well, you'll start tomorrow at 7:00 AM sharp."

"Uh."

"Something wrong with that?" She swipes the sweat beads from her temples.

"No. That works." Hell yeah, Crazy, there's something wrong with being at work that early during the summer.

"*Actually*, give me those and follow me." She takes the avocados from my shirt and holds them to her chest, practically babying them. Weird.

She comes to a halt, stares down at the fruit I murdered, and turns her head back at me. "Did you *step* on this avocado?"

"I have no idea what you're talking about," I lie, trying to conceal a grin.

My poker face must be awesome because she moves on and I follow her inside—her sneakers caked in fresh mud leave trails of brown behind her down the short hallway. She comes to a halt and pulls a plastic bag off a roll attached to the wall, then places the avocados inside and points me in the direction to pay.

"You never really know. I just needed to make sure you didn't take off with them."

Doesn't trust me with the avocados yet trusts me to take a job? All right... "O-kay. See you tomorrow." Strange little person.

Up ahead, I spot a circular wooden barrel separated by dividers and filled to the brim with different kinds of nuts. I grab a plastic bag and fill it up with pecans—Ezra's favorite. There's a heavy-set man with specks of gray sprinkled into his dark hair working the cash register.

My body is already starting to grow weak again, and I probably should have eaten first. After I pay, I stop by the restaurant up front where Flor is busily chatting with an older lady wearing a baggy floral dress.

I place an order for a burrito and churros. Flor brings them to the register with a smile. "Did you find that something extra special outside?"

"Well, I got a job here," I say and swipe my card.

Her shoulders slump, and she frowns. "That's it?"

"Yeah, and the avocados I wasn't supposed to pick." I hold up the bag.

"Hmph. Well, maybe another time." She perks up. "When do you start work?"

"Tomorrow." I stuff a churro in my mouth as the room starts to feel dizzy.

She appears surprised but then winks. "See you then."

A job isn't something I necessarily wanted for the rest of the summer, but it beats sitting in a new house that doesn't feel like home while thinking about Francisco possibly becoming a new family member.

I stand outside and finish the churros, then take a few big bites of the burrito until I start to feel back to normal. Or whatever normal is. Blowing out a deep breath and pulling the shirt away from my clammy skin, I make my way back to the house.

Once in the driveway, I finish the rest of my now afternoon lunch before I head inside. Ezra's curled up with a sheepskin blanket beside Lach on the couch, watching TV.

I toss Ezra the plastic bag of pecans. "Here."

"And me?" Lach asks, eyebrow arched.

"There's enough."

In answer, he digs right in.

Mom's in the kitchen drizzling a red sauce over

enchiladas and sprinkling shredded cheese on top with her other hand.

"Back, honey?"

"Yep." I place the bag of avocados beside her and start to walk away.

"Dacre?" she asks, concerned.

"It's fine."

"Is it?"

"Yes," I lie. "I'm also starting a new job tomorrow at the avocado farm, so I'm going to be busy with that."

"I didn't know you even wanted one right now. But that sounds fabulous!" Her eyes widen in surprise as she wraps her arms around my shoulders and pulls me in for a tight hug. All I get a whiff of is that new scent she's wearing. I want the smell of my old mom, from before I left for Dad's.

Having a new guy living here that Mom has known for less than a month is dumb in itself. And it looks like I have to deal with it, like I do with my disease.

"It's looking good, Paige," Francisco says as he enters the room. When I glance at him, I'm not sure if he's staring at her ass or the food, and I frankly don't want to know.

Leaving the two of them alone, I find Lach in the living room, and I need to get out. "So, when are we leaving for the club?"

4

Sal

just offered Tía Matilda's job to a stranger.

Which is totally not me. I was planning to plan a plan. Ugh, no, no. I thought about a "Hire Tía Matilda's replacement" plan involving the internet and interviewing people. But, no, I just blurted out, "Do you have a job?" to this tall American guy who speaks perfect Spanish, and who I thought was an avocado thief. So, according to Pa, I'm a robot, but now…

I'm an impulsive robot.

Enough about robots.

It's almost noon—time to check on my newest little baby trees. With a sigh, I trudge toward the area opposite the shack, where Flor made out with her boyfriend last night. I can't believe she's been using it to—whatever she is doing in there. Maybe she cleaned it up and it's now all cozy. I stop and look over my shoulder. The shack sits nearby, at a shallow dip by the skirts of a brown hill. I haven't checked it in months, because it makes me feel sad that she isn't there reading her magazines, writing in her journal, or even just chatting with me. I mean, it was part of the farm when Pa bought it, and since Tía Matilda was struggling at the time, he asked her to come work for him, the shack being part of the deal. So, it'd been Tía Matilda's house since the previous millennia, before I was born, and before the internet, the global economy, and electric cars.

I miss Tía Matilda so much—her smile, gentle gaze, and the way she called me, *"mi niña,"* as if I were her daughter.

Daughter … I wish … I wish I knew my ma better.

I wonder how my parents would look together now.

Wonder about my ma.

I was so little when she died, I don't remember her around at all—I wish I did. If she hadn't died, would I be different than how I am now? But living with a single parent, a father, who happens to love *futbol* and all fatherly things, has made me independent.

Pa's shown me old pictures of Ma, and she looked like me, or I look like her, except I have my pa's thick eyebrows and nose. He's also shown me Polaroids of them, dating and honeymooning. I especially love this picture of Ma, where she stood by a small stove, wearing an apron, pointing a spatula toward the camera and smiling wide.

I imagine my pa saying, "Smile, Eloisa."

And she points the cooking utensil and replies, "No, no. I look horrible, and I'm cooking, Gregorio."

"You're always beautiful," he'd answer.

Okay, I didn't imagine this—Pa told me about it when he showed me that photo.

Enough about reveries because the sun is making me sweat. But now that I've thought of the shack, I wonder if Pa is still thinking about demolishing it and using its land to expand the farm and honor Tía Matilda. I haven't reminded him about this ordeal, but maybe I should? And I should also conquer my fear of going there and check it out to see if it's covered in spiderwebs and dust.

Pivoting, I head toward the clay pot area where the baby avocado trees grow, waiting to be planted with the "grownups" when they're tall enough.

"Hello, little ones," I say to the baby trees in the pots. They can hear me, and I love talking to them. I don't care who thinks I'm crazy.

Bending down, I touch an avocado plant, sliding a finger over a leaf, looking for bugs who love to devour them. "You're doing great."

I scoot to the next plant and repeat the operation. "You're in fantastic shape!"

Since our farm is all organic, we avoid pesticides, so checking the baby avocado plants is an exhausting task that has to be done systematically and with perfection—no room for error.

Like a robot, the robot inside me says.

Whatever.

One small mistake can turn into a catastrophe of pandemic proportions. These tiny red bugs mean business.

So, I keep checking my little plants-in-a-pot, and by the time I'm done, my stomach growls, demanding food. Any kind of food. I drag my feet on the dirt toward the house-grocery-store-restaurant combo.

"You're filthy," Pa says when I enter the restaurant. Cold air and the aroma of grilled beef, serrano peppers, and onions welcome me. He scoots out from behind the small counter.

"Good afternoon, Pa." I kiss him "hi" on the cheek, his stubble grazing my skin. I want to add that I hired a stranger on the spot, but no. Later.

He motions to the restroom area. "Wash your hands and face because we have customers."

"*Sí, señor.*" I salute him.

"*Sí, señorita.*" He slaps my back with his heavy hand, making me stumble a bit.

I lock eyes with his and give him a wide smile.

His semi-serious expression crumbles, then he sighs, which makes his chubby cheeks deflate a bit. "I love you, *mija.*"

"I love you, too, Pa." I smirk. "Even if I'm a robot."

He shakes his head. "I didn't say you're a robot—just relax, be more like other girls your age."

I frown and make finger quotes. "Be more normal."

"I…" He rakes a hand through his hair. "That's not what I mean."

But it is—we've talked about this countless times. He wants me to hang out at the main plaza and do what "normal girls" do—look for a boyfriend. But what would I do with an infantile guy who babbles about video gaming nonstop? It's like most boys my age are not really my age, but six years younger. Take my last boyfriend and dalliance, for example—*avocado pie*. Besides, they are so stupid, and they all ask the same question, "Why do I never see you in a dress like the other girls?"

To shut them up, I reply, "Why don't *you* wear a skirt like the Scottish?"

Dresses—so impractical for farm work. That's why I only own a handful for special occasions.

Now, I snap out of my thoughts and say to Pa, "I'm too busy with the farm to waste my time hanging out in the main plaza."

He glances toward the people sitting at the tables and benches. "It's summer, Sal. There's plenty of time to relax."

"I don't want to relax." I grip my hands into fists. "I *can't* relax."

He stays silent for a long moment, then exhales and gives me a little nod, the kind he uses when he knows it's time to stop with a particular topic. He averts his gaze to the restaurant kitchen. "It's late. Are you eating now?"

Even with this small discussion, my stomach reminds me it needs food. "Yeah."

"Let's eat then." Pa grabs my face and kisses the top of my head, then wipes his mouth. "You taste like dirt. Go and wash."

I rush into the restroom, feeling a little weird about the full convo. After I scrub my hands, I splash fresh water on my red cheeks. My head is full of doubt. Do I really need to be more 'normal?'

I do want to be normal.

I want to be less of a robot.

Normalcy is not about dating or anything. It's more about … what? Pa wants me to get out there and meet people, not just boys. And wear dresses and … I don't know. Besides, after the last boy was a failure in my eyes, I'm not feeling like meeting anyone new and… Do I need a dumb boyfriend? Am I being too hard on boys?

Boys. Boy.

The avocado thief boy.

God, I need to tell Pa about the one I hired. What was his name? I never asked. And I hired him on the spot. I guess his exposed abdomen distracted me, not that I was staring or anything. He's just an average American guy.

I'm just gonna call him Mark for the time being.

Heading out of the restroom, I search for Pa, but he isn't here. I guess he already grabbed the food and went to the house. So, I stroll toward the restaurant exit, passing by Flor.

"Hey," she calls from behind the counter.

I stop. "Yeah?"

"Cute, handsome, and super-tall, right?" Flor fans her face. "This place got hotter."

I'm not sure what she's talking about, but knowing her, she's talking about a guy. Maybe her boyfriend from last night. Is he her boyfriend? I never know—she likes so many guys. I search around for cute-handsome-super-tall guys and find none. "Who?"

She shimmies around the counter and elbows me. "The new hire."

"He isn't hot." He looks like a guy who's taller than most here.

"He is." She elbows me again. "What's his name?"

"Mark," I lie, just to get this out of the way. I motion to the counter. "Go back to your cashier duties."

Flor moves back to her station and props her elbows on its shiny surface. "He can help me count here on the counter." She winks. "I'm not that good at math."

Rolling my eyes, I exit the restaurant and take the few steps to my house.

Opening the door, I find Pa setting a plate on the dining table. Without a word, I take out silverware and put it by the plates. Two Tupperware bowls sit on the center of the table. I open one, and the aroma of *fideo* soup enters my nostrils. I try the other—spicy pork *guiso*.

When everything's ready, Pa sits at the head of the table, and I take a seat next to him. We've been sitting the same way since I can remember. I like it this way.

"Let's say grace." He puts his hands together and prays.

I take a moment to also say a prayer, to thank God for the food and the avocados and everything here.

We eat our soups in silence, as if the discussion we had back in the restaurant is still lingering in the air, cutting our tongues.

"So," I finally say, if only because I can't stand the silence.

Pa looks up at me, spoon midway to his mouth. He sets the utensil down and gives me a go-ahead nod.

I point my chin in the restaurant's direction. "About that."

"That," he echoes and bobs his head.

I take a deep breath. "Normalcy."

"Normalcy," he repeats again.

For the tiniest of moments, an image pops in my head—a robot repeating every word it hears. No, no more mechanic things. "My being more … relaxed. Normal."

He gives me a half-smile. "I don't want to impose anything on you."

"I'll give it a try." I bite my lower lip. "Maybe?"

He takes his spoon and points it at me. "Let's eat."

I take mine and clank it against his. "Let's fight."

He chuckles.

We spoon-sword-fight for a minute before going back to eating.

Now that the tension between us has evaporated, I think it's time to tell him about my little impulsive action. I clear my throat. "Um, Pa?"

He also clears his throat. "Um, Sal?"

"I…" I glance down for a moment. "I need to tell you something."

Studying my face, he says, "Relax."

I open my mouth and close it, unable to utter a word. *C'mon, Salbatora Tames, tell him!* Here goes nothing. "I found Tía Matilda."

He cocks his head, eyebrows jutted in confusion.

Ugh. That came out wrong. "I met a guy and…" I can't say it.

Leaning back, he scratches his earlobe, a thing he does when nervous. "Are you dating him?"

"No!" I shake my head. "No. No, no, no. *No.*"

"You met a guy you aren't dating and something about your tía Matilda?" Pa crosses his arms. "Clarity, Sal, clarity."

The last time I got this nervous when talking to him was when I failed a math test in seventh grade. I shouldn't be nervous. "I met a guy, and I hired him as Tía Matilda's replacement." I cover my face in shame. "It's wrong. I know. I should have interviewed several people properly."

Pa pushes my fingers apart, his face making an appearance. "About time."

I drop my hands to my lap, not having to ask what he means. About time we hired someone else. He didn't have the heart to do it until he mentioned expanding the farm. In my mind, I raise a fist.

"Did he give you his résumé?" Pa becomes all business. "Any work references?"

Okay, time to lower the triumphant fist. "I don't even know his name," I say, ever so slowly.

He frowns. "Who *is* this person?"

I explain to him how I thought the boy was stealing avocados, and how he said he was a customer, and how the idea of offering him a job popped in my mind.

Shaking his head, Pa's expression relaxes. He grabs his spoon and continues eating his soup.

We dine without any more words, the tension back like an invisible wall between us. Each bite I take tastes wrong, spoiled or too bland or, I don't know, like nothing. When we're done, he stands, and I watch him stroll to his bedroom. Although we had a late lunch, he never fails to take his usual siesta.

I never take one, but right now, with all of this, I feel like closing my eyes and erasing what just happened.

But I can't erase it.

And I can't just stay here.

The farm work must go on.

I put the dirty plates, silverware, and bowls in the sink, and after doing the dishes, an idea strikes me. With that in mind, I step to Pa's bedroom and poke my head in. He lies on his bed with his hands wrapped around his protruding belly.

"Are you sleeping, Pa?" I ask.

Turning to the side, he shakes his head.

"Maybe you met him?" I ask.

Lifting a brow, he gestures for me to elaborate.

"The boy. He bought avocados." *Slow down, Sal.* "You were at the grocery counter—he must've paid you."

"There were so many people." Pa sits on the edge of the bed. "But since you hired him, I want to meet him again for an interview."

"I can do that," I say. Tomorrow, when he comes for his first day of work, I think but don't dare say it.

"Good," Pa says and yawns, going back to his siesta position.

I exit the house and walk to the farm, where I find Flor smoking a cigarette, her back to me.

I tap her shoulder. "That'll give you cancer."

She jumps in place and spins to face me. "You just gave me a heart attack!"

"Sorry," I say and motion to her. "Did I fry your heart?"

"It's hissing!" She smiles wide.

I jerk a thumb to the side. "Time to check on the 'cados."

She drops her cigarette to the ground.

My index finger points at it. "You know that kills the soil."

"O-kay. Time for me to cashierize." With an eye roll, she picks it up and heads inside.

Still feeling full after having lunch, I stroll toward the trees on the far end, hot air crashing against my face. A minute later, the dirt-covered, brown hill and the shack come into view.

An invisible force pulls me toward it, and as I pass the last row of trees, I say to them, "I'll be right back."

A gust of wind makes their leaves sway, or perhaps they heard me and are nodding their consent.

As I advance, the shack grows in size, anticipation taking hold of me. I mean, Tía Matilda's house is there, and I can go anytime I want to. But since she died, I just can't do it, and now this new energy pulls at me.

Maybe it's the energy of Tía Matilda's soul.

Maybe she *is* pulling me.

I stop and look up at the cloudless afternoon sky. "Tía Matilda?" I ask in this tiny voice, feeling afraid and excited and weird at the same time.

Nothing.

"Are you there?"

5

Dacre

"A friend for some play time?" I groan and slip on my helmet.

"Hey, well, it's true," Lach says as he puts on his and hops behind me on the moped.

In a few months, I'll be eighteen, but Lach just turned sixteen so in Mom's eyes he's still a baby. When I was his age not so long ago, I didn't get swathed and coddled the way he does, even with the diabetes.

"Where's this place at anyway?" I ask.

He rattles off the directions and I pull the visor on my helmet down.

On the way to the club, we pass by several streets with neat and tidy houses until they become old and worn. The road eventually leads us to a shopping strip, where most stores look to be closed. A hair salon, electronic repair shop—the tattoo shop is open, though. Just past that is

Angel's Saloon.

I park near the curb and set my feet against the pavement, pulling up my visor. There are beer bottles and trash scattered all up and down the street, graffiti covering all the building walls. "What is this?"

"Angel's Saloon," Lach says as he removes his helmet, unfazed by how rough the area appears to be.

"I can read that," I reply and study the frumpy place. "But I thought you said a club." Maybe I was expecting loud music and flashing lights. Well, there is music traveling out from inside, but it's not something I would consider club music.

"It is. You just have to go inside."

Maybe it would have been a better idea to have just stayed at home and read one of my books. But then I would've had to be around Mom and her new boyfriend. This place just seems like bad news.

"You might want to move that moped closer to the door, or it may grow legs and walk away," a man in his early fifties calls over to us as he turns to head inside Angel's.

"Great choice for this place." I shoot Lach a look but go to move my moped and park it near the door.

Once inside the front of the building, a large bouncer with hair to his shoulders and biceps bigger than my head pats me and Lach down, making sure we have no guns or drugs. He pulls out the syringe from my backpack and inspects it, rolling it back and forth between his fingertips. I'm so tired of having to explain to people over the years why I have needles with me, or why I'm poking my finger to try and get blood out just to get a reading.

"Diabetes," I say, since he's taking too long analyzing

my things.

"Sounds like a good cover, kid." The beefy man pulls the insulin bottle closer to his face and squints his eyes to read the words. "You're clear. Go on through." He may have searched us pretty good, but the man didn't card either one of us.

Farther inside, the place is as rough as it was outside. There are people dressed in *Norteño* clothing *everywhere*.

"What the fuck is this?" I elbow Lach in his leather jacket. He looks more like he's dressed to go to a punk show—throwback 1978—than this place.

"It's something new. You've got to be open to more than three bands—you're always blaring the same ones."

"So are you, idiot!" I shout, but he barely hears me over the Mexican Banda beats.

He shrugs and fiddles with his septum ring.

We take a seat at a small table chiseled in with lovers' names and drawings of skull faces. I set my backpack with my diabetes stuff on the back of the chair.

"I'll be right back," Lach says and heads in the direction of the bar. I stare out at the crowd, watching the three rows of people in the middle of the floor line dancing to the music. There are a lot of hip rolls in the wrong places, some trying to sing along to the tune, and a very old couple getting a bit frisky.

It's bad—bad music, bad dancing, bad atmosphere. I scan the rest of the crowd, searching for a buzz cut and green eyes that'll match Juan. But for a moment, I think maybe he sent fake pictures to Lach. What is that shitty show? My a-ha moment comes at the same time I recall the name—*Catfish*. Ezra watched old episodes on repeat at Dad's while reading his comics.

My insides clam up and my heart thumps rapidly inside my chest as I try to find my baby brother, thinking maybe he *has* been catfished. Dammit, I shouldn't have let him wander off. The only time I really worry about things is when it has to do with Lach, Ezra, or my mom.

I stand from my chair, darting my gaze all around the room. A sudden tap on my shoulder makes me spin around.

"Why do you look all nervous?" Lach asks as he plops down into a wooden chair with two glass bottles of beer in his hands.

He shoves one at me and I shove it back, dropping down on my seat again. "Dude, what are you doing? Where did you get that?"

"At the bar."

"You don't need to be drinking."

"Why? You do," he says and takes a swig from the glass bottle.

"Yeah, but for one, I'm driving, and for two, I'm watching out for you," I say. Even then, I wouldn't be drinking at a place like this—I might not get home, period. And the last time I drank, it had been too much, causing my blood sugar to drop ridiculously low. My ex-girlfriend had to somehow coax me to drink a couple of Hi-C juice boxes before I came back to myself and could hold the third one on my own.

He sighs and presses his lips together. "I'm practically an adult and can take care of myself."

Yeah, if he didn't act like he was twelve.

"Lachlan?" a deep voice interrupts from behind us.

"Juan?" Lach smiles at the new guest.

Relief fills my chest because at least the guy isn't fifty

and matches his eighteen-year-old pictures.

"This is my brother Dacre." Lach points his thumb at me.

"Nice to meet you," Juan says and reaches out a hand to shake mine. He may not be wearing the complete Mexican cowboy get up, but he does have on a snap-button western shirt, tight jeans, and chestnut-colored boots that come to sharp points.

I grip his hand and say, "Likewise."

Juan turns his head back to Lach. "Dance?"

My brother shoots up out of his chair, finishes his beer, and snatches my untouched one. I'm about to rip it out from his fingertips, but since I'll be driving, a little buzz won't kill him.

After a long while of sitting here and zoning out, a headache starts in the middle of my forehead. My stomach rumbles even though I'm pretty sure my sugar is high, but right now I won't be able to eat anything they have here. If they even have food at all. Right when I'm about to get ready to check my sugar in the restroom, a girl around my age takes a seat beside me, and I don't say anything. She's wearing a *Norteño* shirt tied above her belly button, so her full stomach is showing. The top few buttons are open, putting the curves of her breasts on display. Her jeans look to be several sizes too small, and they show off her legs amazingly well. But her face is plastered in too much makeup.

She leans toward me, and I inhale a coconut scent. It's a little overwhelming, to be honest. "You looked like you needed to dance."

"No, not that kind of dancing," I say, shifting my eyes to Lach in a silent plea for a rescue. Only my younger brother is without his beer, instead nursing some other alcoholic drink—and way too engrossed in Juan to notice my discomfort.

"We can make up our own. It's not a law to dance like that here." She smiles. "And, it looks like you need to live a little."

The other girls I've dated I've always known first—moving usually always ended things for me before I had to. But maybe this opportunity to pretend like nothing exists is better in the end because I wouldn't have to text her after. She wouldn't have to find out I had diabetes, then she wouldn't have to look at me differently, be concerned when my sugar is low, frustrated when my sugar is high, asking me why my moods constantly shift. I can just be Dacre for once—no disease attached. *It's only dancing, Dacre, not sex.*

I can't deny she's attractive. "Maybe just a few songs." Her face is becoming a bit blurry, and I have to take a piss. Every time it's high, I have to keep urinating. The pain at the left side of my head is starting to pound fiercer. "Can you give me a moment? I need to use the restroom first."

"Sure," she says, still smiling.

I haul my backpack over my shoulder and hurry to use the urinal. The restroom is nasty, and I zip up my pants as quickly as I can. A lot of brown covers the walls that probably shouldn't be there.

No one is in here but me and my reflection. I wash my hands with only water because there's no soap, and I should have expected that. My light brown eyes stare back at me in the mirror, tired, and no one in my family seems to notice but me.

Dacre, this disease doesn't define you.

With the lancet, I prick my finger and press the drop of blood to the test strip. The meter gives me a reading of 340. "Dammit." Annoyed, I give myself a shot in my left arm and hope the insulin kicks in soon. I took one right when I got home after the avocado farm and a little after that because my blood sugar was still high. Some days it's fine. Some days it's constantly low or high. Some days I just don't want to be here.

"What am I doing?" I ask myself. Here at this so-called club when we just moved to this new town. I check the time on my phone and it's already almost time to bring Lach home. I'll tell the girl I've got to leave and grab my brother.

Since I don't have the ocean waves here to calm me down or my friends from Texas and my old homes in Mexico, I'll dive into my book where I can be *healthy*. In retrospect, it's what I should have stayed home to do in the first place.

The sound of gunfire breaks through my thoughts and I freeze. The door flings open and two middle-aged men and a woman rush in and hurry to the back of the room.

"What's going on?" I demand, eyes wide.

"A gang fight broke out in the street and they took it in here," one of the men says, breathing heavily.

"Lach," I whisper.

Despite where my thoughts are leading, I dart out of the restroom like there's a fire at my heels—and in some way, there is. More rounds of shots are fired, and I duck as low to the floor as possible. People are fleeing in all directions, and I try to spot chin-length, curly blond hair and a leather jacket.

I don't see my brother and I don't see Juan. Oh my God, if something happens to him, if something happens to him because I brought him here, I can't… I just can't… My eyes fill with water.

"Lach!" I shout. No one can hear me over all the loud screaming. Another bullet escapes a gun, and I can't see where it's coming from, but I visualize inside my head of it striking its mark. The bullet went straight through his skull—he's gone, no movement, no twitching. My brother. My head spins. I shake the false image away.

I want to run out and make sure no one's hurt. But I have to find Lach. Two arms wrap around me from behind and I elbow the shit out of the person's ribs.

"Ow," Lach's voice reaches a high pitch right in my ear.

Whirling around, I see his ghost-white face, cringing in pain. I throw my hands around his arms and shoulders, holding him tight. "Fuck. I thought you were someone else. Are you all right?"

"Yeah." He rubs at his ribs. "Me and Juan are okay."

When I pull all the way back, Juan grabs hold of Lach's wrist. The gunfire has quieted, but the blare of police sirens takes its place. I try to search around and see if the girl I was supposed to dance with is somewhere, but I don't see her. Hopefully, she's gone somewhere safe.

"You guys better leave," Juan says, hurriedly. He kisses Lach's cheek and guides us out the back door.

Without any hesitation, Lach and I hurry around the building to my moped. I sweep my gaze up and down the street but don't see anyone shady. Or at least no one with guns out in the open. We don't even take the time to throw on our helmets as I haul ass on my scooter down the street.

Lach's hands tremble around my waist, and I try to control my shaking by gripping the handlebars more firmly. My head is still throbbing and it would've been better for Lach to drive, but he appeared more shook up than me. I should've turned around as soon as we pulled up to that place.

This isn't the only time I've been around a gang violence scene. The first was when I was fifteen in one of the old towns we lived in. We were inside the house, but outside, two bodies were gunned down. So seeing a dead body wouldn't have been my first rodeo, but it wouldn't have made it easier if I had.

I come to a stop in front of our house, and Lach steps off the bike, swaying back and forth. The adrenaline must have left him, and his drunkenness is now settling in. He stumbles as we go up the porch steps, and I wrap my hand around his waist to help him stay balanced. I shouldn't have let him drink—I shouldn't have taken him there. But we're okay now. He's safe. And he will not go back to that part of town. Don't care if he wants to see Juan. The guy can come here.

"Just act casual," I whisper. "I'm going to get you up to your room and Mom will never know." I've done it plenty of times with myself, but Lach doesn't seem to be good at faking it.

The door swings open before my hand touches the silver handle.

Francisco stands there without a shirt and barefoot, wearing only his jeans. "What's going on?" he asks hurriedly and pulls Lach from around me.

Lach straightens and slurs. "Hi, Cisco."

Couldn't he just keep his mouth shut?

"He's *drunk*?" Francisco's head whips to mine, jaw clenched.

I scratch the side of my head. "Yeah."

"You're lucky your mom's in the shower." He looks up the stairs. "She's going to be upset."

"There were guns going off on a shooting spree," Lach mumbles, not knowing when to stop talking.

"Where the hell did you go?" Francisco demands, eyes wide.

"None of your business." He's not my dad.

"It is my business if it affects Paige."

"Angel's Saloon," Lach finally says.

"*What?*" Francisco hisses. "That's the worst part of town you can go to."

"How the hell was I supposed to know?" I seethe, anger building. "We've only been here for less than a day."

"Look"—Francisco runs a hand through his hair while supporting Lach—"I'll help get him up the stairs but if your mom asks me anything, I'm letting her know."

I nod because the last thing I want is for Mom to see Lach like this.

We stumble up the stairs, mostly because Lach can't keep his balance. I help set him gently on his bed and tell him to stay there.

Francisco doesn't head back down the stairs, though. Instead, he follows me straight into my room. I whirl around on him. "What do you want?"

"I get it. You don't like me." He holds up his hands. "But I like your mother, so you're going to have to deal with it. I've dealt with plenty of teen boys when I was—"

"Yeah, like only a few years ago when you were in high

school, right?" This guy needs to get real here.

"Grow up, Dacre, and I can see they haven't changed. It's about what's inside here." Francisco gently points at his chest. "And what's in your mother's heart."

"Drop the Hallmark card bullshit," I growl. "We both know you're with her because she has money and other physical things I don't want to even think about." I could punch him right now just for me having to say those words about my mom.

Francisco glares, and it's a little on the frosty side. "I'm done arguing with you." He leaves the room without another word, closing the door behind him.

"Whatever," I shout to the wall just to get the last word in, because I'm petty like that.

The door opens, and I spin around to tell Francisco to fuck off, but instead, it's Lach in just a t-shirt and his boxers.

"Seriously, dude, didn't I just say to stay in your room?" I snap, still reeling from Francisco. "Even Ez listens better than you."

"You're not my dad."

"You don't even listen to our own dad," I bite back.

He brushes past me and crashes onto my bed, curling up under the covers. "I'm sleeping in here tonight."

"What are you, a baby?"

"I didn't know it would be like that, all right? And neither did Juan."

"Well, Juan is an idiot since he lives here and he should've known that area was like *Scarface*."

"He texted me a minute ago and said it's not as bad as people gossip about. They haven't had a shooting in months."

"Wow. That's it?" I stare at him with my mouth agape. Because, *come on*.

"I—I thought I might have lost you." Lach tears up and my anger dissipates.

I take off my shoes, turn off the light, and slide in beside him. "Well, here I am."

"I'm serious." He sniffles.

"Me too."

"I know I never say it, and I try to joke around all the time to ignore the real things, but ever since your diabetic coma when we were younger, I've been scared. I never want to lose you."

I want to tell him how panicked I was at the thought he could've been lying dead on the floor of the dance club. But I bottle it up. As much as he annoys and frustrates me at times, I couldn't live without him either.

With a sigh, I roll to my side to try and not think about it—to not imagine his eyes open and unable to ever blink again. He slings his arm around me like I may disappear if he lets me go, as if he's thinking the same things I am, but about me.

Sal

hy?

I don't understand this. I really don't.

Why am I thinking about Tía Matilda? Why do I feel this impulse to go to the shack? I don't get it. I think the discussion with Pa about expanding the farm to fulfill her dream affected me in the weirdest of ways.

Think, Sal, think, my robot says.

I've never believed in the paranormal.

Ghosts. Really? I'm an idiot. Paranormal is all just pretend, like people living forever. And I'm thinking too much—I just need to find out what's going on in Tía Matilda's home. I glance up at the sun. By its position, it should be around four in the afternoon—I better hurry.

When I arrive at the shack, I gasp at its crooked wood planks, which, from the distance, look browner than this ugly gray. One of the four window panels is broken, as if someone threw a rock at it. Washed-down, beige curtains hide the inside. It's like it's been abandoned for years not months.

Taking a deep breath, I twist the rusty door handle, expecting it to be locked. It isn't. I push the door open, and it creaks. A mildew stench lingers in the air, combined with a pleasant aroma. Air freshener. I guess Flor used it in her little adventure last night. I really need to tell her to stop coming here.

A stove stands on one side. On the other, a bed with what looks like clean sheets—Flor's doing, I guess. I don't know why this place feels smaller than the last time I was here. Tía Matilda didn't like me to visit her, stating that it was just a big room, but it's more than that.

A *Virgen de Guadalupe* picture hangs from the wall in the back, just above the bed. The wall at the right has two paintings, fake ones—a fruit bowl, and cats playing dominoes. A solitary calendar hangs on the other wall.

Glancing at the dirt floor for a second, I sit on the bouncy bed. *Bouncy.* I spring up, as an image of Flor and her boyfriend "bouncing" on this mattress pops in my head. Gross. I have to make sure she stops coming here—it isn't right.

What am I doing here?

I pad to the calendar, which shows a date circled in red.

The day I was born.

I asked Tía Matilda why she drew that circle, and she answered because I was her favorite niece—an easy thing to say to her *one and only* niece.

Moving my eyes around, I look for clues, something that tells me what I'm doing here. But I find no signals or anything. And I have to do my afternoon chores. I exit the shack, but before closing the door, I take one last look. It's like the place wants to tell me a story, or possibly warn me about something. I don't know. Only thing I know is that it's wrong for Flor to bring her boyfriend here.

Walking fast toward the rows and rows of avocado trees, I reach the oldest one. According to Pa, when he and Ma moved here, this tree stood here by itself. They used to eat its fruits, but it had given so many avocados, they decided to sell them. And that's how this solitary tree started the avocado farm back in the day, when they barely made money to bring food to the table.

Shaking the thought off, I keep moving.

I spend the rest of the afternoon doing my tree rounds and checking their leaves and fruits. By sunset, I head home, take a long shower, and go into my room. As I'm playing with my laptop, the front door opens.

"*Hola*, Sal," Pa says after a few seconds, poking his head in. "How are you?"

"Good." I smile.

He checks his wristwatch and jerks a thumb over his shoulder. "Want to watch a movie?"

"On one condition," I say, because his movie tastes aren't my cup of tortilla soup.

He gestures for me to elaborate.

I smile at him. "That the movie isn't a chick flick or an over-dramatic telenovela."

"It's a thriller," he says with a smirk.

A moment later, we sit on the couch in front of the TV, and Pa fiddles with the remote and brings up the movie.

"This is a thriller?" I ask fifteen minutes into the

movie.

He shrugs. "It thrills me to watch it."

Oh, Pa. I don't know why he loves cheesy, romantic movies. "Did you and Ma watch these kinds of movies?" I scoot closer and place my head on his chest.

He kisses the top of my head. "Your mother loved them."

I look up at him. "When was the last time you went to Tía Matilda's house?"

Pa pauses the movie and focuses his dark eyes on mine. "Where did that come from?"

"I went there this afternoon," I say, casually, shrugging a shoulder.

"Oh." He points the remote to the TV again and resumes the movie, signaling the end of the topic.

"Why is the shack in such poor condition?" I ask a little too loud.

He pauses the movie again and frowns at me.

"When was the last time—" I start.

"It's hard for me to go there," he interrupts.

"I know." Since Tía Matilda died, we have stayed away from the shack, until today when I felt the pull to the shack. "Have you thought about tearing it down to expand the farm?"

His chest rises and lowers as he sighs.

I smile at him. "It'll be an homage to Tía Matilda, you know? New life, where…" I stop there—what I was about to say sounds weird.

"I'm still thinking about it, *mija*." He points the remote to the TV again. "Can we watch the movie?"

"Wait," I say, and when he turns his attention to me, I add, "Tía Matilda's replacement is showing up for work tomorrow." I bite my lower lip. "You can interview him then."

Pa blinks. "That won't be necessary." He caresses my short hair. "I trust your judgment."

"You do?" I ask, because he didn't trust anything this afternoon.

"Sometimes your maturity scares me." He shakes his head. "To me, you're still my little girl—you always will be."

I press my ear against his chest and listen to the *thump, thu-thump* of his heart. "And you'll always be my pa."

"Okay." He resumes the cheesy movie. "Let's find out what happens to Beatriz Celeste and Alberto Pablo." He peers at me and smiles. "Will they fall in love at the end?"

"Oh, the mystery," I drawl.

As the romance develops on the screen, my eyelids drop, and when I open them, a guy with a big mustache kisses a girl in a body-hugging red dress. My eyes close and open again. The TV now shows a mature woman discussing with the girl—some drama about … I don't know what the drama's about. I yawn and feel like going to bed, but I don't want to leave Pa alone. I lower my head a bit and use his belly as a pillow. My lids shut by themselves, and when I flip them open, excessive light makes me squint.

I fell asleep.

And this time, Mr. Rooster didn't wake me with his cringe-worthy singing.

Stretching and yawning, I glance at the clock hanging from the wall—6:30 in the morning. I drag my feet toward my room, but before getting inside, I check on Pa. He's already at the restaurant, I guess.

I slap on color-matching khaki shorts, a t-shirt, and a bandana. *Shoes.* Mmm. Today feels like an open-top-sandal day, so that's what I put on. I head to the kitchen and have a healthy-not-really breakfast consisting of coffee and two *concha* pastries.

A strange noise, like *potato-potato-potato*, makes me snap my head toward the door. I step to the window and brush the curtain aside as the sound dies down. Out there and to the right, where the restaurant is, a guy wearing jeans and a long-sleeve, button-up shirt jumps off a magenta scooter. After taking off his coal-black helmet, he sets it on the scooter's handlebars, then rotates his shoulders. He stretches his arms up, making his shirt slide up, showing his stomach.

I know that stomach.

The avocado thief I hired yesterday.

Rushing outside, I wave at him, but he's looking in the other direction, raking a hand through his short, brown hair, like a male model in a shampoo commercial. Not that he's my type of model material.

"Hey," I call from the door.

His head swivels in my direction, and he strolls toward me. "Hi … *you.*"

"Hey…" What *is* his name? I hired someone and don't even know his *name?* "Mark," I finish. Mark Twain is the first American name to pop into my mind since I've read a couple of his books.

He glances over his shoulder. "Who?"

"You look like a … a Mark I know. He wrote some American books or something." I wrinkle my nose. "Never mind. Hi, you."

The guy formerly known as Mark nods.

We stay put, looking at each other. Awkward silence.

He scans me, from pixie cut, khaki shorts, to exposed toes. He snaps his chin up and smirks. "Where's the safari?"

I roll my eyes. "Why aren't you dressed for the outdoors?"

He yawns into his hand, appearing a bit tired around the eyes. "You never told me what to wear."

Crossing my arms, I say, "And you figured farm work required overheating."

He shrugs, rolls up his sleeves, and unbuttons the top two buttons of his shirt. "Better?"

I shake my head and pinch the bridge of my nose. "Anyway, my pa wants to interview you." As soon as I say it, I remember Pa said he'd trust my judgment. "No, no interviewing—he wants to meet you." I wave him on. "This way."

We enter the restaurant. From the kitchen, Polo, the cook, says "Hi" to us, waving a knife. He kind of looks like Diego Luna, including dark-brown hair and eyes. That is, if the actor were younger and held a weapon.

"Who's that?" Avocado Thief asks.

"Polo, the resident serial killer." I stifle a laugh.

Stopping, he opens his eyes wide in mock horror, then smirks again. "Okay, where's your father?"

"This way." I know exactly where Pa is.

I march with purpose toward the back with this boy on my heels. We enter the kitchen, pass by Polo, and head to the walk-in pantry.

Poking my head in, I spot Pa in his usual lumberjack outfit—even with the excessive heat here, he loves flannel shirts. He examines the food-covered shelves lining the walls, taking inventory. I sneeze, not knowing why the aroma of condiments, vegetables, and whatever else creates an allergic reaction.

Pa pivots to face us. "You fell asleep last night, *mija*."

"Not really. I was watching the flick with my eyes closed, Pa." I wave him over. "The new guy is here."

Nodding, Pa trudges out of the pantry.

"Pa," I say, motioning at our new employee, "meet…" God, I need to ask him his name, but not now. "Mark."

"The third." The guy rolls his eyes.

Pa exchanges a glance with me. "Nice meeting you, Mark. I'm Gregorio Tames."

"Delighted to make your acquaintance, sir," the guy says, stretching a hand.

They shake like businessmen.

"So, I'm gonna show him the ropes." I point at the back door.

"Go ahead," Pa says.

Mark and I leave the restaurant and enter avocado-farm territory.

"Hey," he grunts from behind me.

I come to a stop and whirl around. "Yes?"

"I forgot something in my scooter." He jerks a thumb over his shoulder. "Be right back." He walks away and disappears through the restaurant's door.

Minutes pass, and the morning heat intensifies. When I'm about to find out what's going on with him, he appears through the restaurant's back door and heads my way, carrying a backpack. His relaxed expression makes me think he went to the restroom to take care of urgent business. Whatever.

"About time," I say after he joins me. "What's with the

backpack?"

"It has my lunch and stuff." He grips its straps. "Do I need an FBI check or whatever?" His tone comes out sarcastic.

"No." I motion to the restaurant. "There are lockers in the break room. Put it away in one of them."

"Now?" he asks.

"No, next Christmas." I feel like shaking him by the shoulders. "Of course now."

"Will do, boss." He throws his hands in surrender, his backpack swaying a bit. But he doesn't move.

"Just—just do it," I say after a few long seconds, gritting my teeth.

"Sure." He takes off with a smirk.

A moment later, he comes back and rolls up his sleeves. "Show me the ropes." He glances around. "*Are* there any ropes?"

I shoot him a not-funny glare, and he shrugs. "Let's start with the easy stuff, Mark."

He frowns. "Why are you still calling me Mark?"

Dropping my shoulders, I say, "Mark Twain came to mind."

A brow slowly slides up. "The author? He's dead."

"Sorry, best I could do because I didn't know your name."

"I don't know yours, either."

I cock my head, aligning it with his. "You go first."

With a half-smile, he grabs my hand and shakes it. "Nice to meet you, You-go-first. My name's I-go-next."

Apparently, I hired a clown—a bad one. "Ha. Ha."

He clears his throat. "It's Dacre."

"Dacre," I echo. "Another joke?"

His expression goes stony—not a joke.

"Dacre who?" I ask.

"Vinson." He drawls out the last name too long.

"I'm Sal." I try not to smile at his hardcore expression.

"Sal who?"

I try not to roll my eyes. "Tames."

"That's … cute…" The way he says it makes it sound like cute-weird.

"O-kay."

I head to a nearby row of trees, and he falls into step beside me.

"How are you today?" I sing to the trees as I stroll in between the rows.

"I'm here, I suppose," he says.

I huff. "I'm talking to the *trees*." I don't care if he thinks I'm crazy. "Pay attention to them—they're listening to you."

He clasps his hands behind his back. "Sure, they can."

I stop by a tree. "They can!"

"Prove it, then." He motions to a low-hanging avocado.

Yep—he thinks I'm bonkers. "There's nothing to prove—it's a fact."

Dacre scrunches up his whole face.

Most people never believe plants can hear us—time to change the subject. I stand on my tiptoes, trying to reach a branch, then look up at him. "Can you do something for me?"

He nods.

I point up. "I think this branch is sick."

"Sick," he repeats. "How can you tell?"

"It doesn't have enough leaves, and its natural color is

a little off."

He crosses his arms and takes a step closer. "Are you some kind of tree doctor?"

I ponder that. "I guess I am."

And so goes the rest of the day, with me showing him the ropes. Although Dacre's a little slow when it comes to "doctoring" the avocado trees, he's a fast learner, but I can't tell if he really is interested or not. What baffles me the most is his constant breaks.

What's with this boy and restrooms?

7

Dacre

I step out of the shower and wrap a towel around my waist. Even with the help of the scalding water, my body still feels so sore from yesterday, as if I got run over by a truck. But no, it's from moving around about a hundred bags of dirt for Sal's "babies."

Not to mention being the idiot I am, I showed up wearing jeans and a long-sleeve, button-up shirt, thinking I was going to be working inside. But there hadn't been any mention of what to wear or anything else, really, besides the time to be there.

I wipe the steam from the mirror, my eyes not as tired this morning as yesterday. And there's a touch of sunburn butterflying across my nose and cheeks.

After discarding the towel, I throw on a pair of my shorts and a t-shirt, feeling slightly better than the day before. When I woke up to my phone alarm yesterday, it was like traveling through a thick and heavy fog. I had left Lach in my bed and constantly had thoughts ticking back and forth with myself—starting with what if something had happened to him.

But it didn't.

And I'm going to try and not think about the shooting at the club anymore. The avocado farm was a good distraction, minus the fact that my sugar was so low most of the day. I had to say I needed to piss—repeatedly—so I could go check my sugar.

When I go downstairs, everyone's still asleep except for Ezra. He's in front of the TV, reading his comic book.

"You're up early again," I say, heading into the kitchen to check my blood sugar and give myself my morning shot. *Repetitive.*

"Yeah, I like waking up before everyone." He shrugs and meets me at the kitchen table.

The numbers on the little device don't bode well for me, and I wince. "Want something to eat?" My question is meant for Ezra, but it's really meant as a distraction from the needle I jab into myself yet again. Might as well get that dose and have a balanced sugar level before eating—or try to.

"Pancakes, bacon, and eggs," he replies.

In answer, I pour him a bowl of cereal. "When I'm off work next, I'll make you a fancy breakfast."

Before Ezra can dive in, Francisco strolls into the kitchen, shirtless and wearing a pair of checkered pajama pants. He takes one look at the measly bowl of cereal and wrinkles his nose. "I got it."

Of course he does. He's already pulling out a brown carton of eggs and all kinds of assortments to make some sort of magical omelet like he had the previous day.

I have to admit it did look good as hell, but I refused to eat one.

"Dacre, how do you want yours?" Francisco asks, pulling out a large frying pan.

"Sorry, I have to head to work."

"I'll wake up earlier tomorrow then and have one all ready for you."

This is too weird—I've got to jet. After our argument the other night, Francisco has been acting like everything's fine again. He may be a lax person, but I'm not. I hurry and eat the rest of my bowl of cereal and fruit, then finish getting ready to leave.

Mom comes out of her room already dressed in slacks and a blouse just as I grab my backpack and am heading down the stairs.

"Leaving already?" she asks, tugging me back by my arm.

"Yeah, I'll see you after work, Mom."

She wraps me in a hug and kisses my cheek. "Francisco and I will make something extra special for dinner tonight."

Oh, right, the new cooking tag team. "Sounds perfect." I smile, but it probably looks more like a grimace. It had always been me and Mom, or one of my brothers in the kitchen helping her before.

Oblivious, she smiles warmly back at me.

Once I get on my moped, I'm feeling good, prepared for a day of sweat and doctoring *trees*.

When I pull into the parking lot at the avocado farm, it's still closed for another hour, so only a few of the other workers' cars are here.

I fiddle with my backpack as I head toward the entrance. My eyes dart right and left, but no weird, sassy shadow clinger pops out at me today.

No, wait, there she is.

"Hey, Dacre. Ready?" Sal leaps out from the doorway, her *Karate Kid* uniform in place around her head—red today.

"Can I at least put my things up first?" I ask, hauling my backpack off one of my shoulders.

She stares at my bag, eyeing it with suspicion just as she had yesterday.

Releasing a sigh, she finally says, "Yeah, do you need me to show you where it is again?"

"I've got it." I walk in and the break room takes like two seconds to get to.

Yesterday, Sal followed wherever I went unless it was me saying I needed to go to the restroom. Sometimes I would use it as an excuse just so she wouldn't be right there in my face.

Without waiting for her response, I head inside, where I find Polo, the freaky cook guy, playing with the tip of his knife. He lifts his hand and does his signature wave with it in the air at me. I give him a small nod in return.

In the break room, I drop my backpack off inside one of the lockers and place the key in my pocket.

"Ready?" Sal asks as soon as I exit.

"Shit." I startle. The shadow returns.

"Sorry, it's just we're on a time crunch"—she taps repeatedly at her phone screen so loud with her finger I think the glass may break—"and have to do some of the chores quickly. There's a small order this morning we have to fill, so I'll be showing you the basics of a delivery."

"An avocado run?" I ask.

"Yep, this will be your first trial before we have to gear up for the big one coming soon."

I have to crane my neck to peer down at her. She's finger counting in the air to herself.

"Sorry, I needed to think about something." She pauses midair. "Okay, never mind, let's hurry and water the trees, then gather the avocados that are ready to be born."

"Eaten, you mean, since they're already *born*." I arch a brow and step around her while keeping my focus on her face.

She gives me an expression that could be best described as the stink eye. I lick my lower lip and smile because this girl is too tense. And needs a shell breaking.

"Come on, Dacre," she grunts and moves past me.

"Sure you don't want to go back to calling me Mark Twain?" I shout after her.

Without turning her head over her shoulder, she says, "That joke is so irrelevant—Mark was yesterday's news. Get with the program."

I roll my eyes and follow her outside.

Despite the bright sun's hot rays, there's a breeze that takes the scorch out of the air. For now. Sal hands me the long reddish-brown hose, and I immediately start to water the trees as she gathers the avocados into baskets. A branch dangles right beside my head with a fruit barely hanging on. She tries to reach for it and fails.

I pluck it and fling the avocado up and down in my hand. "Is this the one you wanted?"

She tries not to smile, but I throw it to her—she easily snatches it.

"Maybe you should join the baseball pros with that catch." I chuckle.

"I don't like sports." She tosses it up and then places it into her basket.

I want to tell her she just shook her baby, but I keep my mouth shut.

Sal goes to grab the heavy ladder, and I can tell she needs help carrying it because the metal keeps hitting the grass with soft thumps. I hurry to her side, watching as each little dent the ladder makes in the grass could be ruining her *children's* soil. Or is it only the avocado trees that are that?

"I've got it," she says, adjusting the ladder so it pulls from my grasp.

I realize that while she may need help with things in the tree yard, it's obvious she doesn't want it. She's one of those people who wants to be in control—do it all herself. If she were to allow someone to help her, it wouldn't be the exact formulation that Sal has organized in her mind. So I don't say anything, but make sure there are no branches in the way that could cause her to trip.

"I'm going to the restroom," I call.

"Already?" she asks as she spreads apart the ladder.

"I can go against one of the trees if you need me to," I say with a serious expression.

"*What?*" She stumbles, and the ladder almost falls.

"Chill, it was just a joke, Sal."

She lets out a small laugh that makes me smile a smidge. "Sorry, someone's actually urinated on the trees before."

I wish I could have been here to see her expression when it had happened.

She pulls her phone from her back pocket. "Anyway, we're about to leave for the delivery so just meet me out front."

Nodding, I walk inside to grab my bag from the break room. Flor is putting her purse in one of the lockers, her hair pulled into a loose and messy bun.

"You made it to the second day." She elbows me in the arm. "Sal hasn't run you off yet?"

"No, here I am." I flash jazz hands beside my face.

"Perfect." She smiles up at me.

"We're about to go on an avocado run," I say.

"Oh yeah, El Mundo needs a box." She taps her chin. "You should take Sal on your scooter. She kept telling me yesterday how much she has been wanting to ride one, especially yours."

"Really?" I don't believe that for a second, but I get what she's doing now. She's not flirting with me—she's messing with me again and wants me to break Sal out of her avocado shell.

"Yeah. She thinks yours is so badass." Flor pauses and seems to think. "*And* you get compensated for fuel. The van hogs so much gas. Totally worth it." She grins.

"Yeah, maybe I'll take her back to my place after. You know, to thoroughly discuss avocados and maybe show her parts of my moped that she can't see." I smirk.

Flor pokes me in my chest where I feel her sharp nail. "Listen, you little jerk, if you try to take advantage of Sal, I'll rip your moped part right off."

A deep rumble of laughter escapes my throat. "Seriously, chill, I was just kidding. Also, you need to quit whatever you're trying to do with me and Sal. It ain't happening."

She lets out a huff of air. "Ugh, you caught me."

I rumple her bun. "Maybe the next hired guy will work out better with operation 'Find Sal a Date.'"

Her expression shifts as if she's already planning ahead. I leave Flor to her thoughts and head into the restroom to check my sugar in the stall. It's low. Of course it is. I stuff some glucose tablets in my mouth and chug a bottle of water to take the chalkiness away. It's not that I don't want to tell these people about my diabetes because I don't care if they know I have it. But it will be the constant questions: are you okay, do you need some sugar, do you need to sit down and rest? I don't need any more mama birds. I've had that in the past with the ex-girlfriends, friends, and teachers. I don't need that again.

When I exit the restaurant, I find Sal holding a small box of avocados. While Flor's plan may not have worked, Sal does need to try something different.

"What took you so long?" she asks.

"Just needed some water, too."

"That long drinking water?"

"Yeah, I was *really* thirsty," I say then change the subject. "You do a whole delivery just for that?"

She straightens the box so it's perfectly perpendicular with the ground. "Yeah, the owner purchases a large supply, but occasionally they run low and just need a bit to finish out the week, so we like to help out."

"How about we take my moped to the restaurant?" I start walking backward to it.

"What?" she stutters. The box of avocados tilts and she hurries to correct it.

"It will save on gas," I say.

"No, that's all right."

"You haven't been on one before, have you?"

Her eyes narrow, and I bet if she wasn't holding those avocados, her hands would be right on her hips.

"Your fingers are fidgeting—you totally haven't. So if you're that scared, we can just take the van then." I shrug.

"No, we'll take the scooter." She shoves past me.

I hand her the extra helmet before taking the box from her hands and placing it into the storage bin on the back of the moped.

"Why did you choose this color?" she asks, poking the aluminum.

I hold up a finger. "I chose it because magenta is awesome. In our old town, the girl who lived down the street was getting a new car when she went to college, so her dad sold it to my mom. Mom gave it to me for my birthday because she knew how much I was lusting after it."

"Lusting over a scooter?" she asks, incredulous.

"I like cars, but damn these are beautiful." I give the handlebar a gentle squeeze.

"You're weird."

I chuckle, because Sal doesn't even know the first thing about the definition of weird, even though she seems to define it. Not in a completely bad way, but still odd.

Sliding my helmet on, I hop on the moped and pop the visor up to stare at Sal since she's still just standing there.

"You do have to get on in order for you to travel with us."

"Us?"

"Yeah, me and your children … that we're selling to

get eaten." I smirk.

That does it. She grits her teeth, shoves down her visor, and hops on behind me, rattling off directions on how to get there. The little daredevil. She leaves her arms by her sides but as soon as I back up, her arms fling to the collar of my shirt in a death grip, practically choking me. I mean, we literally only moved an inch.

Coughing, I rip her hands from my shirt and put them around my waist. Maybe they were better off where they were because this feels worse. Her fingertips are digging into my stomach so tightly I may hurl right here.

Ignoring the annoying grip, I take off down the long and narrow road. Each time before we have to make a turn, she taps my back as if I may have forgotten how to get to the restaurant. There's that need to stay in control again.

Purposely, I fluctuate the speed of the scooter up and down, just to make Sal a bit nervous. Can't be in control of everything.

When we pull up to El Mundo, I make sure to take the avocados out first and hold them dearly to my chest as I follow her inside the restaurant. The smell of green peppers and onions travels in the air.

We approach a tall, slender woman with streaks of gray in her hair standing next to a register. The restaurant is filled with small round tables and a set of four chairs pushed in at each. Maps of different countries are framed and nailed all across the walls.

"Sal, you are such a dear. Thanks for bringing the avocados in on such short notice." The woman looks at me and perks up. "And who is this young gentleman with you, a boyfriend?"

"What? No!" Sal practically shouts. "This is my new co-worker. He's replacing … he's new. Dacre."

"Oh." The woman's face falls as she takes the box from my arms and sets it on a round table. "Hopefully, you do as great of a job as the last employee," the woman says, the creases at her eyes becoming deeper.

Did this other co-worker die or something? Not like I'm going to just ask that.

As soon as we get outside, I turn around. "Did someone die?"

Sal freezes, lips pursed. "I don't want to talk about it."

"Was it while she was delivering avocados?" I ask.

"I said I don't want to talk about it!" She looks away.

I drop the subject because it's obvious I hit a nerve. Silently, we get on the moped and head back. Sal's annoyance is obvious through her stiff arms around my waist. After arriving back at the farm, I'm unsure of what to do when I step off the bike, but I attempt to break the tension when she hands me the helmet.

"So, *Sally*"—I smirk—"there's this dystopian book, and in it, one boy and one girl get chosen to basically kill each other along with other kids to become the winner. The point is I'd rather not have you do that today."

"Seriously, don't ever call me Sally again. *And* are you really talking about *The Hunger Games* right now?"

"You've read it?"

"No, but I watched it with my pa."

"You missed a lot then." I smile, riling her up. "Anyway, I feel like you're in a Katniss mood and you need to snap out of it."

"You're definitely no Peeta for that matter."

"Definitely not. But possibly the faun from *El*

Laberinto del Fauno would be more accurate."

She shakes her head and rubs at her temples. "I think I hear my children calling for me. Let's go."

As we walk to the side of the building, I feel my blood sugar dropping again. I probably should have eaten more tablets or something else. "I need to use the restroom first."

8

Sal

When Dacre shows up for work in farm-proper shorts and a t-shirt, Pa intercepts him. "Good morning, Mark."

"Good morning, sir." Dacre nods at him. "By the way, my real name is Dacre."

Pa lifts a questioning brow. "O-kay. Nice to meet you, Dacre."

After they shake hands like businessmen once again, I ask Dacre to follow me to the tool trunk by the house.

I take out a pair of pruning shears—the ones with the long handles and thick tips—and hand him the tool. "This is for you."

Dacre studies it for a long time, then gazes at me, waggling the shears. "Who am I supposed to use these on?"

I produce another pair of pruning shears. "The dead."

His forehead wrinkles and his nose pinches up.

"Dead tree branches," I add, pointing my tool toward the trees for effect.

His expression relaxes, and he moves the handles out and in several times, making the tips snap. "I'm ready." He gives me a wide smile, like a kid watching *castillo* fireworks.

"This way." I march with a smile on my face, thinking about Dacre's transformation. No, that's not quite the right word to describe it. I mean, two days ago, he was this tired guy, and yesterday he was this less-tired guy on a scooter that freaked me out. But today, he seems more normal.

"Are we there yet?" he asks after a few minutes of padding behind me.

"Are you turning seven this year?" I ask in a playful tone without looking back at him.

He falls into step. "No, but I'll be a year older by the time we get there." He comes to a stop, and I follow suit. He swipes a few beads of sweat from his neck. "Where exactly?"

"Up ahead." I motion a hand toward the trees at the back of the row.

He glances up at the scorching sun. "Okay."

When we reach the trees, I tell him which branches to cut, choosing the tallest ones.

Dacre cranes his neck. "Shit, I need to go to the bathroom."

This is an ongoing theme. Since day one, he takes breaks all the time. "Do you have a bladder problem?" I blurt out what I'm thinking—hate it when my mouth moves without my permission.

"No," he says, the tone of his voice letting me know the question is none of my business.

"Sorry, I wasn't thinking." I sigh. "I'll wait for you here."

He takes off, and I lift my chin and spot more dead branches way up above my head.

"Dacre!" I call.

Spinning around, he asks, "Yeah?"

"Can you bring back the ladder we used yesterday?"

"Sure." He turns to leave.

Getting to work, I cut a gray tree branch, then another. And another.

Dacre comes back carrying the aluminum ladder, and I instruct him where to put it.

We spend the rest of the day working under the scorching sun, and he keeps taking breaks here and there. And I avoid asking him about it.

When we have two trees left, he lowers his shears and wipes sweat from his forehead. "What time is it?"

I stare at him. "Do I look like a time keeper?"

"I don't have my phone with me." He peers at the sky, late-afternoon sunlight illuminating his face, which seems paler than usual.

I look at the sun hovering above the mountains. "6:42 PM."

"Really?" His gaze drops, and he catches me smirking—it's not even five. "Whatever." He points at the restaurant in the back. "So I'm going to call it a day if that's all right."

Although we have those trees to work on, his expression tells me he's done for the day. "Sure."

I watch him pad away, pruning shears in hand. A

couple of minutes later, his scooter's *potato-potato-potato* sound tells me, "Dacre has left the farm."

Turning my attention to the freshly-pruned trees, I examine them. Healthy. Tall. Tons of fruit. I pat myself on the back for a well-done job. No, not done, because I have more trees to prune. Sigh.

By the time I finish this task, it's a bit dark outside. Dragging my feet, I head to the tool trunk by the house and put my shears away. Then enter a now crowded restaurant, hats all around, the aroma of pastor tacos and *chorizo* permeating the air.

I wave "hi" to my pa, but he's too busy with a customer.

Before leaving, I spot Flor standing behind the counter. She examines her fingernails, as if they hold the answer to the meaning of life. I need to tell her to stop going to the shack—Flor and her boyfriend in it is wrong.

I trudge toward her, contemplating what I'm going to say exactly. "I need to talk to you."

She puts her elbows on the counter's surface, leans toward me, and wrinkles her nose. "You're covered in sweat."

I'm tempted to ask her if she and her boyfriend were covered in sweat the other night but decide against it. Instead, I take off my bandana and glance down at my dirty t-shirt, shorts, and, well, everything me. "I really need to talk to you."

"No can do." She flutters her lashes. "I have a date."

I don't know why her answer makes my blood boil, but it does. "Cancel it."

Flor leans back. "I'm not canceling—"

"Flor, *all* your dates are after midnight." I stifle an eye-roll. "Look for me at my house—it won't take long." I walk away before she answers.

"Some of my dates *are* before midnight," she says behind me, her voice icy.

Pretending I didn't hear her, I wave bye over my shoulder. "See you later." I scurry out and rush into my house.

I take a long shower to relax my muscles and then put on a set of clean clothes.

Right after eight, someone raps on the door. I open it to find Flor with her arms crossed—as if a mere peasant has requested a goddess to arrive. Well, we're both clean now, Flor.

She rolls her eyes. "Well?"

"Come in." I step aside.

She stomps inside and drops onto the living room couch. "Whatever this is, make it fast."

I eye the clock hanging from the wall. "I promise we'll finish talking before midnight."

Flor slouches down and crosses her arms again. "Tell me."

Sitting on the loveseat across from her, I meet her gaze. "It's about the shack."

"What about it?" She straightens herself.

"I want you to stop going there," I say, pursing my lips.

She studies me for a moment and gives me a half-smile. "You're messing with me."

"No" I take a deep breath. "It's wrong to bring your boyfriend there and do … whatever it is that you do."

For a long minute, she doesn't move—doesn't reply. "You're jealous."

"Give me a break. I don't even know your boyfriend."

"No. You're jealous because no one thinks you're girlfriend material." She steps closer and motions at me. "You're always filthy and wear no makeup." She breathes hard, like a bull ready to attack.

I scoff. "How am I going to wear makeup in the 500-degree heat? I'd look like—"

"There's such a thing as waterproof mascara, Sal." She shakes her head. "And…" She stops and shoots me a death stare.

I stand and glower at her. "And?" As I spew out this word, it strikes me that I unleashed the monster inside tame Flor.

She waves me off. "And to think I tried to set you up with a guy."

I shake my head. "I didn't ask you to do that."

"Well, I'm glad it didn't work out." She scans me over thoroughly. "This boy is too handsome for you."

I think she wants me to ask who this mysterious guy is. "I don't care," I say with a shrug.

"Yes, you do." She glares at me.

"Oh, right, I do." I pause. "*Not.*"

"Oh, but you do, Salbatora, you do." She raises a finger. "His name is Dacre."

"Dacre," I echo, then freeze because I know the freaking name. "You can't be serious—he works for me!"

"And you know what else?" she asks.

I fold my arms across my chest. "Enlighten me."

"He totally said no." She wrinkles her nose in disgust. "He doesn't like you."

As if I care. Besides, are we in middle school? I count to ten in my head. "Are you done?"

"No." She jerks a thumb over her shoulder. "I'm

going to the shack tonight."

"Don't—" I start but discussing anything with her will take me nowhere. "Look, Flor. There's a strong reason why I don't want you in there."

She stomps to the couch and drops onto it. "'Enlighten me,'" she says, making fun of what I've just said.

"First of all, you know Tía Matilda lived in the shack until she…" I can't bring myself to say it. "Do you understand what I'm trying to say?"

"But that was last year. I thought—"

I hold out a hand. "You thought wrong."

With all the patience I can muster, I explain to her about my trip to the shack and the plan to tear it down to expand the farm in Tía Matilda's honor. And as I tell Flor that in my aunt's memory, she should stop going there, her mouth opens, as if not believing what I'm saying. To her credit, she stays silent, absorbing it all.

"That's it," I say when I finish, feeling mentally exhausted.

Flor stays mute for a long minute, where the mosaic floor becomes the most interesting thing in the world.

"Say anything." I gesture at her.

She looks up and blinks, then rubs a dyed-red eyelash. "So you and your pa want to honor your aunt and… What are you going to do?"

"I told you—tear it down." I narrow my eyes at her. "But in the meantime, do you promise not to bring your boyfriend there?"

"I … I don't have anywhere else to go." Flor glances at her lap. "I want to be with him alone, and my parents won't let me date."

"I understand," I say, thinking she should do something about it, "but you can't go to the shack anymore."

"But after midnight, everything is closed and we—"

The door swings open, and my pa's belly enters first. "Hi, *mija*." His whole body gets in, and he peers at my friend, who is now looking at him differently. "Hello, Flor."

She springs from the couch. "I was just telling Sal I'm leaving."

Before Pa answers, she scurries out of the house, closing the door behind her.

He glances over his shoulder before showing me a couple of plastic containers. "Look what I brought for dinner."

I force myself to smile, because this whole conversation with Flor left me confused. "Cool. Um, I forgot to tell Flor … something."

"I'll get the table ready." He steps to it and sets the food down.

Rushing out of the house, I spot Flor walking in the distance under the orange streetlight. I dart toward her.

"Hey," I call.

She turns around.

"I really, really want you to stop going to the shack." I take a breath. "Look, you need to tell your parents about your boyfriend."

"You know how they are." She shakes her head. "They'd ground me forever."

"Threaten to leave the house," I start. "Give them something to think about."

She lifts a brow. "Like eloping?"

"No, not like that." I pause to think. "They don't want

you to date because they're being overprotective."

She smiles. "That's an understatement."

"Give them something to think about."

Silence.

"Well?" I narrow my eyes at her.

Flor looks up, as if trying to decide, then lowers her chin. "Okay."

"Promise you won't go to the shack anymore?"

She hesitates for a moment before nodding, as if unconvinced.

I gesture at her. "Say it."

She sighs. "Yes, I promise."

After she walks off, I stroll back to my house, where I find the table ready. I sit next to Pa, and as we have dinner, he tells me about his day, but I'm not really listening and just nod here and there. When we finish, I do the dishes and head to my bedroom.

Dropping onto my bed, I wonder about Flor. She has such a hard time seeing her boyfriend, spending her days at work, and with her strict parents who don't let her date.

But now, she'll confront them, and will have to stop going to the shack.

Enough about Flor's drama. I have to make a plan to teach Dacre about the million things Tía Matilda used to do at the farm. She helped so much and was so energetic, pushing through the day as if it was nothing. Her weathered skin showed how hard she worked.

I remember the day when a swarm of beetles invaded the farm, and Tía Matilda didn't panic the least bit. "*Ten paciencia,*" she told me with that crooked grin of hers. "One avocado at a time."

We worked nonstop all day and way into the night

until we were drenched in sweat and satisfied.

A smile stretches across my face as I think of her.

I think … I think I've covered for her okay, but we do need the help. Producing a notepad and pen from a drawer, I scribble a one-task-a-day list:

1) What to do with the dead tree branches.

2) How to properly water the avocado trees.

3) The mysteries behind avocado pits.

4) Which dirt is the best.

And so on.

By the time I'm done, I have more than two weeks' worth of chores.

So, the following day, I execute my plan, starting with the dead branches' business.

"Didn't we do that yesterday?" Dacre complains, examining the branches spread on the ground.

"Not the putting away part."

He looks at me with a frown. "More like throwing away."

I shake my head. "That goes against the rules."

"Rules," he repeats, crossing his arms.

I take a breath. "Recycling rules—this farm is organic, remember?"

He turns his head to the side. "Where do you put the dead branches?"

"Up ahead." I point toward the end of the trees. "We pile them up into little houses."

"Houses," he repeats.

He can't be this dense. "Habitats for the local fauna. They protect the animals from the rain," I say, feeling like a teacher.

"O-kay." He throws a fist in the air. "Let's save the

world, one dead branch at a time.”

Next day—day two on my list. Watering.

After I tell Dacre about the day's task, he rakes a hand through his short brown hair. “I've already learned how to do this.”

“No,” I say. “I watered the trees and you sort of watched.” I follow with an explanation so long, it leaves him with a confused face.

“All that, huh?” he asks.

“Yep.”

Day three. Fetuses.

“Fetuses?” He lifts a brow, locking his brown eyes with mine.

I cock my head. “Avocado pits—they're like fetuses, you know?”

Dacre stares at me for a long second before shaking his head. “You're weird.”

Days turn into weeks, and he puts in the effort, and kind of fails, far from mastering everything Tía Matilda did. During these weeks, he becomes a friend, I suppose, but I keep wondering about his trips to the restroom. I mean, some days he goes very often, while others not quite. And sometimes I swear his skin is paler than other days. It's like he has an urge to … what? What is it that he does in the restroom?

I shudder as a horrible thought crosses my mind.

What if he's doing drugs?

9

Dacre

I've been pruning trees near the restaurant most of the morning, the sun's rays beaming with intense heat, making me sweat more than usual. Over the past several weeks, Sal has put her trust in me with the avocado trees. Or, at least, she isn't shadowing me anymore.

I clip a small branch and let it plummet to the earth while moving to the next one.

"Dacre?" Sal calls my name when she walks out the back door.

"Yeah," I say, tilting my head down to find her standing below.

She rubs a dirt-covered hand across her violet bandana. "Pa just informed me that the big avocado delivery got moved up to this Saturday. I know it's short notice, but are you able to make it?"

"It's the two-day trip you originally told me about,

right?"

"Yeah, that's the one."

This is actually the best news I've heard in a while. Delivering avocados may not sound like the most interesting thing in the world, but the chance to get away from Mom and Francisco for a few days is a relief. I've only been at the farm a few weeks, and it's starting to feel like a second home—even though Sal does give me weird looks every time I say I need to go to the restroom. The day before, my sugar was pretty high and I kept having to drink and piss—really piss that time—so I just ignored her little side stares.

"I can go." I climb down the ladder and continue holding on to the side as I step to the grass in front of her.

"You sure it isn't too late of a notice?" she asks.

"Nah." I know it may bother her because she likes to stay organized, but I can live on spontaneous moments.

"You'll have to put up with me for a whole two days." She smiles.

"Eh, I deal with you longer than that during the workweek." I tug off her bandana and spin it around my index finger.

Yanking it out of my hand, she places her uniform properly back in place. She reaches up to wipe the sweat from her forehead, pretending like she's going to rub it on my face and I easily move away.

"Can't you shrink a little?" She huffs.

"Can't you grow taller?" I chuckle and lightly shove her shoulder.

The back door to the restaurant swings open, and a person I'm not expecting to see until this evening strolls out. Lach. I move toward him and leave Sal behind.

His blue eyes catch mine and he's smiling, but it's not his usual smile, it's a fake one.

"What's wrong?" I ask after walking the short distance to meet him halfway.

He tugs at his band shirt, his face falling, but he doesn't say anything.

"Did something happen?" I ask, my voice growing more concerned.

He just nods, his eyes growing glassy.

"To Ezra?" My heart speeds up in my chest. I look around, trying to spot Ez's small face and glasses. "Where is he?"

"No, Ezra's fine," Lach says, staring down at the ground. "Mom's fine, too."

"Well, where's Ez?"

He lifts his head to look back at me. "Oh, he's at home with Francisco. His job today got canceled."

My shoulders relax. "Then what's going on?"

Rubbing at his septum ring, Lach then lets out a cry that sounds like he's suffering from a fatal wound. He throws his arms around me. "He—he broke up with me."

Before my arms fully wrap around him, I pull back and place my hands on his shoulders, annoyed. "Did you really come up here during my work shift because your boyfriend broke up with you?"

I know Lach isn't used to relationship situations, but he could have texted me, and I would have called him on break.

"Yes, he did it after we … after we…" Another crack of sobs come out, tears spilling down his cheeks. "I hadn't before…"

Oh shit. Juan's going to be dead. I turn around, remembering Sal is somewhere farther behind me. She's still there, observing the clouds, badly pretending like she hadn't heard the entire conversation.

I gently squeeze his shoulder and lower my voice to a whisper. "The first time is always difficult. You'll be okay."

"It happened to you, too?" he asks, waiting for me to tell him a sob story I don't have. I even think about lying to him just to make him feel better, but I change my mind.

"No, I broke up with her because we were moving. It happened a few times like that."

"So you're just like Juan?" He backs up as if I'm Satan in disguise.

"No! I just wasn't going to do the long-distance thing with anyone. I couldn't predict every time Mom would move!" Sometimes it felt like a blessing because in the long run, I knew I'd have to break up with them anyway because a lot of the time, relationships and diabetes don't jive.

His glare slowly fades away. "Yeah, Mom has made us move a lot."

"Sorry to interrupt," Sal starts, "but we really need to plan the two-day trip for this weekend." I didn't even hear her usually loud feet approach us.

"Two-day trip?" Lach's eyes widen. "Does Mom know?"

"Yeah," I lie.

"You can't go." Lach's deep voice comes out as a squeak. "I need someone to hang out with this weekend."

"Seriously, stop being needy." I roll my eyes.

"Do you have a job?" Sal asks, focusing her attention on my brother.

Oh, I know exactly where this is going. And I wouldn't trust Lach to clean up my room—or any room for that matter.

"No," Lach says, before I can speak up.

"Since Dacre and I will be gone, I'll need someone to help take care of the outside and keep things tidy inside the store and restaurant. Interested?"

"Really?" Lach perks up, no longer a wilted flower.

"Yes, but one rule"—Sal holds up a finger—"you *cannot* touch any of the trees. You'll water them, and then my pa will tell you what to clean inside."

"I can do that," Lach answers, straightening his shoulders. Maybe the workdays will do him good—they're a nice distraction for me, anyway.

"You can go show him around and then meet me back out here," Sal says to me. By her sympathetic expression, it's obvious she's giving me time to make him feel better.

I tug my brother inside the restaurant and try to bring him straight to the break room, but not before passing Flor and the cook. Polo is busily twirling his knife, waiting for a customer, and his eyes meet ours.

"Who is that?" Lach asks, not taking his gaze off him.

"The freaky cook, Polo," I mumble. *And please keep your mouth and hands to yourself for the next few days,* I think.

Flor leans forward across the counter, her red hair pulled into a high ponytail. "Who do you have with you, Dacre?" She grins, displaying her full row of crooked, pearly white teeth.

"My brother," I say. "He'll be working here a few days, apparently."

"Nice to meet you, cutie." Flor bats her eyelashes as I tug Lach to the break room.

I release his arm. "Dude, seriously, you could have texted me. I get how you feel. I mean, maybe not about that, but I get down about shit, too. It's life."

"But I thought I loved him…" He runs a hand through his blond hair and grips it.

"Love is … I don't even know. I mean, I love you and Ez, but people aren't always who they say they are. Or maybe they are but then they change. Maybe he just thought he felt the same way and then after, he didn't." Regardless, if he comes near my brother again, I'll tell him to screw off.

"Juan never told me he loved me—I initiated it," he says, guiltily. "After the shooting at the club, I felt as if life could be taken at any moment, so I wanted to."

"Then you should know that sometimes unless you fully discuss it beforehand, and even then, it may not work out." I've had times where I knew it wasn't going to work out, but I tried to stay longer. Sometimes, it's just better to move on. But since it's my brother, I'm pissed as fuck at Juan.

It makes me wonder about love, and if there is truly such a thing where both people have the same amount equally. I don't think they do, but that doesn't mean it's not there.

"I can't wait to tell Mom about the new job," Lach says, his mood already switching to a new one. "Do you think they'll hire me permanently for weekends?"

I hope not.

"Also, look, I lied out there." I rub a hand across my jaw. "I didn't tell Mom I was going on this road trip because she'd throw a shit fit for no reason. She can find out after I leave."

"What?" His eyebrows slide up his forehead.

"Don't worry, it's a straight shot. We'll stop somewhere for the night, deliver the avocados, and come back." I've been away on longer trips camping at the beach with friends back in Texas.

"Mom will realize you're gone when you aren't there for dinner."

"Okay, then just say I'm working late with Polo or something." I shrug.

"Ah, yes, Polo."

"Knock it off." I lightly tap the back of his head. "Feeling better?"

"Yeah, I'll be okay. Just needed to let it out to you."

"One more thing"—I look toward the doorway—"you can't mention my diabetes up here either."

"And why not? Is someone going to be a bully? Because I'll kick their ass." Lach marches toward the door, and I drag him back by his collar.

"No, I just don't like people hovering or looking at me differently." I've had that too much. Teachers patting my shoulder, kids asking why I got to have snacks and they didn't. It's just easier this way. "So *don't* do it."

"Fine." Lach relents. "See you at dinner."

I walk him to the front door and watch as he heads for his new cerulean moped Mom just got him, knowing that he'll be okay. If I felt that it was really the end of the world for him, then I would stay home from the avocado delivery trip.

Before I go out to the back, Sal's Pa, Gregorio, calls me down the hall from the grocery area. "Dacre, I need to speak with you a moment."

"Yes, sir," I say and stroll over. He's a man of very few

words—I've talked to him maybe twice.

"I know you're going with my Salbatora Saturday morning." He pauses, and I'm ready for him to tell me I better keep my hands to myself or he'll chop them off. "I'm going to put my trust in you that you will keep her safe."

"I will," I say, a bit surprised.

His eyes look sad for a moment. "Sal hasn't told you about her aunt Matilda, has she?"

I try to think if she's ever mentioned the name, and she hasn't. "No."

He lowers his chin, releasing a heavy sigh. "Matilda, my sister, was the one who would do the long run, and Sal joined her since she was around twelve. I'm not going to go into too much detail, but Matilda was like a mother to Sal. She died a little while ago from complications with diabetes."

My lips part and my breathing increases. "Type 1?"

He shakes his head. "No, she had Type 2. She didn't keep up with the disease as well as she should have. Sometimes she wouldn't worry about checking her sugar, other times she'd eat things she shouldn't. I wish I'd been able to help out more, but I'm not the healthiest eater either."

Type 1 and Type 2 are similar in a lot of ways but they are completely different in others. For one thing, Type 2 is milder and doesn't have to use insulin. It makes me wonder what Sal would think if she did know I had diabetes. It's better she doesn't know then, especially if it could remind her about her aunt Matilda.

"I probably told you too much," he says, "but sometimes Sal doesn't say enough. I'd make her stay here, but she would find a way to sneak up on that truck anyway."

"Don't worry, sir, nothing will happen to her." I don't know how much of a bodyguard I can be, but I'll watch her back.

"Thanks, son." He pats my shoulder.

I wander outside, where I find Sal with a large blue notepad, writing things down.

"All right, so this is the list." She goes over our trip in fine detail, even plotting the gas stations, restaurant, and hotel we will be stopping at along the way. We then gather some more avocados to be bought inside the store.

After the last avocado is in the barrel of fruit to be sold, I head home to find everyone already seated in the living room. Mom's home early from work, fidgeting with a crossword puzzle.

"You want to wash up, Dacre?" Mom asks, adjusting her sundress. "Francisco's taking us out to dinner tonight."

"No professional cooking tonight?" I ask. Every night since I've been here, Mom has either cooked with Francisco or he's done it on his own. I hate to admit it, but that part has been kind of nice. Mom's food used to not be so great. But I would take Mom's shitty food over this strange dynamic any day.

"Francisco's been promoted to manager at the moving company, so it's more of a celebration." She beams, stroking his bicep. He has on a shirt, thankfully, a green button-up.

"Mmm." Keeping the rest of the comment to myself, I walk upstairs to wash all the grime and dirt from my body in the hot shower.

I still don't like Francisco, but I'm becoming more

immune to the relationship between him and my mom. Like a person who has to tolerate ants in a yard because no matter how much pesticide you use, there's still insects crawling around in the dirt.

After I throw on my clothes, I head into my room to get my shoes. I find Lach sitting on my bed, fidgeting with his leather jacket.

"Are you all right?" I ask, thinking we had already solved this earlier.

"Not really." He tilts his head to the side.

"It was a dumb question, wasn't it?" I laugh. "Look, you're young, I'm young. I know you want to fall in love and all, but don't rush it. If I see Juan ever again, I'm going to punch him in the face."

"Nah, I'll do it." He smiles. Easy fix for now.

"Come on, baby brother," I say. "Let's pick the most expensive thing on the menu, since it's on Francisco's peso."

"God, you're such a dick to him." He shakes his head and chuckles.

"I can't help it." I shrug. All I know is I feel good. My blood sugar has been great today, which is a rare occurrence.

Lach jerks his head to the door, and we walk outside to pile in Francisco's car. I keep to myself and stare out the window with my forehead pressed against the glass. I close my eyes and listen to Lach making jokes with Ez about his comic book. And I'm just glad he's sounding better for now.

I open my eyes when Francisco turns into a parking lot. The restaurant is nice from the outside, a two-story, chestnut-colored building. Tan paint surrounds three large windows on the second floor—each one has a small balcony set in front of it.

Once inside, the young hostess with her hair pulled into a single long braid takes us to the second floor. We head to a large round table near the balcony window. An orchestra plays over the speakers as we sit down to look over our menus.

After a few minutes, a young waiter appears, asking what we'd like to drink. He's in a button-up, white-collared shirt, with a black apron wrapped around his waist. I tell him a Diet Coke and give him my food order.

Leaning over my chair, I pull out my black pouch from my backpack. "I'm going to run to the restroom really quick," I say to Mom.

"Sure, go ahead." She waves me off and a throaty laugh escapes her lips at something Francisco just said.

I take the glossy wooden stairs down to the first-floor restroom. There's another on the second floor, but I'm trying to waste time, not wanting to hear Mom laughing anymore at Francisco's jokes. I want to feel comfortable about it, but I just *can't*.

Inside the restroom stall, I check my sugar and it's still good, but I give myself a shot in my arm because it will go up after the meal if I don't.

I wash my hands and open the door to head back into the hall. The women's door opens at the same time, and I see a familiar face—or possibly not so familiar. Sal's wearing a black Mexican styled dress that hits right at the knee, a red belt at the waist and various shades of flowers printed along the top.

"Looks like you're definitely a *Sally* now," I say, quirking my lips.

She stops in the hall and just blinks at me, as if she can't believe we could be at the same restaurant. Her face has a little bit of makeup, making her look the same yet a little different.

"Didn't I say not to ever call me that again?" No annoyance in her voice this time, just a small smile.

"I see you moved your uniform up, too." Her bandana—now black—is folded on top of her head, making it more of a headband than when she has it tied across her forehead.

"Pa says it's too much to wear it like I normally do when we come here," she says it in a tone that makes me think she wished she were wearing it how she usually does.

Her gaze falls to the black case in my hand. "What do you have there?"

"Just my stuff." I sure don't feel like having a medical conversation here in the hall and not one that might make her upset.

"Okay." She pauses for a moment, her eyes locked on mine. "You know you can talk to me about anything if you need to."

"Are you hitting on me, Sal?" I ask, to distract her from asking me more questions.

"No!" she whisper-shouts. "Ugh, I knew I should have talked to you about that weeks ago. I *do not* like you like that. Flor is ridiculous."

"I'm just messing with you—I knew what Flor was doing. Lighten up," I say and stroke her headband. "I'll admit this looks cute, but I much prefer it the other way, regardless of how fancy the restaurant is." I tug it down into place to where she looks more like Sal. "Perfect." The left side of my lips tilts up as I stare at her.

She gives me a warm smile but then her eyes fall to the kit in my hand and it falters a bit. I don't understand why.

"See you Saturday, Dacre."

"Bright and early, Sal."

10

Sal

A hand touches my shoulder, making me flip my eyes open to the light coming from my bedside lamp. A man in a lumberjack shirt and jeans stands by my bed.

"Good morning, Sal," Pa says.

"What time is it?" I ask with a yawn, sitting up. "Did the rooster lose his voice?"

He chuckles. "He's still sleeping."

"So, what time is it?" I stretch.

Pa smiles at me. "Time to ax the shack."

I think I heard him wrong. Blinking, I try to get rid of my drowsiness. "Come again?"

"Time to ax the shack." His eyes avert to the window.

Okay, he did say that. I sit on the edge of the bed, grab my phone, and look at the time—4:00 AM. "Why this early?"

He rubs his forehead. "I've been thinking about what

you told me."

I wait because he seems to have more to say, and I hope he's referring to our previous conversations about the shack.

"You're right." He nods. "Tearing down the shack to plant new avocado trees will fulfil Matilda's dream."

"Oh." My heart feels as if it's going to burst because he *finally* came to a decision—we're expanding the farm! Before I get too touchy-feely, I smirk. "Now that you're listening to me, you should get a smartphone to replace your clamshell from the nineties."

Pa caresses my hair. "One thing at a time, *mija*."

"Maybe two things?" I smile at him.

He shakes his head. "Don't push it."

"Okay." I drop onto my bed because as much as I want this to happen, my energy level is on the low side. "I'll wait for Mr. Rooster to sing sweet *cock-a-doodle-doo* nothings to me."

"We need to do this now, Sal," Pa says, firmly.

"But I still have two more hours of sleep," I complain, sounding like a little girl.

"That's not going to work this time," he says.

"Can I go back to sleep?" I smile. "Please?"

He grabs my hand and pulls me up. "Get up, *dormilona*."

Okay, my trying to charm him failed. "Why at four in the morning?"

"Today's a big day, and tomorrow's a bigger day."

"Big day?" I echo like a robot. "Tomorrow? Huh?"

"*Sí, mija*." Pa steps to the door. Before leaving my bedroom, he says, "I'll wait for you outside." He exits without another word.

Big day.

Then it hits me—I need to prep for the delivery to Palenque, Chiapas. The task list I made yesterday pops in my mind, and there's so much to do. The biggest item is to collect the avocados. I mean, for a delivery with so many crates, finding the right avocados will take hours and hours.

Pa's right, so I put on my usual shorts and t-shirt, then slap on an orange bandana over my head, because I feel fiery today—big day, as Pa says. Actually, a big-big day that will kick off the farm's expansion. Lots of work, and new baby trees! With my heart filled with excitement, I exit the house to a dark sky and enter farm territory. In the distance, a flashlight points my way. I trudge toward it.

"Ready?" Pa asks when I join him.

"As ready as I can be." I squint at the light. "Can you point the flashlight somewhere else?"

Pa peers down. And now, without the excess brightness, I realize he looks more like a lumberjack, wearing a helmet with a headband light, and carrying another one and a couple of axes. He hands me the helmet.

This one lacks a flashlight. "How do I look?" I ask after putting it on.

"It's too big for you, but it'll do." He offers me an ax. "Here."

I grab the tool. "It's lighter than I thought."

He lifts his chin, his flashlight blinding me. "You were eleven years old last time you used one. Remember?"

Not a super-nice memory, because he asked me to carry the tool, which at the time weighed a ton. I followed him, dragging my feet, holding it with two hands. He stopped at a dying avocado tree. You can imagine the rest. It still depresses me when a tree dies.

"*Mija?*" he asks, pulling me out of my reverie.

"I remember." I lift the tool. "Let's ax the shack."

He pauses for a second before turning around. "This way."

Leading the way with his helmet's light, he ambles toward the shack by the hill, as if his feet weigh a ton. I follow behind him, because I think he needs the space— I can't even begin to imagine the thoughts and memories going through his mind. Besides, it took him a while to reach this decision, but it's for the best.

When we reach the abandoned house, Pa lets out a heavy sigh, and I wait for him to say something, anything. But he just stays there, studying the shack, swiveling his head ever so slowly. His helmet's flashlight illuminates the wooden planks, broken window, and flat roof.

After a long minute, I clear my throat. "Are you still okay with this, Pa?"

"I … I'm…" As he says it, his voice breaks.

Walking around him, I stare at his face, but his helmet's light blinds me again. "We can do this another day." I keep my voice soft, touching his hand.

He looks down, his flashlight making the dirt on the ground visible, tiny broken fragments that must resemble how Pa feels inside.

Pa lets out a little sob.

Another one.

I didn't know the shack affected Pa this much—he hides his feelings so well. I know he's remembering his sister and how she lived and breathed here for years and years. My heart shrinks in my chest, like grabbing a mature avocado and squeezing it tight. Pa … he's as hard as an avocado pit, and he rarely breaks. But here he is now, showing a whole different side of himself—a melancholic piece of him I wish I could toss into the ocean, so it would never find its way back to my pa. A lump rises in my throat, but I choke it down because, right now, I have to be his pit.

"Pa?" I ask.

He inhales deeply, exhales, and wipes his face, then gives me a little nod—just that, at a loss for words.

I can't stand seeing him like this. I raise my ax and lower it. "Ax. The. Shack," I say in a robotic voice—I move my tool again. "I. Am. Programmed. To. Ax. The. Shack."

He chuckles, his fingers gripping the ax a bit firmer. "I love you, Salbatora."

Before we get too sentimental, I say, "Robo-Sal. Cannot. Love. Back. Ax. The. Shack."

Engulfing me in a bear hug, he kisses the top of my head, then lets go and grabs my shoulders. "Let's ax the shack."

I blink and blink.

"Don't cry, Sal," he says.

"I'm not." I point at the helmet's light. "This robot cannot see."

He turns his head to the side. "Better?"

"Yeah."

Pa pads to the shack's door. "Here it goes." He raises the ax high with both hands, then lowers it with such intensity that I feel as if my own bones are shaking. The door cracks with a dull thump. He tries again. And again. Until what's left of the door crumbles down. He glances over his shoulder, blinding me again. "Your turn."

I step to the side and peer at him. "Destroy. Destroy." I can't help being a robot—I'm prepared to be one. I must be one to be able to accomplish this task without breaking inside. Striking the wood planks, I feel them in my tool's handle. I try again, this time with more force, and crack them apart.

As we continue axing the shack, it occurs to me I'll never forget this moment with him—a father-daughter "quality time." I imagine myself in the future, telling my children—my *human* ones, "Then we axed the shack, and all those trees you see down there are part of the farm's expansion, the one Tía Matilda dreamed about."

When weak sunlight appears on the horizon, part of the shack is a pile of debris, the old stove and bed buried under the wood.

Pa lowers his ax, turns off his helmet's flashlight, and wipes the sweat from his forehead. "I'll hire some workers to finish the job and clean it up."

"How do you feel?"

"Exhausted, but good." He rotates his shoulders.

"Good, as in great good?" I drop my ax and massage my now sore arms. "Or just plain, ole' good?"

"Great good."

"Now that you did this," I smirk, "it's time for you to buy a smartphone."

"*Salbatora.*" He frowns at me for a second then gives me a gentle smile. "Let's go back home."

We pad back, side by side, carrying our helmets and tools, which feel much heavier than before. But somehow my chest feels lighter, the burden dissipating.

"Dacre," Pa says as he puts the protective hats and

axes away in the tool trunk near our house.

I step closer. "What about him?"

Pa turns around. "He seems like a good boy."

"But?" I ask after a moment.

"Just that." He shrugs.

"'Seems' is not the same as 'is.' What is it?"

"It's a long trip." He scratches his ear, a thing he does when nervous, then opens his mouth and closes it—something's bothering him.

"If you're worrying about Dacre trying to make a move, it won't happen." I drop my tense shoulders. "I know him well now, and he's not that type of guy. And, he's not my type of guy, either."

Shaking his head, Pa says, "It isn't that."

"It'll be fine, Pa."

He glances at something over my shoulder. "I don't know."

Silence.

Once in a while, Pa becomes this quiet person, and the only way to get him out of this mood is to bombard him with questions. "Is it Tía Matilda? You're afraid of Dacre's driving? Do you think the avocados will go bad? Do you—"

He holds out a hand. "None of that. The *Selva Lacandona* worries me."

Pa and I went on vacation to the lush Lacandon jungle a while back. Sitting in the middle of Chiapas state, fierce animal predators and dangerous insects inhabit it. Luckily, we went with a group and the tour guide helped us avoid the dangerous parts. "It'll be fine," I say, as an image of a huge, gold-colored cat with black spots appears in my mind. "Actually, I'm looking forward to meeting the jaguars.”

“Don’t joke about that, *mija*.” He puts a hand on his heart. “It’s just a bad feeling.”

“Really, Pa—it’ll be fine.”

“You’re right. Tearing down the shack left me a bit on the emotional side.”

“I understand.” I smile. “But think about how proud Tía Matilda would feel.”

“*Sí*.” He smiles and looks up, as though searching for my late aunt in the sky.

“Okay,” I say after a long moment, “time to go to work.”

Pa lowers his chin and takes a deep breath. “Yes.”

He goes in the restaurant’s direction while I walk toward my avocados to start my morning inspection. I stop by a tree and stand on my tiptoes, trying to reach a sick fruit. “Can you help me with this avocado, Dacre?” As I ask, it dawns on me it’s too early for him to be here. Besides, it’s his free day. I miss him—his sarcasm makes my days a bit more interesting.

Dacre’s grown on me. I mean, when I met him, he was this guy who knew nothing about the farm. Now, he helps me everywhere. This makes me think of school, which starts in about a month. Pa will have to hire extra help or something.

The rest of the morning and part of the afternoon zoom by, and now I have to pick the most suited avocados for the delivery. But I can’t do this alone, so I step into the restaurant, searching for help. The aroma of grilled peppers and pastor beef welcomes me. The place is semi-deserted, and only a man with a handlebar mustache sits at a table, eating a *carne asada* stuffed avocado.

Flor sits on a stool behind the counter, reading a magazine. Although she isn't busy, she's the cashier, so she can't help me.

Entering the kitchen, I find Polo and the line cook, this slim girl in a chef apron. She's new, which isn't a surprise—when it comes to cooking, Polo is a perfectionist. He isn't as tall as Dacre, but he'll have to do.

The girl raises a big kitchen knife and drops it down, splitting a pork chop in half.

"Good," he says to her. "But not quite perfect—not yet."

Her lip quivers as she gazes up at him.

"Buzz-buzz." He motions at her. "Try another one."

I clear my throat. "Are you busy?"

Polo jumps in place and presses a hand to his chest. "You scared me, Salbatora."

The girl bows her head, as if I were royalty, making me feel weird.

"Are you busy?" I point a thumb over my shoulder. "I need help picking avocados."

He crosses his arms. "Not quite my area of expertise, darling."

Glancing at the almost empty tables, I say, "It won't take long."

Polo drops his arms, then rubs his chin.

"Well?" I ask after a minute.

"Keep on chopping the chops," he demands to the line cook by his side.

"Sure, sure, boss," she replies.

Taking off his apron, he dillydallies toward me. "I'm ready."

We leave the restaurant, and I ask him to help me carry

an aluminum ladder while I transport a wooden crate. I lead him to a row of trees. Looking up, I inspect them until I find a good candidate.

"Here." I put the crate on the ground.

Polo sets the ladder by the tree. "I'm already tired."

I take a good look at him—about my age, average build, and his skin is a shade paler than mine.

"I tell you what," I begin. "You pluck the low-hanging avocados while I use the ladder to pick the ones farther up."

"I like that idea." He reaches to the closest avocado, then peers at me. "Is this one good, darling?"

It dawns on me I haven't told him which avocados to pick. So I explain to him how to find the best fruit, and he just stares at me with a dumbfounded expression.

"It's not that difficult," I grumble.

"This isn't quite my cup of shrimp soup." He studies the tree. "What color again?"

"Pale to dark green." I point to an avocado hanging higher up above us. "Like that one."

"What about this one?" He reaches to one hanging a little higher.

I shake my head. "That'll be ripe in about two weeks."

"Good."

After a while, we fill up the crate, so I rush inside to the restaurant area. When I come back with another crate, I find Polo up on the ladder near the top.

"I'm back," I announce.

"Good." He cranes his neck down. "If you don't mind me asking, who's the guy that came with Dacre yesterday?"

"His brother—he'll be working this weekend, actually."

Polo grabs an avocado and climbs down the ladder. "They don't look like brothers." He shakes his head. "He'll be working here? What's his name?"

"Yeah. Lach."

"Lach—it's just a click of the tongue." He puts away the avocado in the crate, seeming too concerned over Dacre's brother instead of gathering the fruit.

Polo and I spend the next hour collecting the right avocados and putting them away in the wooden crates, longer than necessary. It makes me miss Dacre—even with his frequent breaks, he's faster than Polo. By the time we fill up the last crate, it's already dark, and we drag our feet to the restaurant. He scurries to the kitchen while I stroll up front, looking at the people crowding the tables. Flor's busy with a customer—a man scanning her all over.

I head to my house and take a shower, then put on a pair of pajamas. It isn't that late, but I'm waking up early tomorrow. Again, before Mr. Rooster sings to me.

The doorbell buzzes. Pa? Nah, he has a key, but he'll be here soon. With a yawn, I walk to the door and swing it open.

Flor stands there, smiling. "Hey."

"Come in." I step aside.

Closing the door behind her, we kiss each other on the cheek.

"What's up?" I ask.

Biting her lower lip, a victorious expression crosses her face. "I did it."

"You did?" I don't quite believe her.

"Yes!" she says. "I told my parents about my boyfriend last night."

"And you waited all day to tell me?"

"You were super-busy." She looks at the clock hanging from the wall. "I took a five-minute break—I need to make this fast."

I gesture for her to go on.

She nods and presses her back to the door. "When I told my parents about it, Pa got mad—you should've seen him. And Ma just shook her head. They told me how disappointed they were in me and all those things, you know?"

I don't know since my pa has always been like a teddy bear to me. "And?"

"I threatened to leave the house, and long story short, I can see my boyfriend." She grins.

"Oh." I'm tempted to tell her that Pa and I axed the shack but decide against it.

"I need to go."

After she leaves, a sense of accomplishment pulses through my veins. Today's been all about that, tearing down the shack to start the farm's expansion and collecting the avocados for the delivery.

My mind goes to the long trip to Palenque to deliver the avocados. I'm glad I'll have Dacre with me, not only to help with the drive, but for someone to talk to. We'll definitely keep each other on our toes, or at least I will. I think about my going-away dinner with Pa at the restaurant the night before, when I saw Dacre outside the bathroom. Maybe I'm wrong about the drugs. At least, I hope I am.

11

Dacre

"Rise and shine," a voice whispers in my ear. My eyes flicker open and a second later, the light turns on.

"Dammit, Lach, what time is it?" I say when I see him already dressed in a white tank top and loose shorts.

"Four."

I throw the pillow at his face. "We don't have to get up this early."

"You said to load the truck early, remember?"

That's right. I have to get to the avocado farm earlier than my usual time to help fill up the van.

With a yawn, I toss back the covers and take a quick shower. Downstairs, I find Lach in the dining area, pouring himself a glass of orange juice. Courtesy of Lach, the kitchen smells as if something's burning but there isn't any smoke. He already has a stack of French toast centered on the table with two empty plates beside it. Still tired, I grab a plate and plop a few pieces onto it, wishing I had stayed in bed for another hour.

The French toast is a bit on the blackened side but tastes decent enough, just a bit crunchy. Once finished, I grab my larger backpack for the trip. The other night after we got home from the restaurant, I loaded it up with everything I needed except for food. So from the pantry, I drop in a bunch of snacks, a jar of peanut butter, and a few bottled waters.

A thought hits me—how am I going to be able to hide the diabetes from Sal while on the road for two days? There won't be easy access to restrooms, I can't just whip out an insulin needle without her asking me questions, and what if my sugar drops so low that I need her help? *Cool it, Dacre, you've managed to hide it for weeks at work. You'll figure it out.*

"Looks like you're going to be gone for more than two days." Lach slaps the backpack after placing his plate in the sink.

"Right, you don't have to worry about this stuff," I mumble, zipping up the bag.

"Yet, you're still my favorite older brother." He grins and walks into the living room. "You're a survivor!"

"I'm your only older brother," I call.

Lach glances up at the stairs, his smile growing wider. "And there's my favorite younger brother."

Ezra strolls into the living room, wearing too-tight Wonder Woman pajama pants with a baggy Thor t-shirt, and flips on the TV. "You don't have any other younger brothers, and your loud voice woke me up, Lach."

They bicker back and forth as I finish getting ready. Mom's door is still shut when I exit the bathroom,

Francisco's soft snores radiating from their room.

"Bye, Mom," I whisper softly to the door and wave to Ezra as I walk outside.

Lach already has his helmet on with the visor up, seated on his moped. "You don't just want to take my scooter?"

"Nah." I shrug. "You can keep Mom off my back a little longer by saying I'm still at work."

"Okie dokie." He waggles his eyebrows. "She'll never know."

The road is empty, and the street is bare, no sounds except the hum of my moped's engine and Lach's scooter behind me. As I take a right, there aren't any street lamps to light our way, only the full moon above us and the semi-bright light on my scooter.

The wind hits my chest, and I think about Thursday evening at the fancy restaurant. Seeing Sal trying to be someone different than who she is, me pretending most of the time I'm something other than myself. On the other hand, Lach speaks his mind and knows who he is. In fact, my whole family knows exactly who they are.

I shake the thoughts away. At least with me away for the weekend, Mom can enjoy her time with Francisco without me giving off bad vibes.

After pulling into the parking lot, I wait as Lach leisurely rolls in and parks next to me. The delivery van is already backed up near the entrance of the restaurant, the rear doors of the vehicle ajar.

The restaurant door swings open, and Sal scuffs her feet against the pavement, shakily carrying a huge wooden crate of avocados. I hurry over to her to try to help prop up the box from the bottom.

"I've got it," she says, out of breath, her face tomato red under the orange light radiating from the outside lamps. She places the crate on the van's floor, steps inside, and pushes it to the back.

I fish out my phone and see that it's five until six—the sun is starting to peak its way up into the cloudless sky.

"Thought you wanted us here early to help load up the van?" I ask.

"You were taking too long." She hops from the van and dusts off her jean shorts.

"You told us six." I roll my eyes. "Can't read minds, Sal."

"Although, it's something we can always learn," Lach pipes in, peering over my shoulder.

"You driving or me?" I ask Sal, batting my brother away.

"Do you even have to ask that?" She grins.

Before I help with the remainder of the boxes, I walk to the passenger side of the van and set my heavy backpack down on top of the rubber floor mat. Gregorio comes out carrying a crate of avocados, and one by one, we all start to load them up. Between the four of us, it doesn't take much time at all.

After the last crate is safely positioned on the floor of the van, Gregorio turns to face Lach. "I'll have you start with sweeping the floors and cleaning the restrooms for now."

"Sounds great." Lach sounds a little too enthusiastic about scrubbing toilets, but he's definitely genuine about it. As Gregorio walks around the van to talk to Sal, my brother spins to me. "Be careful. I'm going to text you at least every hour.”

“Okay, Mom,” I say and rock his shoulders.

“Someone has to step in for Mom since she *doesn't* know.”

“Yeah, yeah. Just behave yourself. And seriously, focus on the chores.” I have a feeling he may try to keep most of his attention on Polo, but hopefully not.

“Got it.” Lach strides to the side of the van and invades Gregorio’s and Sal’s privacy. I close my eyes and shake my head before hopping into the front passenger seat.

A few moments later, Sal opens the door, plops down into the front seat, and starts the engine.

“Not bringing anything?” I ask, seeing her empty-handed.

“I already have my bag.” She points behind her. And sure enough, there’s a huge backpack that looks like it’s more for hiking than going on a two-day adventure. After tugging out my phone, I take a quick photo and shoot it to Lach.

“What are you doing?” she asks, amused.

“Just making a point to Lach.”

Me: **Whose bag looks more ridiculous now? Mine or Sal’s?**

Lach: **Yours.**

Me: **Yeah right!**

Jerkily, Sal backs the van up and swivels onto the road for the start of our delivery journey. She messes with a few buttons on a radio station until she stops on one playing orchestra music—it’s basically putting me to sleep.

Turning the music down, I plug my phone into the car stereo’s auxiliary input and place it on the dusty dashboard. A song comes through the speakers from my playlist. Sal lifts an eyebrow at me, as if she's wondering why I touched anything. But she doesn't move to swipe the phone to the floor.

"Just relax—it's good." I nestle back into the seat— the orchestra music was too stressful. "I put it on an older rock song. We grew up on this music with my dad until my mom, brothers, and I left for Mexico for good when I was ten."

"The beat sounds nice." I'm not sure if she means it or not. Knowing Sal, if she hated it, she would have blasted the orchestra music to make it out-win my selection.

"Oh, just you wait." I do a quick air drum movement.

"You're something else." She laughs, focusing on the road. "So how do you and Lach speak such perfect Spanish?"

I stare at the few other cars on the road, keeping my attention up ahead. "My mom was going back and forth between Mexico and Texas for the first ten years of my life. Even when we lived in Texas, we had a nanny who would speak only Spanish with us, so we'd know it. My younger brother, Ezra, has been living in Mexico since he was four, so his English actually has a Spanish accent."

"Interesting."

"What about you? How did you learn English?"

"From my pa. I tried to teach an aunt once," she murmurs, suddenly looking sad. My stomach drops, and I think I stopped breathing for a second, but she doesn't' notice. I can't help but remember the other day with Gregorio—I know she's talking about Matilda. The diabetes. But I'm not going to pry it out of her. When or if she's ready, she can let me know. Or not.

"So my mom is dating this total jerk off," I mumble to break the tension and to not dwell on the thoughts between death and diabetes.

"Yeah?" Sal's shoulders relax as she glances my way. "What's wrong with him?"

"He's twenty-one and my mom's forty-one." I cringe just having to say it.

She studies me for a moment and then focuses back on the road, not saying anything. The only other sound besides the music is the slight shuffle of the avocado crates as the van drives over the bumpy road.

"What?" I finally say when her lip twitches.

She runs a hand across her flowered bandana. "You're a total brat, you know that?"

"What?" My eyebrow arches because I couldn't have heard her right.

"Is this guy a jerk to you? Is he bad to your mom?" Her dark brown eyes penetrate mine knowingly.

"Well, no. But he's only a few years older than me. He could be my mom's *son*."

"But is he your mom's son?" Her lip twitches again.

"Dude, come on," I groan.

"He's well over the legal age."

"Please don't put any sex thoughts in my head, or I'll vomit right now all over your precious avocados in the back." I pretend to unbuckle my seatbelt.

Sal lets out a loud laugh that I've never heard from her before, and I hate to admit it, but I like hearing it.

"If you do that," she says, "you'd have to walk all the way back home."

"Nah, you're too nice to leave me abandoned on the

side of the road." Shaking my head, I unzip the front of my backpack to pull out a book to read.

"Not for tainting the fruit."

Leaning my seat back a little, I prepare myself to read for a while.

"I didn't know you like to read," she says it in a way that maybe she didn't know I could read at all. "I mean, you did mention you read *The Hunger Games*, though."

"There are probably a lot of things about me you don't know." I swat her arm with my book. "For example, I like to surf."

"Yeah? Tell me about it."

I close my eyes to think of a day when everything was good when I felt free—the perfect day, the perfect waves. "There was one day in particular when I was ten at the beach in Galveston with my family, right before they split apart." And before I was diagnosed with diabetes. I leave the disorder part out, though, as I look at her and tell her the rest.

"Lach and I were swimming in the ocean with our surfboards, the waves barely moving. We weren't that good yet, but we tried. Ezra had just turned four and was playing with my mom at the shoreline. Dad came out with his surfboard and plopped Lach on it to show him some moves.

"Stroking my way back to the shore, I found Mom and Ezra attempting to build a sandcastle. I joined in to help, as did Lach and Dad when they came a few minutes after. All of us worked together as if we were one unit by putting a piece of ourselves into that sand. But the thing is, sand doesn't keep its form forever, not when there's an ocean nearby to knock it down.

"Nothing was perfect then, and behind closed doors it was even less. But that day, I like to pretend it could have changed one of my parents' minds. Maybe one of them could have decided to give up their job because family was more important, but neither wanted to sacrifice it. And life should be about sacrificing. Lord knows Lach, Ezra, and I have had to sacrifice our lives for our mom's career—for Dad's new family. And maybe that's why I'm so bitter at times.

"Mom wants to be happy and for all of us to appreciate Francisco, when she took away from us what could have been."

Sal stays silent for a long time, and maybe I told her too much, went a bit too deep—apparently made her my psychologist.

"Grab an avocado from the back," she finally says.

"An avocado," I echo.

"Yes."

Confused, I unbuckle my seatbelt and grab a fruit from a crate.

"My gift to you." She smiles softly.

"You're giving me one of your babies?" She once thought I wanted to steal them, but here she is giving me one now.

"The company can do with one less. We always add a few extra, and you deserve it."

"How generous of you. Are you sure you aren't breaking your bank?" I laugh, shutting one eye and bringing the fruit up to my open one. "You know I don't like avocados that much, right?"

"Give it back to me." While keeping her eyes on the road, she reaches half-heartedly to grab it out of my

fingertips, and I tear my hand away before she can grasp
it.

"Too late—you already gave it to me. It's all mine now,
and I'll cherish it forever."

She shakes her head and I stick the fruit inside my
backpack.

"Seriously, thank you."

"You're welcome, Dacre."

Quietly, I lift my book and read for about thirty
minutes, when I'm interrupted by Sal slamming on the
brakes. My body jerks forward then crashes into the seat.

"Why did you do that?" I groan, rubbing my neck and
then staring out the window. There, I catch sight of a
black plastic trash bag, lying in the middle of the road.

Sal unbuckles her belt and opens the door.

"You know you can just go around the black bag," I
say, smirking.

"Then we might be missing out on the hidden
treasure." She laughs and hops to the ground.

"If garbage is your treasure, have at it."

She shuts the door, and I let out a sigh because I
should go out there just to make sure she doesn't find
dead body parts or something. Body parts have been
found in trash bags before, after all.

I quickly catch up to her. "So, what kind of treasure
are you looking for, anyway?"

"One that will hopefully help me expand the avocado
farm."

We stop in front of the bag, and I reach down before
she does, ripping it open. No point in slowly teasing
ourselves.

"Well, there's your treasure." I roll my eyes, staring at

crumpled old clothing.

"Well, it *is* somebody's," she shoots back.

"Gone now." I check my phone to see what time it is and see a few texts from Lach. Then my shoulders stiffen. I forgot to give myself a shot this morning before I ate. How could I forget that? "Is there a gas station close by?"

Sal snakes out her arms to retie the bag. "Not for a while."

I could just say I need to take a piss really quick, but then I'd have to go and grab my diabetes kit from the van which would just seem ridiculous. It looks to be my only option, though.

Sal glances at me as she lifts the bag. "I'm going to move this to that gravel spot up ahead in case someone comes back for it."

There's a small spot several yards ahead that looks as if it could be a small rest stop for a single car.

"All right." I head back to the van to hurry and dig out the stupid kit. It's too bulky to shove in my pocket so I thrust a needle and the bottle of insulin there instead.

When I turn around, Sal is standing there, staring at my hands.

"What are you doing?" she asks.

"I need to go to the restroom," I say. "Can't really hold it."

"Oh, I thought I saw you shove something in your pocket."

"Yeah, Lach's messaging about work." I hold both my thumbs up. "Loves it!"

"O … kay," she drawls as I turn and walk to find a tree to wallow behind in my idiotness.

12

Sal

Peering at Dacre as he heads toward a tree by the road, I turn around and wait with my arms crossed for him to take care of business, a business he loves to visit way too often, which leaves me completely baffled. A minute later, he strolls back, carefully wiping his hands with a towelette—so convenient of him and good—don't want to shake hands after he did what he did, and touch what he touched.

Ready to get a move on, I get in the van. "Ready to continue our adventure?"

Taking shotgun, he slams the door closed. "Oh, yes, gearing up for the avocado orphans to meet their new home tomorrow."

Starting the engine, I take off, and Dacre doesn't say much as I concentrate on the road. Moments of silence pass, and the toll road appears up ahead. As I join the other cars, traffic slows down to a stop as we approach the first tollbooth.

"Is it always this slow?" Dacre breaks the silence.

"Yep." I turn my attention to him. "Can you get two-hundred pesos from my bag?"

Twisting to the side, he produces the two one-hundred-peso bills and hands them to me.

The cars behind us honk, which makes me look at the road—the lane is advancing now at a decent pace.

When we reach the tollbooth, the woman inside it extends a hand, palm up. "One-hundred and eighty-nine pesos." The serious tone in her voice and her security-guard uniform mean business.

I hand her the money, and she gives me a few coins and a receipt in return. She motions for us to move, and we go through the tollbooth.

As I drive away, we pass an eighteen-wheeler, and the traffic gets lighter. From the corner of my eye, I catch Dacre pointing out the window at the speed-limit sign outside—110 kilometers per hour.

"Texas has faster highways," he says.

I glance at him for a moment. "How much faster?"

"Fifteen miles per hour faster."

Okay, I have to think about that because I'm not used to miles. I do the math in my head—eighty-something miles per hour. "At that speed, cars must fly."

"Yeah, cars have feathered wings and everything." He rolls his eyes at the ceiling. "But, really, you can drive above ninety."

Again, I'm trying to do the math, but it isn't that easy, though I remember this movie where the character was in a Mustang and hitting 170 kilometers per hour—more than 100 mph. It seemed like a good way to die.

"You should go there one day," he adds.

"Yeah." I don't tell him how hard it is to get a US visa. Besides, if I had the money, I'd rather travel to Europe. "Have you ever been to Spain?"

"Nope. Have you been to Australia?"

"I haven't been out of Mexico." I check on him for a brief moment—he has his hands behind his head, relaxing, I guess. "I'd like to go to Spain."

"Where in Spain?" he asks.

"Barcelona—I love Gaudí," I say, concentrating on the road.

"Who?"

I can't believe he hasn't heard of him. "A Catalán architect. His buildings—"

He chuckles. "I know who he is from History last year—I was messing with you. The *Sagrada Familia* temple is impressive. I'd like to go to Spain, too, but first I want to go to Australia."

"Do you have a soft spot for koala bears?" I ask, smirking.

Shaking his head, he replies, "I have a soft spot for big wave surfing."

"That's cool." I imagine him standing on top of a surfboard, his arms stretched to the sides.

"I also want to ride the big waves in Oahu."

"Where's that?" I ask.

"Hawaii. Also, there's California. Oh, and let's not forget Indonesia, Bali, South Africa, Costa Rica, and Morocco." He grins one of the widest smiles I've ever seen on him. "Imagine yourself lying on a white-sanded beach with your eyes shut, listening to each wave speak to you as it strikes the shore. What that is right there, is Mother Nature telling you all her secrets, but we just don't know the language yet."

It's like I uncorked a bottle cap and let his special interest—his passion—pour out. "Do you want to become a professional surfer?" I ask.

"Um, well, I'm actually not that great at it. But it's one of my escapes," he explains. "What about you? What makes you tick?"

I look at him. "I'm not a clock."

"You sure about that?" He smiles "What's your passion?"

I turn my attention back to the traffic ahead—cars, trucks, and the lush trees at the side. "You know what my passion is, Dacre."

"Your children?" he says.

"Yep." I think of our interests—waves and avocados. So different. Maybe not, because avocado trees grow in tropical countries. Not that all of the surfing destinations are in tropical countries, though. But close enough.

I fiddle with his phone. "Do you like Brahms?"

"Who?" he asks.

"You know"—I glance at him—"Johannes Brahms, the famous music composer."

"What kind of music did he compose?"

"Classical."

He sighs. "Like the orchestra music you played a while back?"

"It's called classical music—not orchestra." I shake my head, take a breath, and look at him. "You're right. Orchestras play classical music, but orchestra music encompasses all sorts of genres. It's like calling techno music rock music."

He massages his neck. "That's interesting…"

A sound makes me squint my eyes at the window. Great—a flying bug just splattered against the windshield. I decide against playing classical music because Dacre doesn't seem interested. I don't blame him, because this kind of music is an acquired taste. In my case, I grew up listening to Pa playing old LP records of Mozart, Beethoven, Brahms, and my favorite, Igor Stravinsky.

After endless kilometers have passed us by, I spot a rusty sign advertising a restaurant. "Dacre?"

"Yes, Sal?"

I look at him. "Are you hungry?"

"Starving. I'd even take it to the point and say you read my stomach." He glances down at his flat stomach. I remember what it looks like under the shirt.

"There's this place I found on the internet. It has great reviews."

He nods. "Do you have to plan everything?"

Paying attention to the road, I shrug. "Of course. Plus, the restaurant is close."

A few minutes later, we exit the highway, joining a two-lane black road. A big *palapa* with a sign stands up ahead—our eatery destination. I slow down the van, veering it to the right, so we can enter the gravel parking lot in front of the restaurant.

"Here?" he asks.

"Yep," I say, parking the van.

Dacre steps out first, taking the drawstring bag he always carries with him.

"Leave it in the van," I point out.

He raises a brow. "Don't want it to get stolen."

"Why? Are you carrying precious jewels?"

"Something more valuable." He clutches it against his chest in an overprotecting manner.

"Gold?" I ask, digging, because he never lets go of it, like he's hiding a treasure.

His eyes widen. "How do you know?"

I refrain from rolling my eyes. "Really, what's in the bag?"

"Snacks, hand sanitizer—that kind of thing." Dacre shrugs. "In case of an emergency."

Obviously, he doesn't want to tell me about his mysterious bag, and I'm fine with that. Am I? Whatever he's got in it couldn't be that expensive. Besides, he could shove the bag behind the seat and it would be safe. I mean, this parking lot looks pretty safe. Safe? Now that I think of it, you never know what could happen here, so I let this detail slide.

Together, we stroll inside the semi-crowded restaurant. Metallic white tables with beer advertisements on top are scattered here and there, red plastic chairs surrounding them. In the rear, cooks with tongs stand behind a big grill, the aroma of grilled beef lingering in the air.

A hazel-eyed girl about my age in skinny jeans and a tight blouse approaches us. "How many?"

"Two," I reply.

"This way." She turns and leads us toward a table, swaying her hips like a model on a catwalk.

From the corner of my eye, I spot Dacre checking out her butt, which makes me wonder if he checks out mine. The answer is probably yes—he's a guy. But in the butt department, this girl wins.

"The waiter will be here shortly," the girl says before

walking off.

The plastic chair squishes as I sit down while Dacre takes the one in front of me.

"I don't bite," I say.

"What?" he asks.

I tap the chair next to mine. "Sit closer."

"Uh, all right." He gives me a weird look but takes a seat beside me.

Last week, we talked about how in the US, people like to keep their distance, while in Mexico, there's no concept of personal space—we like it that way.

He glances down. "Why is it that some restaurants here don't have floors?"

I peer at the dirt ground. "That's how all the *campirano* restaurants are."

"*Campirano?*" he echoes.

"For a guy that knows Spanish left and right, you should know what that means."

He tilts his head to the right. "Entertain me with this new knowledge."

"It means…" I have to think how to say it in simple words—got it. "Rustic."

"Rustic it is." He grabs a plastic menu atop the table and inspects it. "What's good here?"

"Potatoes," I reply.

"Like baked potatoes?" He crinkles his nose.

"Kind of. It's actually, stuffed potatoes." I eye the grill in the back. "They're filled with beef, pork, or—" I motion at his menu. "Look it up."

A guy wearing jeans and a t-shirt, carrying a little notepad and pen, shows up. "Do you know what you want?"

"I want an *horchata* and the pastor-stuffed potato," I say.

He jots down my order then turns his attention to Dacre. "You?"

"Still looking." Dacre puts his menu up to his face, staring over it intensely, as if it were Egyptian hieroglyphics.

The waiter—I guess he's one—stands there, waiting.

"Can you give him a minute?" I ask.

"No, I'm ready," Dacre says, then to the waiter, "I want the *asada*-stuffed potato without the potato and a Diet Coke."

"No potato?" I jerk my head toward Dacre.

He shrugs. "Potato tomato."

"It's tomato potato, and this place specializes in potatoes—that's what they're famous for."

"Potatoes are overrated."

"No, they aren't." I nudge his shoulder. "C'mon, eat one—you'll love it."

"No can do."

"Really?" I can't believe he won't at least try this delicacy—everybody I know loves stuffed potatoes. Or maybe he's one of those snobs who thinks he's too good to try some things.

"Am I committing a potato crime?" He rubs the side of his head. "I just can't right now."

"No, for real," I push. "Is this like a religious thing?"

Dacre lets out a frustrated sigh. "It's just food. And I said *no*."

His reply makes my blood boil, and I've never seen him this cranky. I take a deep breath, because I don't want to say something harsh in return. "Dacre, I'm sorry."

The waiter clears his throat. "So, have we decided or do you guys need more time?"

"Do you have anything un-potato?" I ask.

"We have *asada*, un-potato style," the waiter says, tapping a pen against his notepad.

"Sure. That will work." Dacre still has a hand against his temple and won't look at me.

The waiter nods as he writes down Dacre's order then turns to leave.

"You're gonna like your food," I say, trying to lighten up the mood. "Even *without* the potato."

Closing his eyes, Dacre takes a deep inhale. "I'll take your word for it."

"We should go to the restroom now," I utter.

"It smells great there, too?" He smirks.

I nudge his shoulder. "No." I wrinkle my nose. "We should avoid gas station restrooms to the max."

"You're right. When I was younger, I went to one and found this big—"

Holding up a hand, I interrupt him. "Too much information."

Dacre and I head our separate ways to take care of business. *Again*, for him. When we come back to our table, our meals are already there, along with small containers with red, green, and brown salsas.

"Looks good," I say, plopping back down.

"Let's find out." He places a large piece of *asada* between his lips as I watch in anticipation. "It's good."

Peering down at the potato on my clay plate, I point at the different salsas. "It's better if you pour some of these on it."

"I only recognize the *pico de gallo* and guacamole salsas."

He points his fork at a container. "What's that?"

"Not for you," I say. "It's cucumber-habanero salsa."

"Do you think I'm too *American* for it?" He grins.

I scoop up some spicy salsa and pour it over my potato. "Be my guest."

"Sure." He takes the container and drenches his *asada* in salsa.

"Oh, yeah?" I snatch the container and add more cucumber-habanero spiciness to my food.

"Not enough." He grabs the salsa and pours even more.

It's like we're back in middle grade, competing. And it's kind of fun, but I wonder if we'll lose our taste buds in the process. At this point I don't care—I want to win.

He motions with his fork. "Dig in."

"Sure." I spear a potato chunk and eat it. The lime's sourness combined with the habanero spiciness makes me grimace a bit. "Your turn."

Taking the metallic fork by his side, he digs it into the meal and slides it into his mouth. He nods at me, chewing, and a second later he scrunches up his face. "Good," he says as his nose and cheeks turn red. "It's good."

Putting an elbow on the table, I rest my chin on my open hand. "It doesn't look that good."

"It is." His face flushes, even darker, bordering on purple.

I push my clay glass his way. "Try this."

He shakes his head, sweat beads appearing on his forehead.

"*Horchata* has milk." I gesture at the glass. "That should help."

Eyeing my drink, he takes it and studies it as if it were

poison, then sets it down and fans his face.

"Are you too American for this salsa?" I chuckle.

"No." He exhales. "Yes? Yes!"

"Want more?" I lift my plate under my nose and sniff it. "Mmm, mmm."

His eyes open wider, and he curls a hand and puts it over his mouth.

Setting down my meal, I try another piece. "Delicious."

Dacre stands so fast, his knee hits the metallic table, almost making it topple. His plastic chair drops down, and without a word, he storms toward the restroom area.

Maybe I pushed him too hard. Or perhaps Moctezuma's revenge hit him—happens all the time. But no, he's used to Mexican cuisine. Resting my elbows on the table, I cup my head in my hand and sigh. I guess he'll be fine, but I don't think he'll want his meal anymore— such a waste. I eat mine, trying to finish it before he comes back, because the sight of it may cause him to puke. *Is he really puking?* As I think of this, I imagine him kneeling in front of a toilet, throwing up. I gag—not the most pleasant of pictures.

Taking a napkin, I wipe my forehead and cheeks with another towel. This salsa is hot, even for me, but I'll be fine.

My stomach growls.

I cough.

Hotness engulfs my throat.

Grabbing the *horchata*, I drink it down, but something inside me pushes it up, making me cough and heave.

I rush to the restroom and do exactly what I pictured Dacre doing in my head moments ago—puke it all out.

After emptying my stomach, I step to the sink, throw

water on my face, and exhale. I look at my image in the mirror. I'm the definition of *morena* with my brown skin and black hair, but the face reflecting on the silver glass surface shows a paler girl with dark-brown eyes. I shake my head quickly and blink.

That habanero won this round.

After drying my face with a towel, I drag my feet back to our table, where Dacre is already seated. I drop on my chair, and examine his face—skin a tad paler, too. We gaze at each other for a second before downing our drinks.

Dacre concentrates on my face.

"What?" I ask.

"So." He brushes lint from his shoulder. "Are you not Mexican enough for the habanero salsa?"

"Shut up," I say with a smile.

"Should we order something else?" His eyes tear away from mine and toward the grill.

"Hell, no!"

I explode in uncontrollable laughter while Dacre looks at me as if I'm crazy. Wiping tears from my eyes, I point at him, then say to the people behind the grill, "He told me the hot potato joke."

That makes one of his eyebrows slide up. "Don't worry," he tells the staff. "I don't get my own jokes either."

Taking a deep breath, I calm down. Still, my jaw hurts from laughing. "Let's go."

"I'll drive," he says after we leave the restaurant.

"Sure." I hand him the keys, partially glad to take a break, partially not wanting to give up the control.

"We're gonna need to stop at a gas station for food."

"Yeah." I smirk. "Hot potato chips."

Dacre rubs his jaw, fighting a smile. "Habanero

flavored seems the way to go."

13

Dacre

After the dining disaster, we walk back to the van and I turn to Sal. "Can you take over driving?"

She snatches the keys from my hand and stares at me with what might be concern. "Why the change of heart?"

"That salsa did a number on me." Really, it's because my vision still feels a bit blurry from my sugar being high.

Sal clucks her tongue and makes a face. "Don't remind me."

Hours pass as the sky grows dark, and my eyelids start to close when she shakes my shoulders, jolting me wide awake again. "We're here, sleepyhead."

Sal eventually pulls into probably one of the seediest motels I've ever seen—Hotel Carmelita. Okay, maybe it's not bad, but it's still pretty rough. Part of the roof dips inward, and some of the doors on the rooms seem to be missing. I don't know how the building hasn't been shut down.

A couple seems to be going at it in one of the cars with the windows fogged up as we pass, but I don't point that part out to Sal.

"I thought you said *a hotel*," I say.

"I did." She's already looking at her phone after she puts the car in park. "Hold on."

I check my own and see a stream of text messages.

Lach: **Mom knows. Sorry I couldn't hold back when she asked.**

Me: **All you had to do was say I was with Polo.**

Lach: **Well, then she would think you were with Polo and what if I wanted to bring Polo here.**

Me: **Are you bringing Polo there?**

Lach: **No, we didn't talk, but it could happen.**

I inwardly sigh and move on to a text from Mom.

Mom: **You better be home in the next hour.**

Well, it's only been fifty-eight minutes since the text, so I'm good.

Me: **Sorry, it would take a lot longer than that. I'll be home once we finish the delivery.**

Last, there's one from Francisco.

Francisco: **Your mom's worried. Please come home.**

Jesus Christ, they're acting like I'm a runaway who's been gone for weeks. Give me a damn break. I'm seventeen on the verge of eighteen, not nine.

My phone beeps.

Mom: **You're grounded.**

I roll my eyes and glance over at Sal who's still doing something on her phone.

"Well?" I ask.

She shoves the phone in my face and I take it. Hotel Carmelita. I scan through the info about the place. So the first red flag I see is there are absolutely no pictures of the hotel or most of the inside, only one of what may be a room that has a painting of Diego Rivera dangling on the wall, crookedly. Then I see the rating and the reviews.

"It has four-point-three for the rating, Sal, but did you even look at the reviews? There's four, and you can tell most of the customers came for the happy mattress time. And you picked this dump?"

"Give me that." She tears it from my grasp and gives it a hard examination.

"Great choice with food. Even better choice with hotel—correction, motel." I grin, tapping the ends of my fingertips together.

"How was I supposed to know?" Her voice cracks. "The picture looked good! The place sounded nice in the paragraph."

"Maybe the inside will be better." Um, I highly doubt it, but a little self-confidence will get her out of the van. Actually, maybe it would be better if I slept in here, if I didn't have to sweat all night.

"Yeah." She shrugs.

We both grab our bags. The van's parked in the front of the building, so I hope no one breaks in and tries to steal the avocados. But at least Sal does have an alarm on the vehicle.

"You sure you don't want to drive straight there?" I ask. "I can take back over."

"No. The place won't be open anyway."

I adjust my backpack and follow her inside. The lobby's small—a couple of fluorescent-orange chairs sit to our left with a dusty fake palm tree centered in between them. A colorful straw mat is spread across the tile floor, leading us to the check-in desk straight ahead.

When we get to the counter, it's empty. Sal rings the wait-for-service bell. After about a minute of zero response, I continually tap it until Sal rips my hand away.

"Can you stop? That's embarrassing," she hisses.

Heavy footsteps echo from somewhere in the back. "Got the person's attention, didn't it?"

Sal stares up at the ceiling as if I didn't say anything, so I give her a smirk.

A man in his sixties with receding hair and a tropical button-up shirt approaches the mess of a desk. "Sorry," he says with hot pink lipstick spread across his cheeks and mouth. "I had some work to do."

That he did, I think, feeling amused.

Sal just frowns. "I called in the other day and reserved a room. Salbatora Tames, but it will be under my dad's name, Gregorio Tames."

She finishes checking in and the man hands her two cards to the room. As we turn around, a couple strolls in—a woman with her hand around a man's waist. The middle-aged woman wearing tan pants with a matching vest approaches the desk. "We need a room for an hour."

"Great place, Sal," I say as I walk behind her back outside.

"Shut up," she groans.

Chuckling, I find our room number is in front of the building near the van, so we leave the vehicle parked there.

We take the stairs to the room on the second floor. Thankfully, when Sal opens the door, cool air hits our faces.

She turns on the light, and the room looks as though it hasn't had an update since the sixties, if this place was even built here back then. They might have just gotten hand-me-downs from somewhere.

Shutting the door behind me, I drop my backpack beside a cabinet with a small box TV resting on top. I dive onto the bed, the springs making a loud clang. "Time warp."

"Hmm?" Sal asks, messing with the window unit and attempting to turn it up a little.

"Tonight, we're taking a trip back to 1965."

"I guess the unit has no way to up the temperature." She huffs but crashes down on the mattress right beside me.

I take a good look at the room. The old-school, boxy TV on top of a dresser, a small eating table with two rolling office chairs in front of it. And one bed.

"Where's the other bed?" I ask, propping my back against the headboard.

"There isn't one." She rolls to her stomach. "Two beds weren't available."

"What? And your pa was okay with this?" I can't see Gregorio agreeing to that, but I couldn't imagine him letting his daughter go on a two-day road trip with a teenage guy either.

"He doesn't know. They only needed to verify with him for a second on the phone."

"Sal the rebel."

"It's just a bed—we're not naked in a hot tub."

I stare at her for a second too long, and yeah, because I'm a guy, I may have imagined her differently for a second. But I brush that shit away because it's Sal, and she

146

wouldn't need a diabetic on her plate anyway.

Leaning over the mattress, I try to reach for my backpack, but it's too far away. I make a grunting noise as I stretch for it.

Sal gets off the bed and picks my bag up for me. "You can't be that lazy to where you need someone to hand it to you."

"So I was thinking"—I unzip my backpack—"we should have a toast to our lovely stay you picked out and make up for the restaurant debacle earlier."

She peeks over my shoulder into my bag. "Did you bring *alcohol?*"

"No, I think you'll like this better." I pull out the avocado she gave to me in the van and set it on the bed between us.

Sal folds her legs into a crossed position and I do the same.

"That's your gift!" She pushes it closer to me.

"Eh, I want to split it. You did lose your lunch earlier, but then again you did choose the place."

She shoves my shoulder and I bite my bottom lip, holding back a smile.

"Might have to use your hands though," I say. "I didn't bring any spoons."

"Well, isn't it your lucky day. I just so happen to have some." She rolls off the bed and lifts her hiking bag. Opening up a compartment on the front, she takes out a clear Ziploc bag filled with plastic utensils.

"Okay, you're such a nerd sometimes."

"Nope, I'm just prepared." She digs out two plastic spoons and a single knife. Then from her backpack, she fishes out two napkins and salt packets from a separate bag.

I take a napkin and knife from her lap and move to the table. As I sit on one of the rolling desk chairs, I press my hands against the wood, and the table wiggles. I'm lucky both pieces of furniture stay intact. Placing a paper napkin on the table beside a long scratch, I start to slice around the avocado with the knife as Sal silently watches in the seat across from mine.

"Left or right?" I ask.

She closes her eyes and moves her index finger side to side, stopping on my right. "Your right side."

I pry the pieces apart. "Loser," I say, placing the fresh piece of fruit on her already open napkin.

With my plastic spoon, I scoop out the large seed and set it on my napkin. I take a few bites, not as impressed as Sal is with the avocado because hers is already gone. The doctor had once told me that, yes, avocados are a fruit, but they're actually good for diabetics if eaten in moderation since there's barely any sugar in them and the carbohydrates are low. Too bad I can't agree to eat them on an everyday basis.

"Here," I say and scoot the rest of mine toward her, with my spoon sticking out from it. I'm not a huge fan of their bland taste anyway, but I don't want to break her heart by saying it again.

"Sure?" She pours salt out of the packet onto the avocado.

"Yeah," I reply, but she's already digging into my side of the fruit—with *my* spoon, where my lips have been, where her tongue now is. *What the hell?* I shake off where my thoughts are going because I'm becoming a little flustered by possible sex thoughts. I need to go somewhere, away from that spoon and her mouth.

"I'm going to the bathroom." I pause to think about how I'm going to get to my bag to get my diabetes kit to check my sugar. "And brushing my teeth."

"Okay." She gives me a weird look as if my pause was an odd thing to do, which it was.

Taking the napkin with the avocado seed, I stuff them both into my pocket. I keep my back turned to her as I grab the diabetic kit and things for my teeth from my backpack before heading into the bathroom.

The small interior isn't that bad—white floor. But the grout, which should be ivory, is more of a patchy black in areas. I run the water at the sink so she doesn't hear the beep of the meter or me pricking my finger. It takes me a couple times with the lancet device to draw the blood. I ignore the sting of my finger because my sugar is right on track.

From my pocket, I retrieve the napkin with the seed gently wrapped inside. I wash it with the cool water, removing all the fruit residue. Quickly drying the seed, I place it inside my kit for now. I'm not sure why I want to keep it exactly, but I suppose it's a reminder of a deeper conversation that happened in the van—a piece of a gift that's meaningful to Sal.

Someone who is becoming a good friend. *Friend.* The weird thoughts from earlier have been tossed aside.

After I brush my teeth and step out of the bathroom, I find Sal with folded clothes in her hand, a bra and a pair of panties resting on top.

"What are you doing?" I ask, staring at the pink bra.

Her eyes meet where mine are focused. She rolls her eyes and places the shorts on top, covering the undergarments. "I'm going into the bathroom to change and come out to seduce you," she coos.

My eyes widen.

"Seriously, Dacre, I'm going to take a shower."

"Oh, okay, that makes sense," I say, because that's all I can think of. "I'll take one in the morning, then. I'm going to get ready for bed."

"I'll give you a pass since we were in the van most of the day." Her gaze falls to the kit in my hands. "Did you brush your teeth fine?"

"Yeah, extra minty."

Without another word, Sal arches a brow and heads into the bathroom. I tug off my shirt, shoving the rest of my clothes beside my boxers into my backpack. I hop onto the bed, turn on the TV, and grab my book to read for a while.

All that's on is a bad telenovela, a *futbol* game, and a few infomercials. Not many options here—I wouldn't have expected anything less. I watch the end of the game, and then a news report comes on. The reporter rambles about a shooting, drugs, and then she starts talking about healthcare. The screen turns to a man discussing his Type 2 diabetes, and the news reporter then starts dramatizing about how it's the leading cause of death in Mexico. This is the part I don't like to think about because if so many people here die from complications with Type 2, then how easy would it be for something to happen to me if I didn't keep up with the process?

The bathroom door opens after Sal taking an excessively long shower. I hurry and flip the channel because I don't want her to see the news report and have it remind her of Matilda.

She strolls toward the bed without a bandana, short hair wet and combed to the side. She's wearing a lime-green t-shirt, but my attention drops to her shorts.

"Are those avocados?" I ask, fighting back a laugh and setting my book on the table.

"Heck yeah, they are." She rakes a hand through her hair, and her eyes stop on my chest, causing her to freeze. "Why are you *naked*?"

"What?" I look down at myself.

She averts her gaze. "You have *no* clothes on."

"Correction. I have shorts on."

"Yeah, underwear!"

"Hence, not naked. But I can pull a shirt back on if it will make you feel more comfortable. This is how I normally sleep." I could understand if I had on bikini underwear or something, but these boxers pretty much look like shorts.

"No." She waves me off. "I'm fine. If this is how your usual get-up is. Actually, it's a little cold in here." She shivers and tries to mess with the window unit again. "Okay, never mind. Apparently, you still can't change the setting on this one."

Letting out a deep breath, Sal turns off the light and I pull back the covers for her. "If it makes you more comfortable, I'll sleep on top and you can under. I'm not cold at all—actually, I'm practically burning up."

"Try anything and you're dead," Sal says, pushes in beside me, and drags the comforter up to her chin, teeth chattering.

"I promise I'm not making a move." I roll my eyes. "But if you're that cold you can scoot closer. A little skin-to-skin contact never hurt anyone." Why the hell did I say that? Who even says that?

"That won't happen." She laughs and rolls over to her side.

I close my eyes and try to sleep, but I can't. My body's growing warmer and right when I'm about to get up to drink some water, a body tackles me back down—in her sleep.

Sal seems comfortable, but I don't want to wake her up because she would be horrified knowing she was doing this in her sleep, like I am now since I don't know what the hell to do with my arms. She's crushing one, the other is gripped under her arm, and her teeth are no longer chattering. So I close my eyes because sometimes you have to sacrifice yourself for a friend. It's not like I'm a warlock tied to the stake or anything—I want to help her.

A few seconds later, there's a loud mewl through the wall. My body stills. Then a rough growl and groan follow as a loud creaking of the bed rattles from the room next door. I know Sal's awake because her body shifted and then froze against mine.

"Great choice for a motel," I mumble to break the tension because I don't want her to feel embarrassed either.

"Shut up, Dacre." Sal then rolls off me, sounding as though she did something wrong. "I don't know how… I'm sorry."

I sigh and clasp her hand. "It's okay—no need to be sorry. We're friends, right?"

"Yeah," she says, and I can see the outline of her face in the dark, knowing her brown eyes are locked on mine.

"Do you trust me?" I trust her, but it has to work both ways.

"I do." She pauses and then lifts the blanket. "Still hot?"

"No." My hand falls from hers and I go beneath the blanket because she's handing me her trust. We still lay far apart, but I can still practically feel her warmth. And I have to admit, it feels nice. When the sounds from the room next door grow louder again, I may need a cold shower in the morning because all I can focus on and remember is Sal's body against mine.

14

Sal

I open my eyes to sunlight filtering through the old-fashioned flowered curtains covering the window. Dacre isn't next to me, so I sit on the bed and listen to the sound of the shower coming from the bathroom—*found him*. I examine the old furniture and stop at the beige AC unit, which is still stuck on the same low temperature, wasting electricity.

Oh, God, last night. It happened. Me. *Me* cocooning my body against Dacre's when I warned him not to make a move. Stupid robot, where were you? But then, he grabbed my hand and it felt different, comfortable, which was, to say the least, unexpected.

The bathroom door swings open, and Dacre saunters out with a white towel wrapped around his waist. He slides a hand through his wet hair. His skin has become tanner over the past weeks from working outside, and his smile—the one he's giving me now—looks good on him.

"Sorry, I forgot to grab my clothes," he says.

"That's fine," I say in a raspy voice, averting my gaze, knowing he's naked under that towel and not wanting to think about that. Kick in, Robot! "I have to get dressed anyway." I head to my backpack resting atop the little table at the side and pick out my usual shorts and t-shirt. As I dig to the bottom to find a specific bandana, something crunches under my fingers. Scrunching my face, I drag out a metal wrapper and immediately drop it. Freaking condom! I rummage in my bag a little more and find another four. *What the hell?* I spot a small note taped on one of them:

Just in case!
Flor

I bury them to the very bottom of my bag, covering them in layers of clothes. My cheeks heat up as I look at Dacre, who, thankfully, isn't looking my way. With a sigh, I carry my shorts, t-shirt, and bandana to the bathroom.

A few minutes later, I find Dacre sitting at the small table, staring at the wall, as if the meaning of life were written there in big bold letters. But it's just a wall with decaying wallpaper from the seventies or sixties or who knows what decade.

"Hey." I give him a little wave.

He gives a brief nod at me along with a side smile. "Hey."

"So, I read on the internet about this restaurant that has great breakfast food."

He arches a brow and bites his lip.

"What?" I ask.

"Um, maybe we should ask around." Dacre stands and pops his back. "Your motel choice was shitty."

"I didn't *know* better." I cock my head. "It isn't that bad, right?"

"Just complaints from you about the AC all last night," he replies with a half-smile.

"Shut up." I nudge his shoulder. "This motel is semi-doable, with the exception of the AC and the bathroom's cockroaches." And the rundown wallpaper, and the century-old table, and the creaky bed—the list could go on and on, but I don't say it.

"Cockroaches?" he asks, as if he's never seen one.

"I'm kidding, Dacre."

He rolls his eyes and lifts his backpack to leave, and I grab mine and follow him out of the room.

When we reach the lobby, Dacre asks the man behind the desk about a good breakfast restaurant, which happens to be a couple of kilometers away.

After driving in an almost zigzag pattern for a while, we reach an old, one-story, carmine house with a full parking lot. Which is a good sign—busy restaurants are the best. Parking a block away, we move side by side on the narrow sidewalk to the front entrance.

We enter the small, crowded restaurant and sit at a table in the rear, next to each other—the Mexican way. Large paintings of bulls and bullfighters decorate the crimson walls.

A waiter with a permanent frown takes our orders, and Dacre asks for bacon and eggs while I order *chorizo* and eggs.

"Bacon and eggs? Take a walk on the wild side," I say

to him as we wait for our food. "Nothing beats *chorizo* and eggs."

"We grew up in different countries," he says. "Different things. Food is food everywhere. Now for drinks, there's no Dr. Pepper here."

I've heard of that soda but have never seen one in person. "What does it taste like?"

He looks up at the ceiling and places his lower lip in between his teeth.

"That good, huh?" I smile at him. "Do you miss the US?"

"Not really," he says, sighing. "But I miss the ocean, the sand, a place to escape. If you go to Texas, I can show you around, you know?"

"I'd like that," I say, but I don't think it'll happen—so hard to save money for the trip, and then there's the visa thing, which the American government requires to enter the US. It's *so* expensive and difficult to get.

A girl with big green eyes shows up, carrying our meals. She sets them in front of us.

"Hi," I say to her, "can you remind the waiter of our coffees?"

"Not again." She rolls her eyes, as if it's not the first time he's failed. "I'll get them." She hurries away.

"Pretty eyes," Dacre says.

"Thank you." I flutter my eyelids. He's referring to the girl, but I can't help being a bit sarcastic.

"Not yours." He smiles and points in the waitress's direction. "Hers."

"I know, silly."

"You have pretty eyes, too." He stares, as if he's going to tell me something truly amazing. "Like squirrel fur."

I laugh. "Squirrel fur? Hopefully you'll never have to compliment a woman's eyes again."

"Hey, squirrel fur is nice." He smiles at me for a moment, then he starts to eat his mundane bacon and eggs.

I study my meal—scrambled eggs with red *chorizo*, refried beans with crumbled *queso fresco*, and *chilaquiles*. I grab a piece of *bolillo* bread from a basket in the center of the table. Yeah, this is the carbohydrate breakfast of champions. Then, I turn my attention to Dacre, who's eating his eggs and bacon with gusto.

"You should try this." I show him the *bolillo* bread in my hand.

"No, thanks," he says.

I bite into it and moan. "Oh, it's really good."

Dacre leans a little closer and smirks. "That good?"

"Mmm, mmm. The legend says *bolillo* is the cheapest aphrodisiac." A total lie, but I want him to be intrigued and try the bread.

He studies the bolillo in my hand then gives me a perplexed look.

"I'm kidding, Dacre. Don't get any crazy ideas. C'mon, give it a try—don't be silly."

"Nah, I prefer toast."

"There's toast here in Mexico, you know?" I raise a hand to try to get the waiter's attention.

Dacre shakes his head. "Really, I'm fine without bread—not that hungry."

"I thought you were?" I ask, staring at him, because he's acting weird again.

"I am, but not that much." He grabs his fork and points at my meal with it. "How about you focus on *you* eating instead."

"O-kay," I say, letting this bread detail go, because he seems annoyed. I put *tomatillo* salsa over my meal—not a whole lot, just in case, and place the first bite into my mouth. I almost moan one more time as the flavors mix.

Right as we finish our meals in comfortable silence, the waiter shows up and sets the bill on the table. "No rush." The way he frowns at us says otherwise.

Stifling an eye roll, I pull out a couple of one-hundred-peso bills to please his majesty and stand to leave. "Avocado delivery time."

As we leave the restaurant, Dacre walks so slow, I grab his hand and pull him toward the van. "Move."

"I'm moving," he protests.

But let's face it—he's barely walking, so I drag him harder. "C'mon!"

He just chuckles and finally moves.

"Can you drive today?" I ask, since yesterday he changed his mind about driving with the excuse that he was too tired. That was partly my fault with the salsa fiasco, but he shouldn't have been *that* tired.

"Sure."

I hand him the keys as we reach the truck.

"Where to?" he asks once we're inside.

Sliding out my phone, I bring up the map app and enter the address. The girl on the app instructs him when to turn while my eyelids drop, the extra *bolillo* bread I ate taking its toll. But no, I shouldn't let that happen.

"Hey," Dacre says.

I open my eyes to black asphalt—three lanes each way, the highway. "How did we get here this fast?"

Gripping the wheel, he peers over at me. "I've been

driving for half an hour, Sal."

How did I sleep for that long? "Sorry." I wipe my mouth and inspect my hand—no drool.

"In one kilometer, take exit 41 toward Palenque," the GPS's robotic female voice states.

"We're close," he says to me.

"Do you want me to drive?" I ask, straightening up and blinking a few times.

"Nah, I got it. You relax."

A minute later, we exit the highway, then turn onto the two-lane road leading to Palenque. And as we drive, the scenery turns brighter with different shades of greens highlighting tall trees that line the sides.

"Trees!" I shout.

Dacre appears confused for a second. "What?"

"Can you pull over?" I point at the side of the road. "I want to see the trees."

"You're so weird," he says, slowing the van and pulling over to the gravel curb.

A flash of heat welcomes me as I open the van's door and step out. I lead Dacre through the jungle of trees until we reach a barbed wire fence. I point at the wide trunks on the other side. "Look."

He lifts his chin. "Are those mangoes?"

"Yes!" I move my finger to the side, to a different kind of tree. "Guess what those are."

"Mmm," he says. "Small mangoes?"

"No!" I grip his bicep and pull him closer. "Plum trees."

"Aren't plums purple?" He squints his eyes against the sunlight, staring straight at the yellow fruit.

"The purple ones are *Ciruelas de España*." I softly

bounce on my feet, motioning at the trees. "These are Mexican plums—yellow and delicious. Have you ever tried them frozen?"

"I've never tested out those kinds of plums."

"Time to try them." I place my hand on the barbed wire and give it a tug. "Gentlemen first."

His gaze slides to mine, a smile growing wider. "Are you stepping out of your avocado shell, Sal? You know this is private property."

"It's just a plum." I pull the wire harder. "C'mon."

"I have a better idea." He chuckles.

One second, I'm on my feet and the next, I'm off the ground, releasing the wire. "What are you doing?"

"Just taking you away from here before you get in trouble. Or do you want *trouble*, Sal? I don't mind a little of that," he teases. "But sorry, I can't have you going and doing that. I told your pa I'd watch out for you, yet I like this side of you so maybe just for a few minutes."

"Hey!" a female voice shouts.

Startled, I turn my attention in the voice's direction and spot a woman in overalls walking our way. "This is private property," she calls to us, sweat covering her red cheeks.

"We're just looking," Dacre says, putting on his best innocent face, batting his thick black eyelashes.

I wave at her. "Uh, we were wondering if we could try your plums?"

She crosses her arms over her chest and scowls in our direction. "They aren't free."

"Can you sell us a bag?" Dacre asks, pulling out his wallet.

The lady continues to glare between us, then relaxes

her shoulders. "This way." She strolls forward, fanning her face as we follow her. Moments later, she opens a little gate on the rusty barbed wired fence, letting us in.

"Wow," I say as we head toward a palapa cabin in the back—large tree trunks hold a roof made of dry palm leaves. I look around at the multitude of succulent fruit. "I love your trees. Do you grow the mangoes and plums yourself?"

"Yes," the lady replies.

"Sal here is a tree expert," Dacre drawls. I'm not sure if he's being serious or sarcastic.

"No, I'm not." I sigh. "I only know avocado trees."

The woman's attention focuses on me. "I tried to grow them a long time ago—it didn't work out."

"What happened?" I ask, interested in all things avocado—dead *or* alive.

"Red ambrosia beetles." She shakes her head and drops her shoulders. "We couldn't control them."

"I know." Pa and I have been fighting these little bugs for years.

As we round a few large trees and step over fallen branches, we make it to the palapa.

She steps to a freezer so old, it seems it hasn't been opened in twenty years, then lifts the lid with a creak and grabs a plastic bag filled with plums. "Thirty pesos."

Dacre pulls out his wallet, but I wave him off. I whip out a fifty-peso bill and hand it to the lady. "Keep the change."

"Thanks," she grunts, giving me the bag in return.

As we leave the mango-plum farm, Dacre softly brushes my hand, the one holding the bag. "How do you eat frozen plums?"

I take one out and give it to him. "Peel the skin with your teeth."

"That sounds a bit sexual." He inspects the plum in his hand.

I choke mid-swallow on my spit and start coughing. And I can't stop.

"Are you all right?" Dacre asks, laughing.

After several more seconds of coughing, I'm able to breathe again. "Not sure peeling off skin with teeth would be considered sexual, but whatever makes you happy." My gaze drifts to his lips, but I move them to my safe zone—trees. "I'd go with primitive." I bite into the plum, yanking its skin with my teeth, then try it—too cold, but after a little while, I can taste it. "Mmm, mmm—so good." I'm not lying.

He glances at the bitten fruit in my hand, then sighs. "Yeah, okay, I guess you won this round."

"Cool." I laugh. As we trudge back to the van, avoiding low-hanging tree branches, the sound of insects accompanies us. By the time we reach our vehicle, sweat covers my skin, and my face feels hotter than usual—too much humidity down here.

"My turn. Keys." I show him my palm.

After he hands them over, I blast the AC to the max as soon as I start the van.

Dacre fiddles with the vent, leans over, and grimaces. "Hot air."

"Give it a minute." I bite my lower lip. "Or ten?"

He lowers his window. "Let's do a four by sixty."

"What?" I ask as I pull from the curb.

"You know, four open windows at sixty miles per hour."

I roll down mine. "We only have two windows. Besides, sixty miles is about a hundred kilometers. So by the time the van reaches that speed, the AC will be primed."

"Okay then," he says.

Joining the two-lane road, I drive toward Palenque, which according to my phone, is just five minutes away.

A minute later, a car coming in the opposite direction flashes its headlights, then another car does the same, and another. And it's the middle of the day. When people do this, it's a warning to slow down because there's police ahead. So I do that.

Right after taking a curve, I spot a blockade.

A large group of people. All of them holding AK-47 weapons. Aimed right at us.

15

Dacre

Why the hell is there a group of people with guns? Sal presses the brakes to the van because she can't turn around and go back. Now, cars block our way.

"What's going on?" I ask, turning my head in every position imaginable.

"I don't know." She crinkles her nose and puts the van into park. "The place is right up ahead to deliver the avocados."

"Are you sure they want avocados?" There's a line of people holding guns—most have low hats shadowing their faces.

"Not anymore."

A tall woman in a pair of combat boots and short shorts, carrying an AK-47, approaches the van. I don't have any weapons on me besides my syringes, but that's not going to do anything. She motions for me to roll down my window.

After it's lowered, I do the only thing I know how to do. "Hey, um … beautiful, is there any way you can move those barricades a bit so we can slide past them?"

I hear a groan from my left and ignore Sal's annoyed face.

The woman lifts her gun higher. "Step out of the vehicle now or we'll pop out your tires and you'll be dead before you can say another word, *Romeo*."

Holy shit. If I had to piss right now, it would be all over my pants. I open the door, thinking that I can open it quickly enough to knock her out. But then I see some beast of a guy striding toward us, possibly the size of three Terminators put together. There goes that plan.

My heart picks up as the girl aims her gun right at my chest. "Put your hands behind your head."

I do as she says, and she backs me to the front of the van. Over the past few years, I've struggled to believe the way I'd die would be from complications with diabetes, not me being a target for bullets. The night at the club with the shooting, I didn't think about myself getting shot because I was too concerned with Lach. Even thinking about that now hits me hard. But right now this gun is incredibly close.

Frantically, I look for Sal who is being led by the beasty guy—he's right up on her. At that moment, I don't care if this lady shoots me—I want to help Sal. I don't want Sal to have the expression that's on her face now, terrified and almost in tears.

While Beasty points the gun at Sal's chest, she finally says in a shaky voice, "We're just bringing avocados for a delivery."

"Avocados?" The woman removes her gun a fraction from my chest. "You're from the avocado farm?"

"Yes." Sal's eyes widen.

"You're early." The woman lowers her gun to her side, giving me enough room to breathe again.

"We made good time," Sal says with a ragged breath as Beasty turns his gun away from her, but not lowering it.

"Hey, Alejandro, we're good, they have the avocados," the lady shouts, looking at Sal and then me. "Sorry about the misunderstanding. We have to keep things safe in there. Open up the barricades!" she screams to the group of people, and they each tip their head at her.

Shaking a bit on the inside, I get back in the van beside Sal. "I don't think this place deals in avocados."

Her hand twitches as she starts the ignition. "I'm pretty sure I know what they're using them for."

They're covering up their shady business with the avocados. "Whatever you do, don't ask, just do what they say until we get home."

"I'm not that dumb, Dacre."

I know she isn't, but this is a scenario where something could've actually happened to Sal. What if she would've died? I don't want to even think about that.

The barricade opens, and we easily drive through, both staying completely silent the remainder of the way. It takes us about five minutes to make it down a curved dirt road to a tall tan building with large covered windows. There are at least ten trucks lined up outside the place, their backs already lifted so I can see most are filled with various crates.

A balding man waves us to a stop. "Open up the back,"

he says after I roll down the window.

Sal tells me to wait, but I don't. We both get out, and I open the back door of the van. One of the trucks backs up until it lines with ours. Two women step out with another man with tattoos up and down his arms. They walk to the van and start taking out the crates of avocados and hastily placing them inside the truck.

"We've already wired the owner the rest of the money, but here's a tip for your discretion," the balding man says, handing Sal some bills. He gives us each a hard stare that tells me if we say anything, we're dead.

Sal and I stay silent again, this time until we're back in the van and re-exiting the barricade. My mind is racing wave over ocean wave with panic. The woman who held me up earlier salutes us with her gun.

"What the fuck, Sal?" I finally shout. "Seriously, what the fuck?"

"I don't know!" she screeches. "This isn't my fault!"

"You're the one who approached and hired me." If she had never hired me, I would still be back at home, comfortably in my bed, reading a book. Did she know about this?

"Yeah, because this was supposed to be an avocado delivery!" She pauses to rub her cheek. "I'll let my pa know when we get back to never deal with these people again!"

"You sure your pa isn't in on it?" Because really, you never know.

If two eyes could turn into knives, hers would have. "Do you want me to send you back to that place with those people? Pa had thought the money was too good to be true, but neither one of us thought anything of it."

"Too soon for jokes?" I start nervously laughing and she looks at me as if I'm crazy. "We have a future story to tell."

"Possible accomplice in a drug deal?" she seethes.

"We don't know that for sure."

"Dacre…" She cocks her head as if I'm the stupidest person on the planet.

"We're alive, it's all that matters."

She laughs hysterically then, a few tears sliding down her cheeks. "I didn't know, and my pa didn't either. I'm so sorry."

To keep my heart from racing, and to pretend as if we'd never been held up with guns to begin with, I play songs for us on my phone as a distraction while we drive for the next couple of hours. It helps because my breathing has become normal again, the farther and farther away we get.

Eventually, down the road, I spot a small sign pointing to the right: *Carnaval Mágico.*

"You want to hit that up?" I ask. Sal looks like she may need a bit of something fun after the avocado incident. Hell, I do too.

Sal leans forward over the steering wheel. "Hmm. I've never been to one of those. It might make us not get back on time, though."

"Do you always have to be on schedule? Don't you want to sometimes live a little dangerously?" I shrug my shoulders. "But … we can go straight home. Get ready for the usual avocado day. The *usual.*"

"Game on." She turns the wheel at the last second, causing me to grab the "oh shit" bar at the roof of the van.

The road is more like a narrow dirt trail with sparse grass blooming in patches. The trees flash by the car as we pass them. There's no sign of a carnival. I'm thinking that maybe the carnival has been gone for a while, and the sign had been forgotten when the traveling caravans left. But then rows of travel trailers begin to appear as trees disappear.

A large open field spread out just ahead is decorated in ornate tents of different colors. One is covered in red and white stripes like a candy cane and others are solid bright oranges, purples, yellows, and blues.

My eyes fall back to the candy cane one with a red triangular flag dangling high in the air. "I'm hungry."

"Let's eat it," Sal says, staring at the striped fabric.

An indigenous man stands several yards ahead, pointing us to the left. His black curly hair falls to his shoulders, and he's wearing a palm leaf hat, a purple scarf around his neck, a long-sleeve white shirt with black cotton pants, and sandals.

"He must be dying out there in the heat," I say. I'm wearing shorts and it felt like death outside just in these.

"No kidding," Sal replies and turns the van in the direction he's pointing. She pulls into the first available opening at the end of the row of parked cars.

Reaching toward the cup holder, she grabs her phone. "It's dead. Stupid me for forgetting that charger! Can I use your phone to call my pa and tell him we'll be late?"

"You going to tell him about what happened back there?"

"Not until we get home. No need to worry him quite yet."

As Sal makes her call, I pull out my drawstring

backpack from the side compartment of my bag and toss my diabetes kit inside when she isn't looking, along with a few candy bars in case I need them.

She meets me outside the van and hands me back my phone. "Have you ever been to something like this?"

"Not sure. I've been to Ren Fest back in Texas when I was about nine, but nothing really out here." I don't think small parties really count.

"So I guess we're both virgins then." She smiles.

"Depends what kind of virgin we're talking about."

"I guess so." Her smile grows wider.

My cheeks heat a little, and I take my eyes off Sal, focusing on the indigenous man up ahead.

"Here for the carnival, I presume," the man says, stroking a satchel resting at his hip made from a ropey rough material.

"Yep," Sal says.

"You're in luck. This is our very last day." He pulls out two ten-peso coins from his satchel and tosses one to the each of us. "On me, you can use these with the fortuneteller." He waggles his eyebrows. "Señora Martinica is quite the woman. I like to help her out as much as possible."

I smile to myself because I bet he does.

"Yeah, okay, we'll look for her," Sal says, slipping the coin into her pocket. I do the same.

"Good day." The man bows and waves us ahead.

"I guess we're entering another time warp." Sal shrugs.

"This one seems a bit better than the sixties at the motel." I wink, then wonder why the hell I just did that.

"Something wrong with your eye?" She scrunches her nose and squints at me.

I rub my eye. "Yeah, got some dirt in it or something."

"I've got eye drops." She fiddles around with her purse and drags out a small clear bottle.

"What other stuff do you got in there?" She always seems to be pulling out something when needed.

"Maybe I'll show you sometime," she teases. "Now bend down, you Jolly Green Giant."

I lower myself to a kneeling position and let her tip my chin with her index finger and thumb. She removes the cap and places the lid in the palm of her hand. Her other hand returns to my chin to make sure it stays tipped up, then her thumb slowly caresses my jaw, most likely unintentionally.

Her touch has the unexpected effect of causing warmth to build up in my chest—and possibly other places. I push those thoughts away.

"Hold your eye open!" she whisper-shouts.

"I'm trying!" Desperately.

Sal's hand leaves my chin, and I'm already missing her touch. Her fingers stretch open my eye so hard it may pop out, which I won't miss *that* touch. She pours two drops in each eye. A pointless adventure since my eyes never had any dirt in them to begin with.

"Thanks," I mutter.

"No problem. Glad they could be of use."

I stand back up, and we walk in silence to the entrance. Biting my lip, I keep looking at her face, at the yellow-and-blue-checkered bandana.

"Yeah?" she asks.

"Nothing. Just like the bandana today."

"Gotta keep in uniform, of course."

We continue the rest of the way to the entrance where

a young indigenous woman stands barefoot, wearing a long brown skirt and a white top covered in colorful stitched-in flowers. She's shaking a set of green maracas. And to our right, a small boy around ten beats loudly against a small wooden *güiro*.

"You may enter," the boy speaks robotically, bowing his head. The woman, who might be his mom, gives a bright smile.

"I wonder how long they can do that for," Sal says as we wander past the golden silk curtain.

On the other side of the fabric is a second entrance, where a small white and brown trailer with an open window sits. A paper sign reading fifty pesos for the carnival entrance is taped below the window. As if on cue, a woman appears with her dark hair separated in two braids with red cloth interwoven in between the locks. She holds out her hand, her wrist covered in handmade, vibrant-colored bracelets up her arm.

After we pay, a short man wearing a wooden beaded necklace opens the gate for us. As we walk through, I stare up ahead, not seeing much of a crowd. Maybe all the customers already came the previous days, or maybe a lot of the people didn't know this carnival was out here. It *is* buried in the forest.

"You want to stop by Señora Martinica's booth?" Sal points at a violet tent with matching beads dangling from the door. "That small tent over there has her name on the outside."

"Might as well give these pesos to her, I guess," I say, producing the coin from my pocket. "Watch this." I quickly put my hand behind her ear and show her my peso. "I'm magical. Maybe I should work here."

"You're ridiculous," she says, strolling to the tent.

"Ridiculously magical, right?"

As Sal pulls the beads back, making a clinking sound as they swish together, something pounces on her shoulder.

She lets out a high-pitched scream that I'm sure the entire carnival heard. I don't move an inch, just stare at the small Capuchin monkey sitting on her shoulder.

A loud laugh escapes me, and I'm unable to stop as the black and white face of the monkey meets mine.

"Get it off! Get. It. Off," she whisper-shouts.

"It's only a monkey." I hold out my hand for it to crawl across my arm to my shoulder, but it obviously likes the comfortable spot it's sitting on.

"I'm so, *so* sorry!" a woman's voice rushes out as she scoops the monkey up from Sal's shoulder. "Javi sometimes misbehaves himself."

Sal plucks off the invisible monkey hair from the sleeve of her shirt. "Are you Señora Martinica?"

"I am." Señora Martinica swings her thick dark curls over her shoulder and takes a seat at the table, her hands hovering over a deck of Spanish cards that look similar to tarot cards. Red, white, and orange flowers are somehow attached to the side of her head and long blue earrings dangle from her ears. Javi crawls to Madam Martinica's shoulder, peering down at the cards.

Without asking us to sit down, the woman flips over a colorful card. "You two are lovers, yes?" She adjusts one of her sleeves on her frilly white dress that's hanging off her shoulder.

"No, only friends," I say, toying with my lip.

"Perhaps not yet." She flips over another one, staring

hard at the two of us. "There's a certain danger that lies ahead."

"What kind of danger?" Sal asks, probably thinking we've already stumbled across that with the people and their guns. My mind automatically goes to something with my diabetes, like me losing a leg or something. And I shut those thoughts down because these people are usually frauds just out to make a quick buck.

"The cards only tell me so much. Thank you, tips are welcome." Señora Martinica pushes a metal can toward us.

"That's it?" I ask, lifting an eyebrow.

"One card per person, unless you want to pay two-hundred pesos for a full reading."

"No, that's okay." I'd rather save my money. I toss in the coin, gifted from the guy at the road, and so does Sal. When we walk out of the tent, I feel as if maybe I should have just kept the ten pesos.

"You want to get something to eat?" Sal asks.

I check my phone and see that it's already past lunch time. My sugar feels a little on the low side, so at least I don't have to deny her food again. There's also a text from my brother.

"Yeah." I glance up and find a secluded wooden bench and point to it. "I'll meet you back over there. I've gotta go to the restroom."

"Predictable." She chews on her lip as if she's thinking about something. "Anything in particular you want?"

"I'll get a Diet Coke and *carne asada* when I get back."

"Got it." After Sal walks off, I go to check the text from my brother.

Lach: **I think Gregorio is going to hire me full time**

at the avocado farm. **I'm just that good.**

Me: **I probably won't get home tonight. We're making a few pitstops on the way back.**

Lach: **Oh man, I can't wait to see Mom's reaction.**

Mom hasn't texted me since yesterday. I know she's pissed, but she needs to get over that.

When I reach the pitiful outhouse bathroom, I pull out my kit, finding the saved avocado pit inside. I lift the seed and stare at it, thinking about Sal. Lovers? The last girl that I talk-talked to vanished somewhere within or outside the club because of a shooting. The last girl I dated I constantly argued with because she acted more like a mother hen, constantly worrying about my diabetes. Maybe the danger Señora Martinica mentioned is me.

I close my hands around the seed—friends. I slide it into my pocket to keep it close and maybe for a bit of luck. Briefly, I close my eyes, wanting to be completely honest with Sal as friends are, but I *can't*. I don't want her to see me in a whole new way now that I really know her. And she will, especially after a woman who raised her died from the disease.

After I head out, I find Sal carrying two plates with *carne asada* and a soda under each arm.

Rushing to her, I grab the Diet Coke from under her arm and a plate from her hand. "I was going to get mine. You didn't have to pay for it."

"Nah, the company covered travel expenses and the hotel anyway by wiring money early, so you're good." She pauses. "Although, I don't want to know how they're making their money at the moment."

Without hesitation, I dig into the *carne asada* and the meat melts in my mouth. I'm pretty sure my face is covered in grease, because Sal forgot the silverware, but I don't care. It's that damn good.

Once we finish and throw away the trash, we head to a stage that has three long wooden benches in front of it. A man wearing a large headpiece covered in black and blue feathers stands in a straight position. On his forearm sits a snowy-white barn owl.

"We have to watch this," Sal shouts, dragging me to the farthest back bench behind an older couple.

The guy with the owl elevates his arm up and the bird darts our way. I duck my head and pull Sal into me. Then I turn to find the owl now resting on the arm of a small girl around twelve, wearing an even larger headpiece with green and white beads decorated on the front and a fan of feathers across her head going from yellow to orange before bleeding into red.

Sal sits up and watches the bird eat some sort of treat the girl feeds it. The girl lifts her small arm, the same way the guy up front did a moment ago. With a swish of feathers, the owl flies low over our heads, but neither one of us ducks this time as we watch the beautiful beats of the white wings.

The owl flaps and expands its feathered wings as it lands on the guy's arm, and he feeds the bird another snack.

At that moment, I realize my arm is still wrapped around Sal's waist, but I don't remove it.

16

Sal

*P*ersonal space.

That's where my head is now, because Dacre has his arm wrapped around my waist, and we're sitting so close, my hip is practically rammed into his. And I'm confused—part of me wants to scoot away, while the other ... the other I think wants me to do something stupid.

As another owl glides over our heads, Dacre brings me a little closer—if that's even possible, making something like miniature owls, like these, fly around in my stomach.

I don't know what to do.

He's my co-worker, and in the past weeks, he's become a good friend. But this—whatever this is—feels good and weird at the same time. Perhaps I'm overthinking this situation. We're just having a great time.

"Everything okay, Sal?" Dacre asks.

"Yeah." I straighten in my seat.

"You seem a little lost." He unwraps his arm.

A little? That's an understatement. The lost romantic in me liked his arm wrapped around my waist—the closeness of it. But, well, my robot warns me to be cautious, to analyze what's going on.

"See?" Dacre breaks my thoughts. "What are you thinking about?"

"Owls." *Not the ones flapping around in my stomach*, I think, as my cheeks heat up. "They're so cool."

The people surrounding us clap as the performer on stage places a hand over his heart and then touches one of the blue feathers on his headpiece. He gingerly bows his upper body, an owl on each of his shoulders.

Dacre studies him then locks his light-brown eyes on mine. "Very cool."

"Yeah." I turn my attention to the birds and the man and everything not Dacre—I can't sustain his gaze. No, this is just weird, and it shouldn't be. I look at him, right in the eye. "You… You want to check out the rest of the carnival?"

He glances at my mouth for a moment, then shrugs. "Sure."

We stroll without a specific direction, and as we turn a corner, a crowd surrounding a pole appears, its height defying the sky. If I had to guess, I'd say it's about thirty meters tall. A small platform rests on its tip, and a wooden frame the size of a table stands about a meter down. Five men in red pants, white shirts with ornate-stitched cloth across the chest, and knitted caps on their heads trudge to the post. One of them has a small drum hanging on his side.

Dacre motions at the pole. "Hey, what's that?"

"Don't tell me you haven't seen this before," I say, realizing I've only seen this act on YouTube.

"I'm telling you now—I haven't." He studies the drummer, who grabs onto the rope spiraling up on the pole. "What is he doing?"

"Let's get a little closer." I grab his hand and pull him toward the crowd.

"Whoa," he says, squeezing my hand before letting go. "Is he really climbing?"

"That's what the *Voladores de Papantla* are all about."

Hanging on to the rope, using it as a ladder, the man slowly makes his way toward the top.

"The fliers of *Papantla*," Dacre says. "Are they really flying?"

"Mm-hmm," I say, as another man starts climbing.

Dacre points up. "That's crazy!"

"You haven't seen anything yet."

He stares at me, arching a brow. "Don't tell me they're gonna drop and fly like superheroes."

"*No.*" I laugh, then point my chin at the *Voladores de Papantla*. "Pay attention."

"Okay."

The drummer reaches the wooden frame, and when I think he'll stay there, he keeps climbing until making it to the end of the pole. The crowd gasps as he stands on the tiny platform, balancing with his arms to the sides, like a tightrope walker. After settling, he takes out a little flute and a drumstick from his pocket.

"I bet I could do that," Dacre says.

"Just watch. There's more craziness coming," I reply,

studying Dacre's profile, his sharp features.

The man balancing on top of the post plays the flute with one hand and the drum with the other. The music sounds primitive, as if it were composed centuries ago, a basic drumbeat and a few flute notes. And all of this, while the other men climb the pole, making it sway a bit.

Dacre leans forward to talk over the music, his breath warm against my ear. "Is that some kind of ritual?"

"What?" I ask, distracted by how close he is again.

He nods up at the man standing on the platform. "The music."

"Oh. It's just part of the act."

"No Voodoo stuff going on?" He bites his lip.

I shake my head. "No, only Mexican purple magic."

"Purple magic? Is that good magic?"

"Not good—bad, really-really bad," I reply.

"Let me find out, then." Dacre rubs his palms together and turns his attention to the performance.

A second man holds on to the frame, while the other three men climb the pole, too, reminding me of workers repairing electricity posts.

"What are those ropes for?" Dacre asks once the four men reach the wooden frame.

"It's the Mexican purple magic that'll turn them into superheroes."

He chuckles. "Really, Sal. What are they doing?"

Nudging his arm, I say, "Just look."

"Okay." He watches the four men, who're now sitting on the frame's beams, facing each other, their backs to us.

"They're about to shapeshift." I watch with my mouth open in awe.

The drummer keeps playing, *thump-thump-thump—*

while the other men make the frame rotate with their feet, then hang tight on to their beams and bend backward.

"That looks—" Dacre starts.

Pressing a finger to his lips, I say, "Shh."

"Whoa," he says against my finger as the men let go of their beams and end up hanging upside-down from their knees, their arms pointing toward the ground. And all of this while the frame rotates. People clap to the rhythm of the drummer's music and others cheer, but I'm afraid the noise will make them lose their concentration.

"Here it comes," I say in a whisper.

The men let go of their legs, making me let out a little yelp, and when I think they're going to drop to the ground, the ropes tied to their ankles stop their descent. Although I've seen this before, watching it live isn't the same.

"I guess you were right," Dacre says. "The Mexican purple magic is working."

The people around us shout in excitement as the four men fly down in a circle, slowly, the ropes stopping them from falling. And the more they travel toward the ground, the farther away from the pole they are.

"Told you—they fly like superheroes." My head swings to face Dacre.

He leans down, close to my ear again. "Like Superman in slow motion. My younger brother, Ezra, would dig it. He loves comic book heroes."

"Cool." My attention turns to the flying men.

We watch them glide down in a circle. Before hitting the ground, they do a pirouette and land on their feet, making the crowd explode in applause.

"That was …. wow," Dacre says, as people start to walk away. "Let's find something else to do."

"Something less dangerous?" I ask.

He nods, tugging me by the shirt sleeve. "C'mon."

Under the afternoon sun, we stroll toward the tents up ahead, and in the distance, I spot a girl in a decorative dress with a yellow sash wrapped around her waist, throwing little animals in the air—at least that's what it looks like from here.

"Wait," I say to Dacre when we get near her.

The girl stands by a pastel-blue tent with a table showcasing weird-looking animals.

Dacre nods toward them. "What are those called?"

"How can you *not* know?" I ask him.

"They look familiar—I've seen them somewhere." Dacre grabs a small pink rabbit with long blue ears and inspects it. "It weighs nothing." He turns his attention to the girl. "What's it made of?"

She steps a little closer. "*Papier maché.*"

"May I?" I ask the girl, gesturing to another animal.

"Go ahead." She smiles.

I take a blue dragon with yellow wings and a cat head, and study it. Putting it away, I concentrate on the other amazing animals sitting on the table—a maroon fish with a huge eye, a white bird with olive spots, and even an armadillo with a frog riding on its back. But what really catches my attention are the dolls sitting at another table.

"*Alebrijes,*" I say to Dacre.

"Hmm?" he asks, distracted, and sets the rabbit on the table.

Waving at the table, I say, "That's what they're called—*alebrijes.*"

"Yeah, I've heard of them."

"C'mon." I walk to the table in the rear of the tent

and lift an aquamarine doll. "I used to play with them when I was little."

"Ah, the good ol' days," he says in a playful tone.

"Kind of, but now that I think of it, they're quite different than your regular doll." The head and body appear as if fused together without a neck. She looks a bit creepy with her pinched lips, bright-red cheeks, unblinking wide eyes, and painted-over black hair. "Actually, they're freaky, don't you think?"

"I think I'll take her home with me. She'd make pretty good company while I sleep." He takes the doll from my hand. It reminds me of the night before, when I was sleeping beside him. Luckily, he interrupts my thoughts as he adds, "But, the *alebrijes* are definitely my thing."

We admire the *papier maché* creations for a minute until people behind us applaud, making us turn around. Tent Girl throws a lion *alebrije* in the air, then a paper doll, and a skinny dog. Juggling them—so cool.

When the girl finishes performing, she turns to us. "Do you want to buy one? They're on sale."

My gaze flies to the violet doll in the back, which sits there begging to be loved. It's like she belongs to me. But, no—better save the money for the trip back. "Um, maybe later."

Without a word, Dacre takes out his wallet, but before he pays for it, I say, "Let's save our money for an emergency."

"This *is* an emergency, Sal."

"But—"

"I owe you," he interrupts, then hands the girl the money, and she puts the doll in a plastic bag.

"Thanks, but what do you owe me for?" I ask him

once we're out of the tent.

"For letting us stop here. But before you get too teary-eyed," he teases, "you do kind of owe me for the shitty hotel, almost getting shot, making me sick with food, and oh yeah, our theft attempt with the fruit on the side of the road."

I shrug. "Too late."

"Where to now?"

"Mmm." I squint around and settle on a group of people. "There."

As we stride toward them, my heartbeat quickens. I like being here with Dacre—I don't think I've had this much fun with a friend ever. Even with the one major catastrophe—I shake that thought away because I'll talk to Pa about it when we get home.

A couple of minutes later, we reach the group. People stand in a circle, blocking whatever it is they're watching. *Cumbia* music resonates as we walk around the crowd until we find an opening.

In front of us, there's a girl wearing a pink-and-white-flowered headpiece and an intricately designed dress with the sleeves hanging off her shoulders—belly dancing. She moves her hips at the rhythm of the music coming out from a couple of large speakers sitting on the ground. I turn my attention to Dacre, whose eyes are glued to the dancer. And I have to admit she's pretty—long black hair cascading down to her waist, tall and curvy. The way she dances hypnotizes the audience—not only guys, but girls, too.

She saunters our way, swaying this way and that, hands moving in the air, and when she's close to us, the dancer extends a hand to Dacre, inviting him to dance. The crowd claps and encourages him to go with her.

"Uhh…" He looks embarrassed for the first time since I've known him.

"Go!" I give him a hard push while he shoots me a dirty look.

The belly dancer takes him by the hand to the center of the circle, then flings her hips from side to side as she dances in front of him, sliding a hand down his chest. Apparently no longer embarrassed, he smiles at her in such a way that makes me … my … I don't know—something inside me flips. I want her to stop, but she doesn't as she slowly squats in front of him, swaying her hips in a sensual way.

Thankfully, the *cumbia* song ends, and the belly dancer stands on her tiptoes and kisses Dacre on the cheek.

"It's getting late," I call, unable to stop this new feeling traveling through my body.

He looks at me then at the curvy girl.

"We have to go, like, now," I say a little too loud.

"What's going on with you?" he asks after he joins me, glancing over his shoulder at the dancer.

"Nothing." But it's everything—all my insides swirl in circles. Why am I jealous? I just … and he … it's not like we're dating or anything.

He folds his arms across his chest. "Are you mad at me or something?"

Sighing deeply, I try to control this weirdness. I've been jealous before, but not this irrational. So stupid. "No." I fan my face. "It's hot out here."

"Not any hotter than it's been," he replies.

The girl was hot for you, I think, but don't say it. "We need to drive back home, you know?"

He purses his lips and stares at me. "*Sal.*"

I stare back at him. "*Dacre.*"

Our eyes have their own personal battle for a long moment, until I drop my tense shoulders. "I'm worried about Pa," I half-lie, because I don't like thinking about him being alone in the house.

Dacre takes a breath, uncrossing his arms. "Okay."

"Okay," I echo.

As we trudge back to the van, passing tents and people and even stray dogs, my heart feels small. Actually, I feel empty.

I feel hollow inside, like the paper doll I'm carrying.

17

Dacre

I've only been driving for about fifteen minutes when I glance over at Sal. She's staring out the window with her feet propped up on the dashboard.

"Why are you being so quiet?" I ask. "The last time I saw you so quiet was way back when we were at the avocado plantation and you were extremely focused."

Sal brushes her fingertips across her bandana and slides her eyes to mine. "Dacre, we were just there on Thursday."

"That's probably why it seems like only yesterday." I smile.

She doesn't answer.

Sal was fine before the belly dancer, and then after, something changed in her. "You're the one who pushed me to dance with her, you know. I wasn't going to."

"I'm glad you had fun." Something in her tone still

sounds off.

"If you're jealous that she's my new friend, I'll pull over right now and you can show me your belly dancing skills on the side of the road."

"Seriously?" She tries to look disgusted, but there's a bit of a smile there.

"Just kidding, Sal. Or am I?"

Her gaze swings from mine and focuses on the road. "Dacre, stop!" she shouts.

I slam on the brakes before my eyes even make contact with what's ahead. When I come to a complete stop, there in the middle of the road is a body. A body with fur. Not a human body, though. It's a sloth.

I breathe a sigh of relief and put the van in park. In that time, Sal has already managed to run out the door, leaving it wide open. I hurry and meet her in front of the vehicle. One of Sal's hands reaches for the curious animal that is slowly trying to lift its head and body.

I push her hand out of the way before it makes contact. "You can't just touch a stray animal."

She rolls her eyes and steps closer to the animal. "Dacre, I have sanitizer back in the car. We're good."

"What if it bites? I really don't think sanitizer is going to help if your arm gets ripped off."

"It's a sloth," she says simply. "They rarely attack humans. And even if they did, they are like one of the slowest animals on Earth. You can easily dodge out of the way."

The sloth reaches a hand toward me, and I stare at it, unmoving. For one, I'm not going to sit here and Google to see if what Sal said is true. Two, I'm not an animal person and three, the claws are like razor blades that could easily cut Sal. But its face is on the … cute side. I suppose. I'd never seen one in person.

"We can't just leave it here in the middle of the road." Sal looks down at the animal and kneels before it. "Which way do you want to go, buddy?"

"I'm assuming the direction his head is pointing." Unless he wants to spend all day trying to turn himself around.

With what I can only describe as a gentle touch, one she uses with the avocados, she scoops the animal up like it's no big deal. *And* I haven't seen something so sexy in my entire life. I shake my insane thoughts away and hurry up to her. "Here, let me help." Not that I really want to, but if something happened to Sal, her pa would have me for breakfast.

She hands the sloth to me, and it smells like shit. Literally. It would probably be dead by the time it dragged itself to a lake to clean off. But I ignore the stench as I help him wrap his long arms around my neck, and I can't help but feel a little softness in my chest for the thing.

"Up or down?" I ask him as we come up to a large tree. "Up sounds good to me." I try to unstrap the thick arms from around my neck, but the beast stays latched on. "A little help would be nice, Sal." I hear a clicking sound. "Sal?"

"Sorry, I had to take a picture—photographic evidence." She laughs. "I'll give you your phone back when you finish."

What? How was she sneaky enough to grab the phone out of my pocket without me noticing? "We have more problems to worry about. Like me not getting suffocated to death."

"I think a snake does that," she grunts as she loosens and lifts the sloth's arms from around me.

Together, we help him reunite with a new tree to do whatever it is he needs to do, which in reality is still a bath. But he stays glued to the trunk, possibly making its way up one day.

My phone beeps, and I take it back from Sal who somehow magicianed her fingers into my pocket. And I'm thinking more about her fingers in my back pocket, so I brush that away.

Lach: **Mom's pissed.**

Me: **What's new?**

Lach: **Where are you now? I had to tell Mom you were going to be late.**

I look at all the trees around us—wide trunks and large leafy lush leaves with various shades of bright and dark greens.

Me: **On the side of the road by the jungle.**

Lach: **"Welcome To The Jungle"**

Me: **Thanks for putting that song in my head.**

Sending him the picture of the sloth, I chuckle and look up at Sal.

"Ready?" I ask her.

"What's going on?" She must have seen whatever look I had on my face when I was texting Lach.

"My mom's kind of pissed because I left without telling her."

"You *what?*" She takes a step toward me, eyes wide.

"It's fine."

"Dacre, you left for two days without letting your mom know. My pa would be going insane!"

"Well, good for you and your pa, but my bond isn't

like that with my mom." It hits me that maybe I'm a little envious about that, even though I do have my brothers.

"Yeah, but what if your mom had called the police? We could have gotten in trouble for your stupidity!" she seethes.

"It's fine. Everything's okay now. Shit, live a little." I don't understand why she's being so uptight. I mean, who cares?

"You don't have to be a jerk." She leaves me at the side of the road and I watch her hop into the driver seat of the van, slamming the door. I guess it's her way of saying she's going to take control.

With a deep sigh, I head to the van, noticing I'm feeling a bit lightheaded and hungry, but I need to finish this conversation. As soon as I get inside, I set my phone on the dash. "Look, I'm sorry," I say. "It's just my parents aren't like your pa, okay?"

Her lips are in a tight line as she turns to face me. "I get it. But you'll have to let your mom know next time, so my pa doesn't get in trouble. Not that we'll be doing this run ever in the future because I don't want us to end up dead, but you know what I mean."

I move to unzip my bag to grab a candy bar. Before I can give her a response, she starts the van, a loud gurgling sound happens, and then a pile of thick smoke rises from the hood.

With quick reflexes, I let go of the zipper and reach for the keys and hurry to turn off the motor. "Looks like you shouldn't have made me stop for the sloth," I say, avoiding her death glare. "Pop the hood."

Hand shaking, she pulls on the lever by her side and gets out. I meet her at the front of the van and lift the hood, wave off the smoke, and peer inside. My gaze falls to the radiator and coolant, and they both appear fine. Wiring is good—no fire there. Then I get a big whiff of burning oil—the oil pump is leaking. Dad's the one who taught me and my brothers about cars, and right now I'm grateful for it.

Sal's head is all up in the hood next to mine. "Did you find anything?"

"It appears we have some oil leaking," I mutter, trying to keep my concentration steady as my hands start to feel clammy.

"Mmm. How do we fix that?" She leans back so I can close the hood.

"Well, do you have a new oil pump laying around?" That's going to be the only way we're going to be driving anywhere today.

"Yeah, let me go get it out of my backpack." She starts for the van and a bit a relief hits me.

"So you really do carry everything in there." I grin.

"No!" She stops and turns back to me. "That was me being sarcastic!"

She could be an actress because I seriously believed her. "I think we need to work on your sarcasm and this oil pump."

"Dacre!"

"Seriously, just call a wrecker or your pa," I say.

"My phone's dead." She grits her teeth.

I pull mine out of my pocket and text Lach again.

Me: **Can you show this location to Sal's pa? The oil pump needs to be replaced.**

I go to send him our location and right as I press the button, the phone dies. Dammit, I should have charged it last night at the hotel.

"Well, now my phone's dead, too!" I probably shouldn't have been messing with it so much and playing music on it. "I tried to send the message, but I don't think it went through."

"I guess we wait then."

Squinting my eyes, I try to concentrate on what she said.

"Dacre?"

That's my name but it takes me a second to focus on it—on anything.

"My bag," I rush the words out, my limbs growing heavy.

"What?"

"I need my bag!"

Shakily, I follow behind her, knowing my sugar is dropping fast. Sal hands me my backpack and I know what I'm doing but don't at the same time. As I dig through the clutter, I pull things out and toss them to the ground, feeling more confused.

"Dacre, why are there needles in your bag?"

Ignoring her, I find the candy bar and accidentally drop it.

"Are you using heroin?" she squeaks.

Nothing is clicking together right and I can only focus on what my body needs. "My sugar's low. I need help, all right?" I hate saying the words, and I'm honestly not even sure if I said them out loud or in my head. But I must have spoken them because the candy bar hits in between my lips, and I'm not sure if it's Sal feeding me or my own hand holding the bar.

I finish the candy and rest my back against the van.

Sal stays silent as I lean over to my bag, the fog in my head lifting. Blowing out a breath, I fish out a few glucose tablets from the bottle and chew them.

Time passes and I'm not sure how much exactly when I feel better, not completely, but not like a fiend needing a blood dose or an addict needing their drug fix.

Finally, I turn to Sal then, her gaze on me. I'm sure it's been on me the entire time

To break the odd tension growing, at least from my side, I say, "Did you mention heroin?"

Her face contorts into a cringe. "I'm sorry … it was the first thing I thought when I saw the needles."

"Don't you think I'd have heroin scars if I was shooting up?" A halfhearted chuckle escapes my chapped lips. But I get it. If I didn't have this disease, it would have been the first thing to come to my mind, too.

"Are you a diabetic, then? Or possibly hypoglycemic?"

I can't meet her inquisitive stare when the question is about to give me a panic attack. It shouldn't because I've never had a problem telling someone before. "Well, since there are the needles, it would make me a Type 1 diabetic."

"Why hide something like that, Dacre? Especially if something like this could happen? I mean, at work I wasn't sure if you had a 'restroom' problem or were just lazy and didn't want to do the work. Then sometimes there was the shakiness…"

"This is exactly why, Sal!" I yell. "I don't want to be treated different, like I'm incapable, or people thinking I'm *lazy*. It's not like I'm gonna shout to the world, 'Hey, my name's Dacre Vinson, and I have Type 1 diabetes.'" I shake my head. "They're strangers."

"I'm not a stranger, Dacre." She places her fingers on

my bicep.

"I know, and I still didn't want to tell you."

"It's your choice who you want to tell, but we're friends, right?"

"Can we not talk about it right now?"

Sal drops her hand from my arm and looks out to the trees. "Okay."

I wait for her to open up to me about Matilda, and she doesn't. She wants me to spill my life story to her, yet she's not an open book either.

We sit in silence as we wait and wait for someone to pass by, but not a single car does. Sal's fingers are fidgeting against the pavement as she looks toward the trees.

"You all right?" I ask, lifting my head from the side of the van. It's hot outside but luckily not like it has been.

"Yeah, are you feeling okay?" she asks.

"Back to a hundred percent." For who the hell knows how long, though.

"Then I'll be right back." She opens the door and reaches inside for her backpack behind the seat. "I'm going to go in for a few minutes and check to see if the trees have any unusual fruit."

She can't be serious. "This isn't the time, Sal. Definitely not the time."

"I've been here before with my pa on a tour. It'll be fine." She pauses. "Plus, I want to see what kind of fruit they have."

"Then I'll come with you." She can't think I'd let her go wandering off alone inside a jungle. I wouldn't go by myself in one unless I was prepared.

"No, just wait right here in case someone passes by." Sal looks up and down the road, as if a car might be coming right then. "I promise I'll be back in like ten minutes, tops."

What happened to a few minutes?

"You know the Mayans survived out here, so I'll be okay."

"They also aren't here anymore." I don't know where they went exactly, but obviously the jungle wasn't working for them.

"Expand on this history lesson, please." She shuts the door and meets my icy gaze.

I'm not her pa, so I shrug my shoulders. "Yeah, go on with your fruit obsession."

"Whatever." She adjusts her backpack and marches off into the jungle while I stare after her, pissed.

Ten minutes later, or that's my guess since my phone's dead, I slide my hands in my pocket and feel the avocado seed. I know I made a mistake in letting her go alone. The sun already looks as if it's going to be setting soon as the sky grows a bit darker.

I don't want to leave my backpack behind with all my stuff in it, so I grab it from the van and walk inside the jungle. The only place to start is where Sal did, but there's a lack of any footprints, and I'm no detective. A loud squawk high up in the tree radiates through the air. Insects chirp, branches sway, and leaves crunch as I head farther in.

"Sal!" I shout and wait for her to call back. But nothing comes. My heart starts to accelerate as I glance all around. It all looks the same. Except, up ahead, there are trees with figs. "Sal!" I shout again.

"Dacre?" Her voice sounds tiny in the distance, but relief spreads through me at hearing it. She calls my name again, and I head in the direction where it comes from.

"Where are you?" I call.

"This way!"

It takes me a minute, but I finally find her near a large papaya tree.

"Aren't these beautiful?" she says while gazing up at the too-far-up fruit. The tree's top brushes the sky and the green papayas almost look like deformed-sized lemons, but larger.

"Do you want me to scale it for you?" I don't really want to, but the way she's looking up at it, like this piece of fruit is her world, makes me want to grab one for her.

"No, they aren't ready yet, but thank you." Her eyes focus on mine, growing serious. "Why aren't you waiting back at the van? What if someone passed us?"

"You were taking too long. You said ten minutes tops." Maybe I had just thought it felt like more, but I didn't have any way of finding out.

"Well, I found more than I thought." She adjusts the backpack on her shoulder.

"We don't need fruit right now," I say, staring up at the darkening sky.

Her smile fades as she looks down at my feet. "Dacre, run!"

She pulls my hand and I almost topple over. We run in the direction that I think is back, but everything still looks the same, and the sun is setting. We run and run, but it's taking too long.

I pull Sal to a stop and breathe hard, because I don't even know why the hell we're running. "What was it?"

"Snake." She takes in deep, heavy breaths.

"A *snake*?" My voice goes up an octave. "And we ran

this far over a reptile? We could have bounced out of the way. Now I don't know where we are anymore."

Sal ignores me. "Dacre, do you hear that?"

I listen closely, and there's a sound of water falling. Pushing a few limbs out of the way for us to pass through, I spot a waterfall. Sparkling with steady motions under the fading light.

The dark is already coming down upon us, and I don't know how to get us out of this mess. Monkeys sound from the jungle, growing louder as the night begins to make its descent.

I don't usually panic, but I'm starting to now. "Sal, I think we're going to have to stay here until morning."

"*Morning*?" she shrieks and hastily searches around. "No, I know where to go."

"You don't, do you?"

"In the morning, I'll figure it out," she says with determination.

I think about what I have left in my backpack. Two water bottles, a jar of peanut butter, two breakfast bars, and glucose tablets. It's enough.

"Sal, what food or drinks do you have in your pack?"

"A roll of crackers, a bottled water, and the fruit I grabbed." She appears a little nervous as she peers down at her backpack.

"Okay, so we'll be fine," I say, staring at the waterfall. "As soon as the sun rises in the morning, we'll get out of here."

Sal looks at the blades of grass beneath our feet and back at me. "We don't have a tent, Dacre."

"We'll be okay. We just have to stay close by the water, and nothing will come near us," I lie, but think that maybe it could be true. It sounds good at least.

"Why did we have to waste all this time stopping at places?" she says.

"No. Why did you have to come in here, Sal? This is all your fault with your stupid fruit obsession." If she hadn't come in here, we would have both been at the side of the road. Someone could have stopped by now.

"My fault. *My* fault? You're the one who came into the jungle!" She glares at me, inching closer.

I shift even closer, craning my neck down at her. "But you came here first!"

Sal takes a step back and plops down at the edge of the lake. I can barely see her face. "I'm sorry," she whispers. "I didn't come in here because I wanted to see fruit, Dacre."

"Then what?" I ask, still irritated.

Defeated, her eyes meet mine. "I came in here to have fruit in case you needed it—in case your sugar got low. Who knows how long it would've taken for someone to come down that road. And it's my fault for us taking this driving route."

My heart beats an extra thump because she didn't do this for her—she did this for me and my stupid diabetes. If I didn't have this damn disease, we wouldn't be in this predicament now. "It's my fault."

"No, it's the van's fault. How's your sugar? Is it okay?" Her tone's worried, and I remove my backpack and sit down beside her.

"Yeah, I'm fine. If I need anything, I have the fruit. Thanks to you." One night. That's it. Just one night.

She nods.

I squint my eyes, looking for a sign of a person or

possibly an abandoned tent, but it's only us. When my gaze meets Sal's, I say, "If you have to take a piss, you better do it now."

18

Sal

After splashing cool lake water against my face, I inhale deeply and take in the aroma of wet grass and trees. Cedar and mahogany trees, I think. Then I admire the now dark skyline. Stars—tons of them—dot the night sky, and the almost full moon provides enough light to illuminate this jungle, this place full of noises—crickets, cicadas, frogs, the occasional bird chirp, and…

Jaguars.

Standing, I listen carefully for sounds of large cats. Nothing, just the sound of the water descending from the waterfall. But what about snakes?

A warm hand lands on my shoulder. "You've been by the edge for a while," Dacre says, "Are you gonna piss again, Sal?"

I squat and look over my shoulder. "I'm about to."

Dacre kneels next to me. "Well?" he asks after a

moment.

"Well, what?"

He tosses a small pebble into the water. "Do your thing."

"*You* do your thing." I push him to the side.

He drops down on the grass, as if I actually pushed him hard, and puts his hands under his head. "This is … just like a bed." The sarcasm rolls right off his tongue.

Something itches at my arm, and I don't scratch it. Instead, I go to my pack and pull out the organic insect repellent and spritz myself down. After working on a farm for so long, I can't go anywhere without it.

"What are you doing?" Dacre asks.

"Do you want a lot of bug bites?" I hold the can out to him, and he takes it, spraying himself with maybe too much.

I lie next to him, and for a minute, we just stay there, watching the twinkling stars and the moon and the darkness.

Turning on my side, I ask, "Do jaguars roar?"

"Lions roar," he says, rolling my way.

"Do you think we'll come across a wild animal?"

He doesn't say anything for a long moment. "I'm not going to lie, Sal. It's a strong possibility."

"How are we going to find our way back?" I've been here with Pa, but I don't know every single detail about the jungle.

Dacre stares up at the star-lit sky. "We'll figure that out tomorrow."

"Tomorrow…" I think of the broken van, the sloth, the magic carnival, avocados, and Pa. And I wish … I wish I could travel to the past and ask Dacre to drive around the animal on the road.

But I can't change what's happened.

And somehow, I feel trapped here, like the day I locked myself in the kitchen's pantry when I was small while Pa was outside. But, no, this isn't like that, because I have Dacre by my side, and together, we'll find our way back to civilization.

A horrible thought strikes me: What if we have to wait for *days*? Worse—*weeks*. Or hell, *forever*. What about his sugar levels? I want to ask him more about his diabetes, but as I think of it, something inside me crumbles, because if he considers me a friend, then why didn't he tell me? He even trusted me enough to talk to me about his life, his family, and his parents living in different countries. I know enough about diabetes from Tía Matilda—I should have seen the signs. Dacre's pickiness with food, his constant trips to the restroom, and the way he would look pale and shaky at times. I almost hate myself for assuming drugs could have been a possibility.

I sit up and concentrate on the tall trees surrounding the lake and the waterfall, then lie down again and gaze at him. His eyes seem to be lost in the vastness of the sky.

"Are you tired?" I ask.

He turns his attention to me. "Not really."

"Were you devising escape plans?"

"No." I can hear the smile in his voice. "Well, kind of, but my grand plan is to go back the way we came in."

"You're a genius," I say.

"How about you tell me a secret?"

Biting my lower lip, I think about his question. I could tell him something silly, but this isn't the right place or time. "I don't know."

"We all have secrets, Sal. You go and then I will." He shifts closer to me. "What happened to your mom?"

I freeze because I wasn't expecting him to ask. "Ma?" A wave of sorrow travels through my body, and it's so weird, because I can usually control my feelings when I think of her. But when I think of Ma, the sadness is always because of memories that could have been. Her, Pa, Tía Matilda, and I, together at the dinner table eating some kind of food or even us all together planting new trees across the farm. Now that I'm here, in this situation, with Dacre, my state of mind is a mess.

"I can ask something else. It's fine."

But no, it isn't fine. I don't want to forget. I do want to tell him, but the robot inside me tells me not to, so I stay still and don't know what to do. Dacre lies on his back, his hands at his sides, and I do the same, staring at the star-dotted sky. I blink, trying to get rid of this thing inside me, then take a deep breath and clear my throat. I think to myself, *Everything will be okay, Sal. Everything will be okay.* Somehow, the barrier my robotic side created inside me crumbles down, leaving way to this lump in my throat. I'm a mess, such a mess of feelings. I try to choke it down, but I can't—I really can't. And I can't help but let out a little sob.

Dacre slides his arm around me, and I want to turn into his chest. I want to cry and spill the tears that have been waiting to come out, but I don't.

"My ma ... she," I start but my voice breaks, letting out another sob. No, I have to pull myself together. I sniffle. "My ma," I say, closing my eyes. "I don't remember her. Ho-how lame is that?" I swallow hard. "You're lucky—you have a mom."

He doesn't say anything for a long moment, as if my words left him speechless. "Maybe, but my mom and me … we don't connect. As for you and your ma, it isn't lame you don't remember her."

Taking a deep breath, I gather the energy to keep on telling my story. "It's not quite like that. I 'remember' her, but just by the pictures Pa took. It's weird, you know?"

"I bet, but at least you have your pa," he replies in a soft tone.

"Pa told me Ma died from Lupus when I was two years old." I sigh.

Dacre's arm tightens around me.

"It's so unfair," I add. "One day you're here, and the next, poof, you're gone." And somehow, these last words make me think of Dacre, what he's going through and what he has to deal with on a daily basis. No, he *isn't* going to disappear just because.

"I can relate to that—people possibly losing their lives anyway." He removes his hand and averts his eyes, as if lost in thought. "A shooting."

"Back in Texas?" I ask.

"No. Here. Not here, here, but back in your town." Dacre sighs. "Angel's Saloon."

"That place is a dump," I say, wrinkling my nose. "I never go near there." I've heard horror stories about that shady club.

"I wouldn't take you there either."

If we can escape this jungle. "Why'd you go?"

He shrugs one shoulder. "Lach took me to this club— his now ex-boyfriend asked him to meet there. I just wanted to get out of the house."

I want to ask him why he didn't want to be at home,

but he seems to have more to say.

"I was in the restroom when I heard the gunshots," he continues. "The first thing that came to mind was Lach. So I rushed out and searched for him, and I couldn't find him. There was a girl I was supposed to dance with, but I'm not sure if she made it out of there. I hope she did." His words make my heart constrict with contradicting feelings—he was with another girl who may have or may not have gotten hurt. "I'd just met her, though, like literally barely spoken."

"Oh, and Lach?" I ask, knowing nothing bad happened to him.

"Lach appeared behind me and scared the bejesus out of me. He was trembling but fine—not a single scratch."

"Wow," I say. Closing my eyes, I hope I'm not entering dangerous territory when I ask, "How did you meet the girl?"

"It's just, I met her that night and she asked me to dance. That was all."

Something inside me stirs, and I push it back down because the girl could've been hurt, and Dacre feels awful about it. "I'm sure you would've heard about it on the news if something happened to her."

His breathing feels off until he finally changes the subject. "What time is it? Can you read it from the moon's position or something?"

"8:56 and five seconds." I smirk. "I don't know, Dacre!"

"Mmm, that does sound like it could be accurate."

"We should try and go to sleep." I roll onto my back, stretching my arms and letting out a fake yawn. "Big day tomorrow."

Dacre gives me a small kiss to the temple, which takes

me by surprise. "I've got your back, Sal. If you ever want to tell me anything else, don't hesitate."

He's the one to talk. I mean, he's the one who should tell me 'anything else.' "We've all got those."

We lie flat on our backs again, and I place my hand on top of Dacre's, telling my robot that it's okay to let him in. I close my eyes and try to think of nothing. But I can't. It's like my brain is stuck in tenth gear and has no brakes.

"So," he says.

"I can't sleep either." I sigh, thinking about the incident earlier with Dacre's low sugar, and then me being a part of getting us in this mess. "There's something else I need to say, should have said back on the side of the road."

"What is it?"

With my eyes focusing again on the stars, I think of her. "I may not have had my ma around, but I had another wonderful woman who raised me—an aunt. Her name was Matilda, and she died less than a year ago."

Dacre takes a deep breath. "I know, Sal. Your pa told me."

"He did? Did he tell you how she died?" If Pa told him, I'm sure it would've made him feel awful. I really hope Pa didn't say any of this to Dacre.

"Yeah, he did…"

There goes my hope of Pa keeping his mouth shut, but Dacre just told me about his condition, so it's not like Pa knew at the time. "Oh."

"It's okay, Sal, you don't have to say anymore," he whispers.

I wait for my fast-beating heart to slow down because talking about this brings a torrent of emotions—sadness, frustration with not understanding why the world works the way it does sometimes. But I want to tell him. "I just don't understand why that happened. There were signs—clammy, peeing a lot, snacking—but I wasn't expecting her to die all of the sudden. I mean, she was rushed to the hospital because her sugar levels were shooting sky high, and…" I swallow hard. "Tía Matilda … she died a week later. So fast, you know?" *You know, you know, you know?* echoes in my head. My heart becomes this tiny thing because I wish we could've done something, anything. "I … I miss her."

He shifts closer and places an arm around me again. "I wish I had better words to say, but thank you for telling me."

I take a deep breath before saying, "That's how I knew we may need more sugar, why I went into the jungle. I wouldn't want to see anyone go through what she did, especially you. I'm sorry. I should have told you about that earlier." I wipe one of the loose tears that escaped my eye, needing to change the subject. "I'll let you know more about how great she was another time. But you know what? I've got something just for you."

"Oh, yeah?"

"Once upon a time in a distant future," I murmur to every part of the jungle, "on a planet from another galaxy, there was a rusty robot who worked for years-on-end, picking green eggs from tall, multi-limbed monsters. The robot met an alien from another planet. And the alien helped the robot pick the green eggs. They worked together—"

"And this alien didn't like green eggs, right?" Dacre interrupts.

"Do you want to hear the story or not?" I ask.

"Sure."

"Okay. Then the alien went back to his planet, and the robot died of the rusty plague."

"Sounds like my kind of plague," he says in a soft voice.

"Shh. There's more. In the end, the alien wanted more than anything to have his friend back, right? So he replaced all the rusty parts with new ones. With much determination, the alien was able to bring his friend back to life. With her new and improved abilities, the robot was able to pick more green eggs than ever before. And she had her alien friend to thank for that."

"You're totally talking about us. And even lost in the jungle, you can't wait for us to get back to pick more avocados together, right?" Dacre chuckles.

"I've never had a real friend. It feels nice, you know? I mean, there's Flor, but you're the first guy I'm really friends with."

"It definitely feels nice. Goodnight again, Sal." His voice comes out warm and different than he usually sounds.

After a moment, I say in a mechanical voice, "Robot to alien."

His eyes flip open. "Alien reporting to duty."

"Can I ask you something?"

"Of course." He smiles.

"Tía Matilda was forty-two when she was diagnosed." I keep my gaze trained on him. "How old were you?"

Dacre closes his eyes as if he's gathering his thoughts. "I was eleven and went into a diabetic coma. That's how we all found out."

"Oh, my God." Something in my heart deflates, because … eleven years old is way too young to suffer like that.

"I was using the restroom more days prior, but I didn't think anything of it. The transition was big, going from eating what you want to not was emotional for me as a kid. The needles were the worst. My parents didn't even help me with my first insulin shot because they said I'd have to get used to it. That first time, I sat scared shitless on the toilet for twenty minutes before finally sucking it up."

"I may not know on a personal level, Dacre. But I understand." I think I do. It's like Tía Matilda, but worse—much worse. Will he die young because of this? No, I need to calm down and stay positive.

He turns his head to me. "Sal?"

"Yeah?"

"I'm sorry I didn't tell you before about my diabetes. After your pa told me about your aunt Matilda, I thought it would be best to keep it hidden. I didn't want it to remind you of her."

It makes sense—it's a touchy subject, but I'm glad he told me. Something inside me relaxes, because I thought he didn't trust me, but he does. I know he does. "This robot would like to switch topics," I say in a monotone voice, trying to break the somber mood.

"I knew you were weird the day I met you, but it's a cool kind of weird."

I nudge him. "You're one to talk." Again, we relax into the quiet of the jungle. Not absolute silence because of the buzzing bugs, and the occasional bird sound. God, we're in the *Selva Lacandona* at night.

"Dacre?" I ask.

"Salbatora?" he replies.

"Can aliens and robots survive in this place?" I half-joke.

"We'll find our way back. I'm sure of that."

"Good." I don't know what to think of our current situation, but just thinking about it causes me to tremble.

"Are you cold?"

"A little," I lie, not wanting to complain about how terrified I'm starting to feel.

"We already did it once at the hotel." His voice is light with a smile behind his words.

"*What?*" I practically shriek.

He chuckles. "Not *it*. But held on to me when you were cold, remember?"

"In my *sleep!*" I swat him and he laughs.

Without another word, he opens his arm up, and I wouldn't have done this back at the hotel, but I do now. I lay my head against his chest. The *thump, thu-thump* of his heart beats against my ear. His chest rises and falls, helping to shut off my fears. No, not that, but it's a sense of calmness, like being alone on a beach watching the waves.

Waves… Is this…

Is this the calm before the tsunami?

19

Dacre

My body hurts. It feels as if I'm sprawled out on a pile of dirt, and I even taste it. I slowly open my eyes and a bright light blinds me. I'm about to tell Lach to turn the damn light off, but then I realize the orangish color is rays from the sun, and I actually have dirt in my mouth.

I push myself up from my stomach and rotate my shoulders, trying to relax the muscles. Whatever grains are in my mouth, I spit out onto the sparse grass. To my right, Sal is still fast asleep, folded up as if she's lying in her own comfortable little nest. Her bandana is safely beside her forehead, ready to eventually be put back on.

My thoughts circle to the conversation last night. She told me about Matilda—I told her a little about my diabetes. A part of me selfishly wishes it was still hidden from her, because that part of me really likes her. *Friend, Dacre, friend—that's it. All the parts of you like her as a friend.*

Shaking my head, I unzip my backpack and chug a half-bottle of water to get the lingering taste of dirt out of my mouth.

My hands shake as I lower the plastic bottle, and I can tell before I even get my meter that my sugar is low. All the sounds of the jungle blend together—insects chirping, buzzing, twitching. Hurriedly, I find the container of glucose tablets and pop open the lid with a shaky hand.

I toss back eight of them into my mouth and chew up the chalky tablets. This kind is supposed to taste like oranges, but every single flavor tastes like shit. The avocado seed is still in my pocket so I pull it out and place it back in my kit after I fill up the syringe and give myself my morning shot. I don't have many needles left either, so I might have to reuse them even though there is a possibility for a skin infection—a deadly one.

If it would have been as simple as getting to reuse needles, then I wouldn't have had to hear Mom complain over the years about having to buy so many needles, lancets, test strips, and insulin.

As I'm putting the meter into its case, Sal stirs from her slumber, and my hands jerk, spilling a few of the contents. *Old habits die hard*, I think as I hurry and zip it up.

"Good morning, Empress of the Avocados."

"You can say that again when we get home, and I might not have a sarcastic remark in return." She smiles, but her eyes appear worried as they scan the scenery around us. Her tired gaze stays studying the descent of the waterfall as the sound surrounds us. "How's your sugar?"

That's one of the reasons I didn't want this, because

there would always be that question, but I smile anyway. "It's a little low. How about we eat first and then head off?"

She nods and slides out a water bottle from her bag. I take out the two breakfast bars and toss her one. She then pulls out some of the fruit she'd picked just yesterday— one of the main reasons why we're in here. But I'm not going to say anything. And I don't as I grab a guava.

I press the fruit to my lips and it tastes amazingly sweet. Sometimes, I miss the days when I could just eat whatever I wanted. Actually, almost every day. For once, I'd like to have a bowl of ice cream because *I want it*, not because my sugar's low and my body needs it. I can't even remember the last time we went to an ice cream parlor and I got to pick out whatever flavor I wanted without a reason for it.

The fruit resting on my tongue seems to become bitter as I think more and more about it. My brow furrows as I stare fiercely at the ground, watching miniature insects scurry around.

"Something wrong?" Sal asks, dragging me out of my thoughts.

"Not more than it already is," I say in a harsher tone than I mean to, lifting my head up.

"Okay, foul mood this morning it is," she says softly, taking the last bite of her fruit and tossing it to the grass.

"Sorry, Miss Brightside, I shouldn't have acted like an ass. Like I said last night, I'll get us out of here." One small step to get away from the lake, one giant leap to get us out of here. More like several giant leaps.

"You're fine. I'm not in the greatest of moods, either."

Is she sure about that? Maybe she's better at wearing

her mask than me.

When I don't say anything, she adds, "I need to use the ladies' room, so you might want to go to the boys' room before we leave." She points in the direction across from us, near the waterfall where I went to last night.

"Yeah, okay. Good idea." We each strap on our backpacks, not willing to leave them behind—in case someone or something decides to wander off with it.

At that moment, monkeys' screeching radiates throughout the jungle as if a mating ritual is taking place right then. I clench the straps on my pack tighter because I can definitely see a monkey trying to steal one of our bags.

"Meet you back at the lake," Sal says, leaning on her heels before taking a step back.

"Our new safe zone." I turn around and trample past two large cedar trees, pushing a large leaf out of the way. The sound of the waterfall increases as I shuffle in between two large bushes. A small limb scratches my arm, and I lightly rub my hand over it to stop the sting.

As I come to a stop, I'm about to unzip my shorts when I see a toucan watching me from above. It feels a bit creepy, and I know I should just piss, but I can't. So I let go of my zipper and move out a bit farther, stopping in front of a tree with thick olive vines wrapping up the trunk.

Before I head back, I press my forehead against the bark of the tree and stand there to think for a few minutes. I told Sal last night I'd find our way back, but really, how am I going to do that if I don't even know which damn direction to go in?

Despite our situation, I had wanted to make her feel

better, but in reality, I'm starting to feel useless. I probably should have told her that I don't know where to go and there's a chance we could die out here.

Pulling my wits back together, and whatever confidence rests there, I tell myself we can do this. I've been leaning up against this tree longer than I should have, and Sal's probably wondering what I'm even doing out here.

I rub my forehead where the imprint of the tree bark lingers. The smell of the jungle is a unique scent all its own, and I breathe in fresh earth mixed with exotic flowers as I head back to the waterfall. The water drowns out a lot of the other noises which was probably a good thing for Sal last night.

When I push a branch out of the way, I expect to spot Sal near the lake, but she's not back yet. After an impatient minute of staring at the treetops and sky, I whisper to myself, "What the hell is she doing?"

I'm about to go after her, but what if she's still doing personal stuff? After another minute, I say screw it, because we're in a jungle. Privacy be damned.

"Sal," I call, stumbling a bit over a few fallen tree limbs. "Sal!" She doesn't say anything back. Only a few wild birds caw as they fly over my head and dart away. My leg itches from a few bug bites that have swollen but I ignore it as I search around.

This doesn't feel right. My heart accelerates in my chest, thumping harder and faster with each beat. I grab at my hair to calm myself down as I scan the area. "Come on! Don't tell me you went looking for fruit again!" *What if she did go searching for more fruit?*

When I find her, apparently, we're going to have to

stay linked together, even for "potty" breaks.

"Sal!" I yell as loud as I can, my voice cracking.

There's still no sign of her, only bright orange and blue flowers and an abundance of trees. A rustling of bushes comes from behind me. I whirl around to shout at her, stopping my vocal cords from going any further when I see a tapir. It looks almost as if a rhino, anteater, and a mouse were to have had a baby together. Along its body, there's short fur that's a dark shade of brown and almost looks black. The last time I saw one of these was back at the Houston Zoo in Texas. Without moving a muscle, I watch the animal scurry a few paces across the dirt and leaves before disappearing behind a few bushes.

The sun's rays beam down over the jungle, and it's just tree after tree. A large sheet of moss dangles across a limb in front of me. I rip it down and throw it at the ground to help my mood.

What if something took her? No, what if *someone* did? She also mentioned jaguars, but I would have heard one, right? I think back and maybe not, because I was near the waterfall. But I would have definitely heard a growl.

I press my fingers against my temples, digging in as hard as I can. Priority one, finding Sal. Option two, getting out of the jungle so I can find someone to locate Sal. Why am I already overthinking this? I'll find her.

With quick paces, I head back to the waterfall, in case she showed back up there. But she isn't here. The memory of yesterday comes to mind, being held up with guns. There could be shady people in the jungle. Or maybe the Mayans made their great comeback.

"Seriously, Dacre? Next thing you're going to say is that the ghosts of the Mayans are here. Fuck, I'm done.

I'm already talking aloud too much. *To myself.*" I've barely been alone and I'm already turning into Tom Hanks in *Castaway*. What was the name of that damn ball he carried with him? Who cares!

With no way of being able to tell time, I guess it's been about thirty minutes of me apparently needing to be taken to a mental institution. I head back in the direction Sal went earlier, sweat dripping down the back of my neck and back. Despite my nerves on edge, I walk in a straight path, calling her name over and over until my voice is dry and hoarse. And now I'm thirsty as hell.

Unzipping my backpack, I pull out the water and drink the last of the bottle. One left. This is a survivor nature show's nightmare. Well, not a survivor one, because I'm still here!

I plop down in front of a tree, resting my back against it. Time passes and passes. The humidity is driving me crazy.

My stomach rumbles, so I take out the jar of peanut butter. If only Sal was here with those spoons of hers and those crackers. Thinking better of it, I put it back in my bag. The peanut butter would only make me thirstier, and I don't need that right now. If only I had stayed by that waterfall.

Sal could be anywhere. What if she's dead? She's not dead. I decide to go in a different direction because I feel like I'm just going deeper and deeper into deadly grounds versus possibly finding a way back to the van. But it's all just a hypothetical guess in this labyrinth of trees.

Something akin to a growl comes from right above me. Without moving any other part of my body, I slowly tilt my head back and stop when I spot the animal. A jaguar. Its black spots are sprinkled over the orange fur that looks more vibrant in real life than on the nature shows.

My body is frozen as the large cat growls a low and deadly sound again. But its head isn't looking at me—it's staring at a small monkey in the next tree over.

Right as the jaguar leaps from the tree above me to the next, I quickly move away, slamming my backpack hard into a trunk and turn to take off running like there's no tomorrow. My insides are both rattling physically and mentally. To distract myself from the grumbles of the cat as I hurry through the jungle, not once looking back, I think about the ocean I love so much. I pretend like the dirt and grass on the jungle floor are waves, and I'm surfing over them, beating each one. A shark swims up from behind me, but I veer perfectly over the water, killing it, crushing it. The growls either stopped as the jaguar feasts on its meal, or I made it too far away.

I sigh in relief, but don't stop running—that's when I leap over a branch and into something not quite solid. The next thing I know, my body is sinking, and I can't get out.

20

Sal

As I search for the right spot to relieve myself, I remember when I came to the *Selva Lacandona* with Pa a while back. The guide asked us to stay together because the dense jungle made it incredibly easy to get lost. I should've remembered that when I first ventured to find some fruit for Dacre. And my non-robotic side made me dart away when I saw the snake.

It is what it is.

Stopping, I set my backpack behind a thick, rugged tree trunk and peer up in awe. Its branches touch limbs from other trees, like having a reunion … in happiness or possibly sorrow? *No, Sal—be positive*. I take a deep breath, letting the aroma of leaves, bushes, and the whole jungle enter my lungs. If I weren't lost in this vast place, I'd be happy to stand here surrounded by the different shaped trees—each one unique in its own right. Some with gnarled branches, others with newborn limbs. A bug with too many legs crawls up my leg and I flick It away.

Okay, time to take care of business.

After I relieve myself, a low howl echoes in the distance, followed by sounds of bird wings flapping. Squinting, I discover a rainbow. No, not that—a flock of colorful macaws flying away. A black monkey with a long tail appears, hanging from a branch, swatting an arm, as if trying to scare the macaws. He looks down from its spot up in the tree and howls, showing a couple of menacing fangs, which make me jump in place. I step back and hit a trunk. I move around it until I can't see the long-tailed animal. After a few tense seconds, the howling subsides, and I listen intently to the sounds of the jungle—bugs buzzing and the occasional chirp.

Moving around the tree, I take a peek—no monkeys, or macaws, or anything. Just the tree branches intertwined, hugging themselves. I stay in place for a long moment and wait for my heartbeat to slow down, then trudge back to my backpack. When I'm about to lift it, leafy bushes with small berries catch my attention. Curious, I walk to them and inspect one—tiny with red fruits. I don't know what kind it is—doesn't seem edible. But there seems to be something more behind these tall bushes.

Pushing them aside, I lose my footing and slide down into a wide, circular pit.

I dig my fingers in the dirt, but the texture is too soft. Unable to get a grip, I dart down, down, down without any control whatsoever. I hit the bottom. And roll. A rock the size of a golf ball comes down after me, and I have no time to move out of the way. It knocks me on the face. My cheek. Sharp pain. I lose sight of everything in the jungle.

However long later, my head hurts, my cheek stings, and I feel dizzy. When I try to sit up, everything around me spins, making me drop back to the ground. With my cheek pressed against the dirt, I spot a worm crawling my way. I turn to the other side, and with the minor movement, my brain rattles against my skull. *Am I going to die here of starvation or dehydration?*

No, the robot inside me replies.

But for a moment, the image of a vast desert and a woman clutching her throat as she begs for water comes to mind. No—I have to conquer my fears and use logic. The waterfall has plenty of water, and there's fruit all around—along with jaguars, snakes, monkeys, and… No, no, *no*! I'll wait until the world stops spinning before attempting to climb out of the pit. I close my eyes and take deep breath after deep breath.

Dacre.

His name comes to mind and makes me gasp. We're here and he has a limited stash of insulin tablets and shots. They should last him, what, a day or two? I have to escape this deep hole and hurry back, so we can find a way out before he runs out of medicine. Besides, he has to be worried that I've taken so long. *How long has it been?* I open my eyes again and lie on my back, squinting at the big opening above me and the intertwined branches. Then I turn my attention to this huge hole, which must be about ten meters wide. Its walls rise about three meters high, sloping down in an angle—definitely climbable. I thrust myself into a sitting position and get dizzy again, but not as bad as before.

"Dacre," I say in a hoarse voice. I swallow hard.

"Dacre!" He can't hear me unless he's nearby. Maybe he is? "Dacre!" I shout again. "Dacre!"

No reply.

With all the strength I can muster, I stand on wobbly legs and try to keep my balance. My cheek pulsates from the hit, so I touch it and look at my fingers—blood. It reminds me of the time I was running outside as fast as I could when my foot got caught in a small hole in the ground, causing me to trip and fall onto broken shards of glass. Only that hole was a lot smaller than this one. Blood drizzled out from the wound, and at the time, it seemed like rivers. I'd thought the doctor would amputate my arm—it had felt worse than it actually was.

Pa came rushing from the farm and applied a bandage, then took me to the town's Red Cross clinic. And we waited for hours in the emergency room, where I cried on his chest. But the funny thing is—my injury didn't hurt as bad.

Pa. I wish he were here, helping us get out of this jungle. No. Let's be real, Pa isn't here, and I can't cry on his chest like a little girl when something's wrong.

Okay.

I have to get out of this pit and find Dacre. I crawl toward the nearest wall, like a soldier in a trench. The soil sticks to my clothes, arms, and legs. But I keep pushing myself forward until I get dizzy. Again. I look at the dirt wall and now that I'm a bit closer, it seems taller than I thought. A heavy sigh escapes past my lips. *How am I going to get out of here?*

A howling sound makes me look up at a monkey climbing down a tree. I know what kind it is, a howler monkey—so proper. Even in this fearful moment, I chuckle at that. More onyx-colored monkeys appear, and soon, a group of about three follow what I guess is the leader. As one reaches the bottom of the pit, I drag myself backward until I'm at the center of the hole.

The other monkeys slide down the slope from all around, and I don't know why I get this crazy image of fur animals surfing. I laugh in my head at this stupid thought—Dacre would love it. But these wild animals aren't a laughing matter. They're bigger than the capuchin monkey from the magic show, and about a meter tall. As they approach me, their howls grow louder, and I cover my ears. The leader creeps my way and shows me his long canines. As my heart quickens, I close my eyes.

The howling stops, making me uncover my ears.

Grunting. I can hear the leader smelling me.

"*Please*, don't bite me," I murmur more to myself than anything as the hair on my arms stand on end. My body stays as frozen as possible.

Grunt. Sniff. Grunt. Sniff.

Silence.

Stepping.

Taking a deep breath, I open my eyes. The leader turns to leave, and the rest follow. Up they go, climbing the pit's walls with dexterity, digging their nails in the soil, their long tails swinging about. After they disappear from my sight, distant howling resonates all around, as the monkeys search for their next victim.

Dropping my tense shoulders, I force myself up and stand on weak legs, knowing I can do this. I walk to the edge of the wall and look up again—listening to my robot, who tells me it's at about a forty-degree angle, making it totally climbable. So I go for it, mimicking the monkeys, digging my fingers into the dirt. But when I'm a quarter of the way up, I lose my grip and slide back down.

"No, no, no!" I shout in frustration, running a hand through my short hair.

There has to be an easier way. I search around, perspiration beading my forehead, and I find a vine running down the opposite wall. *Yes!* I can use it to climb up. I pad to it and tug at it—it won't give up on me. So, I do the climbing, holding tight onto the vine, one step at a time. And when I'm midway through, I glance back and get another dizzy spell. Without letting go, I close my eyes and inhale, then exhale.

You can do this.

Looking up, I take another step. And another. My knuckles turn white with the effort, but I won't give up. Not now. I push myself harder, going up a little more. My arms and legs burn. *C'mon, Sal.* With a supreme effort, I climb the rest of the slope and reach the top. Dropping onto the ground, I curl and flex my hands, trying to make my blood flow again. I hurriedly search around to see if there are any lingering howler monkeys, but they all seem to have already left.

After a minute of rest, I stand, put on my backpack, and stumble back the way I came, except now filthier with aching muscles. The waterfall appears after I push some bushes aside. If I were in another situation, the water and the lush vegetation would feel like paradise. But right now, it's just a part of the devil's playground.

"Dacre?" I look around, and when I get no answer, I make a megaphone with my hands and yell, "Dacre!"

No one emerges from the lake or appears from behind a tree.

There's no way he's still "taking care of business." Maybe he got lost again. *More* lost, that is, since we're already lost. I sit on a boulder and wait, but I can't just be here. I need to find him, especially if he went searching for me.

If I were him, where would I go? Anywhere, that's where I'd go. Hmm. I pick a direction and enter the jungle again, making sure to mentally file landmarks that will later lead us back to the waterfall. After a few minutes, I spot a few footprints that aren't mine.

"Dacre!" I shout for the thousandth time.

No reply.

Desperate, I pace forward, pushing branches aside, climbing over small boulders. Time passes, and the more I advance, the less this makes sense. After several long minutes, I come to a stop and listen—nothing. I turn around, but before leaving this area, there's a grunt, or maybe I'm imagining things. Still, I pad in its direction and step through thick bushes. I hear my name being called and run toward the voice.

Sand.

I gasp at the sight of a guy buried in it from the waist and down.

"Dacre!"

21

Dacre

My feet are sinking into something. When I look down, that something happens to be quicksand. If my heart could pound any more, it would blow up into an infinite number of pieces. I shift forward to get the hell out of here, but the shit only pulls me down more. My shoes are locked into place.

The grainy texture is rubbing every single inch of me. As I try to move, the liquid sand only becomes more watery and weighs me down. The sandy film is right above my waist, and I'm so frustrated I want to hit something.

At this moment, all my years of swimming and surfing aren't helping a single bit. Each minuscule movement only seems to be making everything worse.

I scream the first word—name—that comes to mind. "Sal!" If she didn't hear me before, she's not going to hear me now. But I try anyway.

"Sal!" I shout, my voice deep with raw nervousness. My throat still hurts from yelling for her earlier, but I don't care.

Sometimes, I find myself at the point where I don't think I'd care if I died because of the diabetes, but right now I don't want to. Not like this, drowning, suffocating until I cease existing. The thought of seeping down into this sand-gate to hell lights my insides on fire—Lach, Ezra, and even Mom will never know where I went. I would be just another mysterious Mayan disaster, the lost life of Dacre Vinson, except not many people will care.

The thick sandy goop continues to shift against my waist. I call Sal's name at least fifteen times in a row, because who else can I call for? The fucking jaguar?

There's a rustling from behind me. The jaguar did answer—I just know it, and here's the part where the big hungry cat is going to finish me off. I clench my fists in the air and prepare to fight back until I die. But then I hear the voice of an angel. "Dacre!"

Maybe not an angel, but it is the person I need. "Sal?" My tone comes out desperate, given the circumstances.

"Dacre!" she shouts, stopping at the edge where the quicksand meets hard dirt. "Oh, my God. How did you get in there?"

"I thought this would be a good place to relax and take a sand bath," I answer, rolling my eyes.

"Just come to me." She quickly waves her hand, holding it out for me to grab.

She's not too far, but I can't reach it. "I've been trying, but the more I move, the closer I am to vanishing." Eventually, the pit is going to consume my entire body.

"Dacre, quit being dramatic. The quicksand isn't like in the movies—just stop moving. Also, I'm pretty sure it's not even that deep."

"How would you know?" I ask in disbelief.

Now it's her turn to roll her eyes. "I've been to the jungle before, remember? Pa taught me a lot. Now relax and go onto your back. But first toss me your backpack, that thing's only weighing you down."

"My feet are stuck," I say but take off my backpack anyway. With one hard toss, it lands beside her on hard earth.

"I know. It's going to help, though."

I do as she says, my feet still planted at the bottom.

"Now roll a little to the side until you free your legs," Sal says softly, as if she's talking to her baby avocados, "and fill your lungs full of air. Keep doing that to help you stay more buoyant." Her clothes and skin are covered in dirt that I just now notice.

What I really want to ask is where the hell she's been all this time, but I'll do that once I get out. So I lie on my back as if I'm in the ocean, the liquid lightly swaying against me. It takes several rotations of me tilting my body to the side, but eventually, my feet finally become free. If I could, I'd yell to the Sandman for helping me get this far.

"Now stay on your back and propel yourself toward me as if you're swimming."

From my peripheral, I see her holding her hand out to me. It feels absolutely nothing like swimming in the ocean as I rotate my arms, building up the movement, trying to keep my lungs filled with oxygen, and move toward her. But then I feel a hand clasp mine, and my heart relaxes a little as she helps to pull me out.

With a deep sigh, I drop to the dirt and have never been so happy to see it in my entire life—I practically kiss it.

Slowly, I roll to my back and stare at the light-blue sky. A head pokes over my face, blocking the sun.

"I almost died." I chuckle, a bit crazed.

"In the two to three feet?" Sal smiles. "No, you may have been potentially trapped there until you died of starvation, but more or less, you would've only gone into a withered state."

"Just let me live out my glory for a moment, Sal." I stop laughing when I remember the whole reason I'm here. "You're about to get yelled at because where the hell were you? *Again*!"

"Oh, let me tell you about *that* story."

My gaze focuses on her, and I get a closer look at her face. There's a long gash along her cheek with dried blood and dirt stains her clothing. I hurry and sit up. "What happened?" I reach for her cheek and lift her chin instead, since my hand is still covered in liquid sand.

Her eyes lock on mine, and she glares. "I wasn't out searching for fruit—*again*. I went to the 'restroom' and somehow fell in some pit about ten yards wide and three deep. It was like the perfect trap for jungle inhabitants."

"*What?*" I look her over to check for more wounds, but she appears all right. She's only covered in dried mud, but there could be bruises elsewhere.

"I don't know, Dacre!" She pulls her face from my grasp and runs a hand through her hair. "Somehow, a rock fell and hit my cheek, knocking me out. Then I woke up in this dark hole and had to climb my way out—which took forever. And don't get me started on being almost attacked by monkeys."

"Damn, you really are bad luck," I say with a half-smile.

"Not usually," she mutters, then pauses. "Well, I guess on this trip."

"Eh, you're my bad luck, so it's all okay." I look around the jungle for which direction to start in. "You want to try getting out of here? If I knew the way back to the waterfall, we could at least wash off."

"Maybe my luck isn't so bad because I remember the way back." She grins, cocking her head behind her.

"You're a lifesaver." I wipe the sand off my palms on the front of my shirt before picking up my backpack.

"I learned to remember which direction I go in from now on."

"No jaguars?" I ask, thinking about the close encounter earlier.

"Jaguars?" Her eyebrows lower in confusion.

"Nothing." No need for her to get frightened. "Just keep your eyes open."

As we trudge through the jungle, pushing thick ropes of vines out of the way, there are growls in the distance. But nothing seems dangerously close.

The sounds of the waterfall draw near, and I'm more than thrilled Sal knew our way back. Now after this, if only we can get the hell out of here.

"You want to go in first?" I ask, staring at her, both of us in desperate need to get clean.

Sal crinkles her nose and scans me up and down. "Nah, I think you need to. Actually, same time."

I lift a brow.

"Going in with our clothes on, dummy."

From inside my backpack, I pull out my last set of clean clothes and set them next to where Sal has just placed hers, right at the edge of the lake.

"What's that?" I ask, staring at the two small bottles in her hand as I yank off my filthy shoes.

"Shampoo *and* body wash."

"I knew I needed you for something," I say, snatching the bottles from her hand. I hop in the lake as she shouts something not too nice at my back.

The water stops right at my shoulders. I turn around and glide backward, farther into the lake. "Just kidding. Come here, and I'll wash your hair for you."

"You're an idiot," she says but splashes into the lake. Sal strokes her way through the water and stops in front of me. I hand her back the bottles and scrub whatever grime I can from my clothes.

"This is stupid," she says, exasperated. "Just turn around so I can take my clothes off and wash them properly."

After a few minutes of her cursing, I guess trying to tug the wet clothing free, she tells me to turn back around. The water's too dark so I can't really see anything besides her bare shoulders.

"Go ahead," she says, swimming back out to the middle.

I stroke my way to the edge, glancing back once at her as she starts to shampoo her hair while she stares at the waterfall.

The shirt feels like it's glued to me, but I get it off. I scrub the rest of the clothes as best I can and toss them on the grass next to my shoes.

"Here," Sal calls, holding out her hand with the shampoo and body wash.

Gliding through the water, I come to a stop right in front of her. Something in my breath hitches when I pull my head out of the water, and my eyes fix on hers. Sal's short hair is slicked back, and the lake's gentle waves swish against the curve of her bare shoulders. It's not like I've never been naked with a girl in the water before, but this feels even more intimate than that.

"You're out of uniform," is all I say as I take the bottles from her hand. My skin lingers against hers for a moment too long.

"I have a new bandana waiting on top of my clothes," she replies, appearing unaffected that we're inches from each other. *Naked.* Then I have the image of her wearing only a bandana coming to mind, and I better drift away, thankful for the water's concealment.

Without another word, I swim to the waterfall and listen to the relaxing sounds as the water cascades down into the lake. I shampoo my hair and wash my body, but even though all the muck is off, I can still feel the graininess of the quicksand. And there needs to be a new word for it, since it isn't very quick at all—more like trapped-sand.

When I turn back to Sal, I find her already dressed and tying the bandana around her forehead. Something in my chest locks up, and I'm glad she's okay. I feel as relieved as I was the night I found Lach intact at the club. And I'm thanking every minute I'm here that both my brothers are safe at home with my mom.

After dipping my head below the water one last time, I swim back to the edge of the lake. Automatically or as she would say, robotically, Sal faces the other direction and heads to her backpack.

I lift myself out, wishing I had a towel, but I have to make do. After picking up my clothing, I throw them on. With the lake water, I scrub as much sandy residue from my shoes as I can before slipping them back on my feet.

Water droplets slide down the back of my neck as I walk to meet Sal. I hand her the two small bottles.

"Thanks," she says and tucks them away into her pack.

"No, thank you. You're a savior by having some of this shit in there."

"How are you feeling?" she asks, chewing on the edge of her lip.

What she means is, how is my diabetes doing. This time around, it's not bothering me as much with the question. "I can feel my sugar dropping." It doesn't seem too low, but I can tell it will get there if I don't eat soon.

"Okay, well let's eat something before we leave. You still have the peanut butter, right?" Sal asks as she pulls out her crackers.

"Yeah, but I only have a full bottle of water and an empty one left." The thought of peanut butter right now is only making me thirsty.

"Mine is almost empty"—she stares out at the waterfall—"but we can fill up with water from there."

"All right." I pause, staring at her massive bag. "So how did you manage to climb out with that big pack?"

Sal shakes her head. "I didn't. I sat it beside a tree, thankfully. Then when I walked through some berry plants, I fell into that deep hole I told you about."

"I can't believe I missed finding that hole," I say, handing her the jar of peanut butter.

She takes out a plastic knife from her bag. "It was still covered pretty well when I climbed back out. If my pack had fallen in, I probably wouldn't have been able to climb out with it."

As she rifles through her things, I pull out my kit so I can give myself a shot. My hand freezes as soon as I unzip and open it.

"What's wrong?" Sal asks.

It must have slipped out when I was caught off guard from Sal waking up this morning and spilled the contents. Frantically, I pull everything out of my backpack, and there at the bottom I spot the glass—broken. My heart thumps too rapidly when I look up at Sal. "My insulin bottle broke." The jaguar. The tree. Me slamming into it.

If it takes too long to get back, Sal might be heading out of the jungle alone.

22

Sal

My blood goes cold at Dacre's words—I can't believe things got worse than they were already. I stare down at his kit. "You … broke … how?" It's like sentences can't form in my mouth.

Dacre runs a hand through his hair. "It had to be when I slammed my back into a tree."

"How?" I ask again.

"I was running from a fucking jaguar, Sal." He closes his eyes and moves his mouth like he's silently talking to himself.

"A jaguar?" Is he joking? By his serious expression, I don't think he is, but you never know.

"Sorry, I thought it was better to keep that part out of my story." He rubs his forehead, clearly upset.

Calm down, my robot says, and I follow its orders, counting to three in my head. "I'm not going to fight about that." I gesture to his kit. "How does this change our…?" I can't even finish asking my question.

"It changes *everything*." He searches around the waterfall and trees before his gaze settles on my face. "We need to find our way out. Soon."

I want to ask how soon is soon, but that would create even more tension, so I refrain from asking. "Let's go then."

After filling up our water bottles, I squint at the sun and think about the best direction to take. *West*. That's the shortest way out because going any other route will lead us deeper into the jungle. How deep are we, anyway? I have no idea and feel *so* lost. No, no, no. We *will* find a way back to civilization, even if it is Hotel Carmelita. That shady place sounds like paradise now, and in other circumstances, this lake could be one, too.

"This way," I say to Dacre, pointing to my left.

He shifts his gaze in that direction. "We sure about that?"

I nod. "West is our best option."

Jerking a thumb over his shoulder, he says, "I say going back the way we came is better."

"Really." I cross my arms over my chest. "And what direction is that? Just back, huh? We could've walked in circles without realizing it, Dacre."

"And walking 'left' is the magical solution, *Sal*?" He frowns at me, which makes my blood boil.

"I don't know!" I throw my hands in the air. "We *are* lost, and the only thing coming to mind is moving toward civilization, which is *west*."

Rolling his eyes to the heavens, or in this case, jungle hell, he breathes deeply. "Fine."

"Fine," I echo. *Calm down*, my robot says, *think logically*. This is a desperate situation and each decision counts. But with Dacre staring at me and the mess we're in, I can't organize my thoughts like a machine.

Without another word, I pad away. Moments later, he comes into view, adjusting his backpack. We enter the lush area again, which is starting to look the same by now—a never-ending sea of cedar trees, shrubbery, grass, and brown soil. And wild animals. We trudge our way for about an hour in silence, as if our previous discussion cut our tongues out and we're unable to articulate a single word. As much as I love plants and trees, this feeling in the pit of my stomach makes me feel like puking.

"I hate the unknown," I say as we enter an area with lichen-covered trunks.

"What?" Dacre pushes a low-hanging branch aside.

"You know what I mean." I gesture around. "Doesn't it look the same to you?"

He shrugs one shoulder. "Not really. Look, it's greener here." He squats to touch a patch of grass, then glances back up at me. "Why's that, Sal?"

Kneeling next to him, I take a breath—the air's damper than before. For a moment, my blood drains as questions strike my mind: What if we're going in the wrong direction? What if his sugar levels drop again? What if—

"Well?" he asks. "You're the expert here."

"I'm not the 'expert,'" I say. "This much green could mean we're closer to the coast. Or that it rains more often in this area since the *Selva Lacandona* is a rainforest." I drop my tense shoulders. "It can be anything."

He doesn't reply, too busy digging his fingers in the

soil, like he's trying to plant a seed. I lean a little closer and shovel a chunk of it with my hand—tiny leaves, ranging from lime-color all the way to dead-brown, and microscopic twigs and stones.

"I could use this for my avocados," I say. "I mean, this is organic fertilizer."

"Avocados…" He propels to his feet, groaning. "That's why I'm here."

I spring up. "What's that supposed to mean?"

"Look, you…" he starts, then shakes his head. "Never mind, Sal."

My brain tries to complete his sentence, but the expression on his face tells me he really wants to spit it out. "I'm looking," I say, sarcasm peppering my words as I bring my hand to a salute position and scan the area extra slowly to prove my point.

He quirks a brow. "Get real here. If you wouldn't have entered this jungle or even offered me a job, I wouldn't be here."

"Really, Dacre? How many times are we going to discuss this?" I shake my head. "It wasn't my fault or anybody's—it just happened."

He scrunches up his face for a second. "You're right. It's my fault for taking the job."

I've never seen him this grumpy, not even after a long workday. Something's off. "Are you okay?"

"I'm fine," he says, touching his forehead.

Either he woke this way, which could happen, or he's feeling sick. "Are you sure?"

He grimaces a bit. "It's my sugar, and we didn't eat before we left." He points ahead. "I don't want to waste time."

"Dacre"—I grab his arm—"anytime we need to stop, we can."

"I'll eat on the move. I don't want to waste time."

Quickly, I pull out the crackers from my pack and as we walk, he dips them in the jar of peanut butter. I dig through my bag and hand him a guava—there are only two of those now left, along with two bananas. Which won't last us long at all.

Shifting my gaze up, I look at the tree limbs and can barely tell the position of the sun. It's past its zenith, which is bad news for us—I won't be able to tell which direction is west anymore. "We better hurry."

Resuming our trip, we stumble our way to wherever it is we're going. Again, I'm afraid of leading us in the wrong direction. We take a pebble-covered trail, but it's too hard on the feet. So we stagger through a cluster of plants with huge leaves—elephant ear plants—and find cedar trees shrouded in vines. About an hour or more later—I've lost track of time, sweat trickles down my armpits, and my legs burn. And a quick look at Dacre's face shows he's sweating, too. Maybe we should've stayed back at the lake, and then what? Wait for a miracle rescue? Or … *Don't think about it, Sal,* my robot warns me.

Dacre drags his feet—I guess feeling tired like me, but we have to keep on going. The aroma lingering in the air changes as we step into an area with different kind of trees. They stand tall, and unlike the cedars, their limbs are closer to their tops and have pear-shaped leaves.

"Mahogany," I say, stopping.

Dacre takes in the view in front of us. "How can you tell?"

"They look different and"—I sniff the sweet

aroma—"smell different."

"Than what?" he asks, taking his backpack off, breathing heavily.

I glance over my shoulder. "Cedar."

"They look the same to me." He fishes out a water bottle from his pack and offers it to me, giving a small smile. Which makes me think his sugar is okay. "Thirsty?"

We filled the empty bottles back at the waterfall, so we have a grand total of three. "Not now—we need to save water."

He puts it away and then focuses on me. "Look, I'm sorry about my shitty mood earlier." He rubs a hand across his jaw. "It's just when my sugar is off, I snap for no reasons at times, and there's the bottle incident."

I would be cranky if my lifesaver broke too. I place a hand on his shoulder because I get it, even though I don't have what he has. "Anytime you need to slow or stop because you don't feel good, just tell me."

He nods. "Do you think we're getting closer?"

My first thought is, *I don't know*, but that would just spark another discussion. "I think so." I gesture around. "Mahogany trees are a good sign," I lie.

Dacre rotates his shoulders. "I'm sick of walking with this damn backpack."

I take off mine and lean it on a tree, which brings images of the pit I fell into this morning. "Yeah, my shoulders hurt," I say, rubbing the back of my neck.

He pauses for a few moments and stares at me before shaking his head and moving closer. "Get over here, Sal." Before I can ask him what he's doing, his thumbs and fingers dig into the tight muscles. And it feels … it feels miraculous—like he's done this a thousand times before.

"Are you a certified masseur?" I ask, as he applies firm pressure to my neck.

He chuckles. "No."

I turn around. "I'm no masseuse, but I can try it if you want me to."

With an almost excited expression—well, as excited as Dacre can get, he faces the other direction. "I'll take it."

"Here it goes." I press my fingers against his shoulder blades.

"*Ow!*" he shouts, shrugging me off. "Never mind."

"It wasn't that hard, silly." I laugh.

He reaches over his shoulder. "Hell, yes, it was. Give me your hand for a sec." I place it in his, and he guides my fingers to his lower neck. "Here."

"Okay." I softly stroke the area after he releases my hand.

"I'd say it's a tad bit better." Without turning his head, he holds up his fingers an inch apart. So I gently stroke up and down, and his shoulders relax.

As I massage his upper back and hard muscles, I laugh after he makes a noise that sounds like an animal growling. My smile falls because I'm liking touching him more than I should. It's the perfect movie moment—I can see it: I release his shoulders, step around him, stand on my tiptoes, and kiss him on the lips, then the film credits roll with a happy ending.

Man, that sounded *so* cheesy, and so unrealistic.

Shaking the weird, pretend movie scene away, I remove my hands. Besides, Dacre only thinks of me as a friend. *And you should think of him as a friend, too*, my robotic side gushes.

"That was good." Dacre turns around and faces me.

"Cool." I feel a bit disoriented, which is funny since we're so lost. I mean, inside me—deep inside—something is aching to break out, but, you know, friendship is the most logical direction. Which, I guess, is *west?* I chuckle at this stupid thought.

"What's so funny?" he asks, fighting a smile.

"You and me. Here. Super-lost."

"Funny isn't exactly the word I'd use," he says, then lifts a brow, as if confused, "but whatever floats your boat."

Taking a deep breath, I nod at the mahogany forest. "Maybe there's civilization on the other side of these trees."

"Let's keep going then. The sooner we get out of here, the sooner we can kiss the cement." He picks up his backpack and slides it over his shoulders.

Dacre and I continue our trip toward the unknown. After a long time, the trees are a tad shorter, the soil gets a little softer, and there's more vegetation, if that's even possible—luscious shrubberies, wild white flowers, and tall grass growing in large circles around the trunks. This area looks similar to the one before, but not quite.

"I'd give my right arm for a map," Dacre says, stopping.

"Like an old-style map to a treasure chest?" I put some pressure on my tired legs.

"Something like that," he replies. "What time do you think it is?"

Weak sunlight filters through the branches from high up in the sky, and I scratch a couple of bites where mosquitoes have leeched out blood. "Later afternoon? I'm not sure—the jungle's too dense."

"I think I need a break." He points at a thick trunk.

I tap at my nonexistent watch on my wrist. "You have six minutes and thirty-two seconds."

He cocks his head to one side, then the other. "Nah, you should have given me a better answer. Six minutes, thirty-two seconds, and forty-four milliseconds. Then you could have tossed in microsecond, nanosecond, and picosecond."

Parting my lips slightly, I stare at him. "You took the joke a bit too far there, my friend."

"So I'm the weird one now?" He chuckles.

"That crown is now all yours." I laugh in return.

"Are you hungry?" he asks.

I nod. "Very thirsty, too."

After drinking only a little of my water and eating the last two bananas, we sit on the ground, our backs firmly pressed against a trunk. More mosquitoes come buzzing around, so I find the insect repellent in my bag and spray us both down. I sigh and close my eyes for a moment, thinking of my trees and home.

"Sal?" Dacre asks, startling me out of my pretend avocado-picking dream.

"What?" I open my eyes and find him squatting in front of me.

"You fell asleep." He pulls up to full height and helps me to my feet.

Still confused, I look around. There's less light, which means I slept for more than a few minutes. "We better hurry and find a place to spend the night—*again*." Again, horrible thoughts cross my mind. How long can he last without insulin? Are we even going to get out of this jungle?

"Hopefully, a place with water," he replies.

We trudge our way to what I hope is civilization, this time Dacre leading the way. He increases his pace and disappears through a group of tall plants with giant peach-shaped leaves.

"Whoa," he shouts, and a moment later, he pokes his head through the shrubbery and waves me on. "You're not gonna believe this."

Joining him, I take a peek and find a small valley with tall and wild green grass. Without thick vegetation blocking my view, I can finally tell the sun is starting to set. But what gets my full attention is a strange-looking brick construction up ahead.

"It's a ruin," I whisper, not knowing why, but it seems this place demands silence, like museums or libraries. I mean, this is real history in front of us.

From this distance, the building looks like a big mound with a small house on top. I move a little closer and realize the mound resembles a dilapidated pyramid with stairs leading to a rectangular building, which appears familiar. I gasp—I've been here before. "I know this place!" Grass protrudes in between where the bricks join, the setting sun bathing the construction in fiery orange.

"You're being delirious, Sal," he says.

"No! I came here with Pa—a tour." My heartbeat increases, and I feel like clapping. "I know how to get us out of this jungle!"

"Definitely delirious." He crosses his arms.

I nudge him. "I'm not lying! Civilization is a couple of hours away."

His eyes study my face, I guess trying to find out if

I'm going bonkers. "You *are* telling the truth. After all this talk about Mayans, we've finally stumbled across their territory, right?"

I nod. "Definitely Mayan, since they dominated this part of the country."

"The jungle gods are always listening," he replies. "Which way should we go?"

Pointing at the trees behind the ruin, I say, "That way."

He peers up at the evening sky. "Maybe we should spend the night there," Dacre says, gesturing to the house. "Unless you think we should go farther."

Gazing around at the trees surrounding us, I realize this may be safer than venturing out right now. I mean, when I was around this area with Pa, the tour guide warned us about the hidden dangers—his words. But then, I think of Dacre's sugar levels and unable to contain myself, I ask, "How long before you need more insulin?"

He glances up for a long moment, as if making mental calculations. "I'm not sure, it all depends, but this walking keeps making it low."

"You'll be fine then."

"As long as no monkeys intervene and rip us apart."

I swat his arm. "Dacre!"

"Kidding!" He chuckles.

Dacre and I climb the ruin's steps, which aren't that many, and reach the top, then creep into the house through one of its three entrances. Nothing much here, just brick walls and a floor. After setting down our backpacks, we relax, sitting side by side.

"This moment would be perfect if I had a sleeping bag," he says.

I touch my backpack. "At least we brought pillows."

"Let me try that." He scoots forward, stretches out his long legs, and lies on his side with his head on his backpack. "Not bad."

Doing the same, I end up face to face with him, about half a meter apart, the hard floor crushing my ribs. "Yeah, not bad at all."

He closes his eyes. "Goodnight, Sal."

"Goodnight." Clasping my hands, I press them against my chest.

Being here in this place makes me think of the people who built this, how they lived and what they did—that kind of thing. I take a breath and concentrate on Dacre's face, feeling compelled to move closer to him. And I do until our faces are a few centimeters away. Warmth radiates from his body as his chest heaves ever so slowly—he's already sleeping.

Because I can't help myself, I kiss him on the cheek and whisper in the lowest of voices, "We'll get out of this mess tomorrow, Dacre. I promise."

23

Dacre

Pound, pound, *pound*. I let out a loud grunt as I reach for the left side of my skull. The pain inside is blazing—an inner fire igniting in my brain. Digging my fingers into my scalp, I feel the sensitive spot where it's coming from.

Slowly, I open my eyes to darkness. I clench my teeth to try to stop the pain, but it won't go away. Then I remember where I am—at some Mayan ruin, which is better than sleeping out in the middle of the jungle. Sitting up, I tear the sweat-soaked shirt from my body.

Fidgeting in the dark, I grab my backpack to find my meter, hoping my sugar isn't high as hell. My broken insulin bottle is resting somewhere in peace because of my stupid bad luck and me not looking where I was going. And I'm not going to lie, I was panicking inside my head for a long while before Sal finally knew where we were.

Earlier when my sugar was low, I acted like a moody

jerk for no reason to Sal. When I'm having problems with sugar on the high or low side, it causes me to snap at things more easily. Since I haven't eaten that much, I don't think it will be high. But the disease is always unpredictable.

After rummaging through my bag, I finally find the kit that drifted down to the bottom. If only I had a light to see something.

"Dacre?" Sal asks, no tiredness in her voice, as if she's been lying there unable to sleep. "You all right?"

"Yeah, I'm fine. I need to test my sugar, but I won't be able to read the screen." I guess I'll just have to play a guessing game with whether it's low or high. I've always had a way to light up a room or place with something, until now. If this was back in the Mayan times, this is what I'd be doing. Oh no, that's wrong, I'd be dead, because there was no insulin back then. I shrug off the morbid thought.

"Hold on a second." A rustling comes from where Sal is, and then I hear the sound of her backpack being unzipped. After a few moments, the light of a small flashlight clicks on, illuminating the bricked room.

"Are you sure you didn't come semi-prepared for the jungle?" I ask, pricking my finger with the lancet, ignoring the thump of my headache.

"You should see it when Pa and I go to the jungle." She smiles, moving the flashlight in-between me and her.

The meter blinks a few times before showing my reading. And it's low as fuck. *Again.* But I hold my emotions back, staring up at the low-ceiling. With a yank of the glucose tablets, I pour them out in my hand and pop them back in my mouth, hoping to neutralize this. I stare down at the empty bottle, my heart thumping a taunting beat. "I'm out."

I catch Sal watching me. "Do you need one of the fruits? I have two left."

"No, I'll be fine and will eat one in the morning if I need it."

"As soon as there's light, we're out of here," Sal says with determination. And thank God she knows the way out, because I honestly don't think I would've found a way. She said it should only take us a couple hours to get back to the road from this location, which I could walk in my sleep with that timeframe.

"How long was I asleep?" I ask, hoping it's already almost morning now.

"Probably less than an hour," she says. "We still have a long while until sunrise."

The annoying pounding is still going off in my head. "You wouldn't happen to have something in your magical backpack for a headache, would you?"

Sal ticks her finger back and forth in the air. "You're in luck." She withdraws a small white container from her bag and hands me two pills.

I drag out my water and swallow them down with the warm liquid, finishing this bottle and only leaving me with the other one left.

Sal puts the pill bottle away, and when she sits back down in front of me, she glances over my shoulder. Her eyelids basically disappear and she appears on the verge of panic. "Look out!" she shouts.

Without thinking, I leap forward, knocking Sal to her back, and covering my body over hers. "What is it?" I hurry and peer over my shoulder.

"A snake!" She pushes at my chest, or more like slaps. "Get off me before it attacks!"

"Shit. Shit. Shit!" I stand up, kicking the flashlight down in the process and ripping Sal from the floor.

I snatch the flashlight and quickly use it to search around the room, coming to a stop on a long, thick … *vine*. "Please, to the holy Mayans, don't tell me this was the fucking *snake*."

Sal purses her lips and blinks. Blinks again. "That's the snake," she finally says. "But better than a real one, right?"

I ignore that second sentence. "A snake again? A vine snake? Remember what happened last time we encountered one that may or may not have been poisonous? I think this time instead of getting lost in the jungle, we'll be forced to walk through a labyrinth in another dimension with *vine snakes*." Striding forward, I rip the liana from the wall and toss it at her feet with a smirk.

"Don't be an ass." She holds out a hand to me and kicks Tarzan's means of transportation away.

"Only stating facts." I shrug, staring at the now decapitated plant. It definitely is better that there wasn't a real snake in here because I really don't feel like having to spend the night outside again.

"Better safe than sorry." She smiles and motions to my backpack. "Go back to sleep." Her pillowy backpack may be comfortable, but mine sure isn't after lying on it for ten seconds.

"Oh, no. Not tired anymore after *that*." I couldn't fall asleep now even if I wanted to. Lowering myself on the floor, I wonder how my brothers are doing. I know Ez is reading a comic book, and I'm sure I've had about a million texts from Lach and Mom. Mostly Lach.

After about ten minutes of staring at cracked walls, and my headache subsiding, Sal asks, "You want to play a game?"

"Let me guess, you have travel games in there, too?" I wouldn't be surprised as I cock my head and stare at her pack.

"Not that! Truth or Dare," she says as if we've just struck the lottery of games.

Truth or Dare can always get a bit daring, though… The last time I played it was about two years ago with Lach and Ezra. It stayed kid-friendly until Ezra went to bed, but then on a dare, Lach had to knock on one of the neighbor's doors in only his underwear and say he'd lost his pants and shirt. The cops almost got called that time.

"Yeah, how about we start with some truths and move up to the dares?" I say, rubbing my hands together in anticipation.

Sal pinches the bridge of her nose while she seems to think, finally meeting my gaze. "If you could live anywhere in the world, where would it be?"

"By the ocean." I stare at Sal, her dark brown eyes flickering from the flashlight. It takes me a while to think of a question. "What's your favorite fruit besides avocados?"

"Mangoes," she answers automatically as if she already knows the first twenty of her favorite fruits in order. I bet she does.

We go back and forth for a long while with easy questions, until I move up to something that I'm suddenly wondering about. "So when was your last boyfriend?"

"About a year ago." She answers that one fast too, as

if she's programmed like the robot she thinks she is.

Not surprised it's been that long, though. Not as though Sal isn't pretty enough, but because she's so consumed by those damn trees!

"But…" she continues, "I decided to experiment with him to see if it was meant to be."

Wasn't expecting *that*. "Hold up, what do you mean by *experiment*?"

She lifts a brow and smiles wide. "Sorry, my turn now. Have you ever been in love?"

"No," I say quickly to get back to this interesting turn of events. "My question—what did you mean by experiment?"

She shrugs. "I mean, I thought we were on the same level with our avocado connection. So I took things to the next level."

Avocado connection? Next level? "Are we talking about the same person here?" My jaw drops. "Organized, avocado-tree-loving Sal?"

She folds her arms over her chest and raises both eyebrows this time. "I may love the trees, but I'm not weirdly *in love* with them, Dacre!"

"Well, there are people…"

"Just stop. You're making me think of weird things." She holds up both hands while I let out a rumble of laughter which makes her smile. "My turn. So, are you interested in anyone since you've moved?"

Why did she have to ask such a loaded question? Couldn't she have just asked how many girls I've been with? I look at her, *really* look at her. She still has on that bandana of hers. It doesn't matter that it's covered in dirt and sweat, because all I can think about is how hot it looks on her. How messed up is that? We're out here alone, lost in a *jungle*, and my hormones are still out of control. I didn't really want to date anyone because of my past with girls treating me like a baby, but something about being around her makes me not give a damn. So I answer, "Yeah."

Apparently, a bandana can be a turn on, but it's not just that, it's a part of Sal. Something sets off inside me that I've been trying to smother. But I push all that away. "Let's move on to dare."

"Well, since you already have your shirt off…" she teases. Or is she? "Howl as loud as you can. Actually, scrap that. We don't want to lure any crazy animals this way. How about … you do the Macarena?"

Oh man… I would've rather her said to run naked outside real quick. "I don't even know if I can do that lame dance. Also, how was that even *ever* cool to do?"

"Do it!" she demands, softly clapping her hands together.

"Or what?"

"Seriously, you're such a poor sport." She motions continuously at the floor for me to start.

"Fine!" I stand up and do the stupid dance, because of course I remember the dumb shit. Lach would do that all the time—at fourteen years old! He'd probably do it right now with me if he was here.

"My turn," I say, plopping back down. "I dare you to belly dance."

"Like the dancer from the magic carnival?" She narrows her eyes.

"No, like the girl who asked me to dance the Macarena."

"God, you're so stupid!" She laughs. "I'm not Shakira."

"Do it!" I echo her demand from before. "Isn't that what you said to me?"

"Fine, dumbass." She gets up and sways her hips. It may be a bit stiff but it's still hot as hell as her shorts ride up a bit.

"I think the belly dancer was closer to me than that, Sal. Come on." I wave her over to me.

"I'm done!" She throws her hands up, but a smile breaks out across her face as she sits down.

"I dare you to skip across the room and sing 'Ring Around The Rosey.'"

Shaking my head, I skip, or try to, in a circle while mumbling most of the song's words wrong but remembering the tune. Her laugh travels throughout the room, and it's the loudest one I've ever heard from her. A real one.

Coming to a stop, I breathe heavily as I stare at Sal, the beams of the flashlight highlighting her face and all her features. Her wide eyes, her Mona Lisa nose, her shapely lips—those lips that my gaze is now glued on. Something inside pushes out everything I've been pushing back down, and I can't control myself.

"Sal, I dare you to kiss me," I whisper softly and don't even regret saying it, despite that she's probably going to say no, despite that I have this shitty disease and am afraid to let anyone in. But I like her, really like her, and I can't ignore it anymore.

"What?" she asks, incredulous.

"You've experimented before. I want you to kiss me." I'm ready to be shot down, but then she stands up in front of me. She slowly moves toward me until she's only a hairsbreadth away.

Before I say that she doesn't have to, her lips are on mine. They're soft and supple and taste of the fruity mints she had earlier. Without hesitation, I lift Sal up and her legs wrap around my waist, molding to me perfectly. I carry her lightweight body until my back collides with the wall. Using the rough brick as leverage, I slowly slide us down, not caring that the wall is scratching my skin. Sal's lips haven't left mine—not once. She opens her mouth again, and I caress her tongue with mine. If this is what the jungle tastes like, I never want to leave it.

As I recline to my back, taking her with me, my fingers intertwine with her short hair.

She pulls back, locking her gaze with mine and murmurs, "I dare you to take off my shirt."

"Are you sure?" I ask, rubbing slow circles on her back.

"Yeah. I'm not a robot anymore." She runs her hand across my forehead and through my hair, my eyes closing automatically.

Despite wanting to keep feeling her hands in my hair, I tug off her shirt, wishing there was more light in the room so I could see every inch of her.

"What's your next dare?" she whispers after kissing me again.

"Well, my shirt's already off." I chuckle.

"We can move to the next clothes item, then." She bites her lip and shrugs. "If you want."

It's about the most brilliant idea she's had while we've been in the jungle. We each take turns peeling off clothing particles, until we're left with her bandana. Since this has become one of my favorite parts of her, I gently remove the cloth for her, and softly kiss her forehead. Then I curse about five times. "I didn't bring anything."

"Did you think I didn't come prepared?" she asks with a neutral expression.

My eyes widen.

Then she laughs. "Oh, just a parting gift from Flor that I found in my backpack at the hotel. Flor thought it was one big joke. But, apparently, we do have them…"

As much as I'd rather be on the beach next to an ocean with her, the sounds of the jungle are truly something else. At this moment, I wouldn't want to be anywhere but here.

"Okay," I say, pressing my lips against hers.

"Okay," she responds and reaches for her backpack.

24

Sal

S*unlight.*

That's what my robot says, waking me up. And, yeah, even with my eyes closed, I can sense the light's intensity, which will be hard to adjust to. But I try, opening an eyelid, just a crack. Tons of gray bricks. Mahogany trees. Very green, wild grass.

The jungle.

I move a little, but the arm wrapped around my stomach stops me, so I peer down and smile. The limb belongs to Dacre, and I have no clothes on—at all. Last night … it happened—not being able to sleep, the games, the dancing. Suddenly, I snap out of my groggy state and squint.

What did you do? my robot asks in an alarming voice.

What did you *do?* I counter-ask.

It's so stupid to be talking to myself. But I can't deny

there's a little sense of guilt for taking it this far, this quick. Yet, another part felt it was the right time, the perfect place. It isn't like I did it on instinct, though. Instead, being in this jungle, hearing Dacre daring me to kiss him, and everything that happened over the past few days, blew a heavy wind that ripped the avocado shell right from my heart. And, you know what? I can't be sorry about that. Being with Dacre was ... nice. More than nice.

Still. Dacre and I have become friends and now ... what are we? A couple? Friends with benefits? Maybe I should be guilty that nothing was verified beforehand. My mind takes me back to the night we spent at the Hotel Carmelita, which I guess started it all. I want to talk to him about last night, but his warmth and breathing pattern—the comfort of it—stop me from saying anything.

Last night, my robot failed me, which right now, I think, is a great thing. With relationships, be it friends, boyfriend, it's all nonexistent. Yes, I'd been with a guy before, but nothing came from that, except me putting my robot walls back up. Somehow, Dacre took them down last night. If he just wants to be friends, then so be it, but I know I can't do the friends-with-benefits thing. That would just open up too many windows inside my heart.

You'll always have your trees. They'll never fail you, Salbatora Tames, the mechanic part of me echoes in my head, like an old man giving wise advice.

Normalcy.

The word pops in my mind out of nowhere. Maybe ... maybe letting Dacre be part of my life could bring normalcy. That, along with making new friends outside of the avocado trees. Am I becoming less of a robot? I think I am.

Robot or not, feelings and whatnot, I have to wake up Dacre so we can scramble our way out of this jungle.

Untangling his arm from my stomach, I lift my scattered clothes from the brick floor and put them on, then pick up Dacre's crumpled t-shirt, shorts, and boxers. A memory from last night slides in, and my body tingles at the thought—his hands sliding up and down my bare body, his fingertips in my hair, his lips on my neck going lower and lower and lower.

Shaking my head to get rid of those thoughts, I squat next to him and say in a whisper, "Wake up."

He doesn't move, looking so peaceful—eyes closed and chest gently rising and falling in a slow rhythm.

"Dacre, it's time to go." I nudge him slightly.

Groaning, he curls into a fetal position.

I can't let him sleep because we really need to move. "Dacre, there's a bear outside!" I shout.

"What?" He snaps his eyes open and blinks, springing up and glancing around. "Where?"

"There are no bears in the jungle." I laugh.

Dropping his tense shoulders, he yawns, looks down, and curses as I toss him his boxers. "Thanks," he says, not looking me in the eye.

"Hurry up and cover your birthday suit so we can jet." I hand him the rest of his clothes, smirking.

"Another game of Truth or Dare?" He smiles and finally meets my gaze.

"We need to escape our jungle prison first."

He throws on his clothes, and I try to avert my gaze, but it's kind of hard. For his comfort, I close my eyes and hear the sounds of fabric brushing skin mixed with distant cicadas' singing.

"It's gonna rain later." With my lids still shut, I point my chin to what I think is outside. "The cicadas—they sing to announce the oncoming storm."

"We better hurry then," he replies. "You know, you didn't have to shut your eyes."

Maybe it was for my own comfort then, even though it was hard not to look. Opening my lids, I find him in shorts, still shirtless, looking like Dacre—my friend and yet something tangible is now there. "Okay. How are you feeling?" I need to know if his sugar will be okay until we reach civilization.

"Good." He slides on his t-shirt and rakes a hand through his hair. "Ready?"

"Yes." I remember he did that when I met him, reminding me of a guy in a shampoo commercial. At the time, I thought he was just some guy, but now I realize it was my robot talking. Somehow, I'm looking at him differently than I was that first day.

Maybe he only wants to be friends with benefits, my dear.
Shut up, robot!

A minute later, we trudge through the mahogany trees toward civilization. The sun's heat strikes my skin in a way that makes it feel hotter than the past few days—I try to ignore it. Now that I know where to go, a weight has been lifted, but the lack of insulin keeps nagging at me. There's also this thing tugging at the pit of my stomach—Dacre still hasn't really talked about what happened last night, besides the short teasing. I haven't said anything either.

"So," I say, like we're starting small talk. I even kick a little at the dirt like an idiot, as if this isn't a big deal.

"So," he replies, adjusting his backpack.

"We're saved." How stupid is that? Here, I am trying to veer myself in any other direction and get lost again—this time in my head. As Dacre would say, *Break out of that avocado shell, Sal.* "I mean, you know."

"Yes, I know." He lifts a giant hand-shaped leaf blocking our way.

It makes a crinkling sound as I duck underneath it. "I didn't know you were such a gentleman."

"I'm not."

Liar.

We keep stumbling through the thick vegetation, and step into an area crowded with fern plants—the ones with skinny branches and long, pointy leaves. I recognize them from the last time I came to the ruins with Pa.

Feeling antsy about the silence between us. I stop and come up with something to say. "Are you hungry?"

While surveying the area, he asks, "How long 'til we reach civilization?"

"There's a trail up ahead." I point in the direction where the path to our salvation is. "Once we hit it, I'd say another hour or so."

"Okay, I'll be fine. I think my sugar feels a little high, and if it is indeed high, I don't have insulin to lower it, so let's leave it at that."

I agree with him, but I can't help thinking about how he'd gone into a diabetic coma once before because of high blood sugar. "All right." As I say this, I can't stop my stupid robot from asking me questions: *Does he have to eat? Or fast?* I really don't know—he hasn't asked for any of the fruits I have in my bag yet. "I mean, are you sure you don't need to check your sugar?"

"I'm sure, Sal." He smiles and walks ahead.

"You aren't very talkative this morning," I say, joining him.

"What's that supposed to mean?" Dacre shakes his head. "Sorry, I'm … about last night…"

"Yeah?" I step on a twig, which makes a crunching sound. He's probably going to say it weirded him out, and I'll have to think of a lie to say about how I'm totally weirded out, too. "Do you want to talk about it?"

He comes to a halt, and when I do the same, he says, "Look, I like you a lot, but…"

And there it is. My heart drops—I'm sure he's going to friend-zone me. "But not enough to date." I cringe at the cliché sentence that just came out of my mouth.

Dacre holds out a hand and gives me a deep scowl. "Don't put words in my mouth."

Really? I narrow my eyes, locking my gaze with his. "Isn't that what you were going to say?"

"No, Sal," he drawls, staring at me.

"Then what?" I say through clenched teeth, feeling so irritated by this—I shouldn't be. If he doesn't want to be more than friends, I'll have to be fine with it.

"Can you let me finish?" His tone is serious, meaning business.

I'm tempted to open my mouth and blurt out what's on my mind, but no—it'd make things worse. I need to calm down. Breathe in. Breathe out. "Go ahead."

"You've become a good friend." He pauses, as if waiting for me to confirm I heard him. "And I really like hanging out with you."

Again, I want to say something, anything, but he said no interruptions. I just give him a little nod.

"Since we started this trip," he continues, "things are becoming different between us, in a good way, you know?"

His words make me smile. "I know."

"Good," he says.

"Good," I echo.

The cicadas' singing intensifies, breaking the silent barrier between us. It's like we have so many things to say, yet we don't know how to articulate them.

Unable to take this anymore, I interlace both of my hands with his, holding them up between us. "I think it may be a fact that we both like each other." The bit of guilt from earlier has dissipated as whatever this is between us is taking a new shape of its own.

"That's the understatement of the week." He bites his lower lip. "I really did like your belly dancing."

"*Dacre.* God, you ruin everything!" I tease with a playful frown.

"*Sal.*" He draws me forward, leans down, and places his hands around my waist, taking me by surprise.

With my arms tightly around his neck, I press my ear against his heart. *Thump, thu-thump, thump, thu-thump.* As much as I like its rhythm and being with him, I have to ask him a question, so I break the hug and peer up at his face. "Whatever happens next," I say, "I'm glad I've met you. Okay?"

He furrows his brow. "What kind of statement is that?"

"I don't know what we are now, or what we will be later." I sigh. I want to say more, but a part of me is just being cautious.

"Come here." Dacre presses his lips to mine in a different way than last night, not as wild but more delicate, as if he's trying to tell me something with the soft kiss.

As much as I'd love to stay here and kiss him all day long, we really need to leave this jungle. "We have to keep going," I say, pulling apart. Unable to help myself, I give him one more kiss on the cheek. "But I suppose Señora Martinica may be a real fortune teller after all."

Dacre holds up one hand. "Lovers?" Then he holds up the other. "Danger? She's the real cause of all this, isn't she?"

I chuckle and shake my head.

Again, we head toward the trail, as if it were the Promised Land. Stepping through a group of plants with dark-purple leaves, I spot movement—a small, furry animal. "Wait," I whisper, stopping Dacre with an arm to his chest.

"Watch out for the cat," he says, a little too loud.

"Lower your voice," I say, studying the cat's fur—tawny yellow with black spots—and big eyes. "It's a jaguar cub. They're never alone—the mother should be roaming around nearby."

Dacre puts a hand on my shoulder. "Already encountered one of those. Should we go back?"

"No—she could be anywhere."

The little cat looks in our direction and meows. As adorable as it sounds, that means he knows we're here. All my blood drains because he could be calling for its mother.

"Do-don't move," I say with trembling lips.

"Okay."

We wait a few moments until the cub meows again, this time a little louder. A cracking sound follows and a majestic cat leaps from the vegetation on the other side, landing on a boulder.

"Shit. Hide behind this tree," Dacre murmurs,

grabbing me by the elbow.

"Too late," I say without moving my lips, like a ventriloquist.

Mama Jaguar glances around with menacing eyes. A deep roar escapes her mouth, showcasing two rows of sharp teeth. Although we're about ten meters from her, I swear I can feel her warm breath brushing against my face. She jumps off the boulder and stalks our way, slowly, moving her strong muscles.

I'm petrified, and I think Dacre is too. My first impulse is to run, but that would be wrong—a sign of weakness. At the same time, we can't dare her or anything like that. Our only choice is to freeze in place and somehow become part of the jungle.

Meow.

The little cat turns around and runs to his mother. She roars again, showing her dagger-like fangs. My heart slams against my ribcage, and I want to look away, but I shouldn't. She bites into her cub's fur, lifts him, as if he weighs nothing, and whirls in the direction she came from.

"Can we move now?" Dacre whispers after the jungle beast and her cub disappear from our sight.

"Wait," I reply and take deep breaths, trying to slow my heartbeat. After a long minute, I turn to him, but I hang on to his torso as my legs buckle a bit.

"Are you okay, Sal?" he whispers.

"I think so." I point ahead. "The trail is up there, where the jaguars went."

"What's option two?" Dacre asks.

I make an effort and try to remember, but I can't recall any other way. Actually, when I was here with Pa, the guide demanded we all stay together and to follow him.

"There isn't one."

"That sucks," Dacre says. "Now that we found our way back, we're totally—"

"Don't be pessimistic," I interrupt. "We'll get there. I promise." *I promise*, the words echo in my head. I said that to him last evening when he took a nap. I meant what I said, and I mean it now. "We better try."

"I know you got this," he says.

"*We* do," I say with a firm voice.

Both of us pad forward, holding hands tight and looking around, searching for anything deadly. Each step we take is a little triumph. Up ahead, there are cedar trees and one, in particular, catches my attention. It has a lot of thick vines sprawled out, some grazing the ground. I remember it, because when I was in this area with Pa a while back, it made me think of an octopus disguised as a scarecrow.

"We're close," I say, trudging toward it, dragging Dacre.

"And here we are," he says, as we enter the human-made trail. "Civilization!"

"Shh," I say. "We aren't out of the woods."

He chuckles. "You mean jungle."

I laugh—can't help it. "C'mon."

With a road deprived of obstacles, Dacre and I increase our pace, but as minutes tick by, he slows down.

"Are you getting tired?" I ask.

"I'm fine," he says, breathing a little hard, appearing a shade paler. His shirt is drenched in sweat, but mine is too.

"We can take a rest, if you want," I say because he seems to be more tired than what he's letting on.

Dacre shakes his head. "Nah, we don't have time for

that business."

"Are you sure?" I ask.

"Yes." He sighs and then smiles, but it doesn't seem like a real one.

"Okay." I let that go. Still, something about him isn't right, like he's being too sure of himself.

We trudge in silence, and as we advance, signs of civilization lay on the ground—a crumpled potato chip bag, an empty soda bottle. In the distance, I hear a faint noise, like a little motor.

"I know that sound," Dacre says as we take a turn and a highway comes into view. He lets go of my hand and takes long strides in its direction.

I join him at the highway's shoulder. "It's a toll road."

Putting his hands on his knees, he nods, breathing heavily.

Cars zoom by, going fast, their engines' sound roaring like the jaguars. I walk to the edge of the shoulder. "I'm going to get help."

He doesn't reply, or maybe I can't hear him over the loud noise.

"Dacre?" I glance over my shoulder.

To my horror, he's on the ground, shaking violently. I rush to him and kneel by his side. "Dacre! What do I do?"

His eyes won't focus on me as he keeps on shaking. The shakes turn into violent jerks, and his breathing is uneven with saliva foaming at his mouth.

"Dacre!" I scream with tears sliding down my cheeks.

25

Dacre

My eyes feel sewn shut, and I try several times to get them to open.

"And there he is," a distinct male voice says. It can only be one person. "I knew you'd come back soon."

I finally get my eyes open and focus on Lach. His blond hair is disheveled, and he looks as if he hasn't slept.

My arm feels strange, and I lift it to find an IV attached with clear fluid seeping into my vein. I try to recollect everything that happened after the jungle, and it's mostly clouded. There was a car ride with a person, but I can't remember if it was a guy or a woman. Sal telling me to hang on until we got to the hospital. Me being taken back and mentioning of a seizure I had on the side of the road.

There's only Lach with me as my gaze flickers around the room.

"Mom took Ezra downstairs to get something to eat," Lach says when I haven't spoken. He has a smile on his face, but his shoulders are a bit stiff, and his fingers tap agitatedly at his knee.

The inside of my mouth is dry, and it may take a whole gallon of liquid to quench it. "And Francisco?" There's bottled water by my bedside, and I reach for it, chugging the whole thing down.

"Already want to talk about him so soon?" My brother sets his phone back down after messing with it, holding up a hand before I can answer. "He's been calling too, and he's the one who told Mom to drive down here. It took a while but that was faster than flying because Sal's pa wouldn't have been able to catch a flight until the following day. So Gregorio rode with us."

"You came with Sal's pa? I didn't think my message went through—my phone had died." My voice sounds a bit hoarse even after the water. The past few days flash before me. The avocado delivery, the jungle, Sal. *Sal.* What a fucking mess.

"Yeah, I got it. When Gregorio told us the mechanic got the van, but you guys weren't there, Mom flipped her lid. But we didn't think you two went into the jungle… We thought you were kidnapped!"

"No. Here I am." I push the pillow up to get more comfortable.

"Tell me"—Lach leans forward, a smile appearing—"how did my big brother wind up in a jungle?"

"I went looking for some fruit for my sugar." I don't want Sal to get blamed for going into the jungle first, even though I did go in right after her.

"Right… Sal already told me what happened, so just

seeing if you were going to protect her."

"Seriously? Just go be an FBI agent." I roll my eyes and my thoughts fall to Sal. Right as I think of her, the door swings open.

Lach darts his gaze between me and Sal with a smirk on his face.

"How did you know I was awake?" I ask her, feeling a rush of something akin to happiness at seeing her face. Sal still looks as if she's walked right out of the jungle with reddened cheeks and her short hair mussed in all directions, but her polka dot bandana is firmly in place. She has on clean clothes from somewhere, though, and jungle debris no longer clings to her skin.

"That would be me." Lach grins. "She's been here a while, and I told her I'd text her a heart emoji when you woke."

"All… right…"

Lach seems to soak up the awkward moment but finally takes a hint when my eyes narrow at him. "Anyway, I'm going to meet Mom and Ez downstairs to tell them you just woke up. I'm yearning for that hospital cafeteria food. Cheerio, big brother."

Glowering even harder at his back, I watch as he silently gives me a quick kissy face with his eyes shut before closing the door.

"How did you get your phone working?" I ask.

"Lach let me use his charger." Sal rotates the phone in her hand as if she's not sure what to do with it. She obviously wants to talk about more than getting her phone working again.

I nod but can't look her in the eye because all I can think about is me having a seizure in front of her—one I can't remember. Then having to be carted off to the hospital, when all I had to do was check my sugar right when I woke up. It had still felt fine in the morning, and I was too focused on hurrying to get out of the jungle. I didn't know my sugar was going to drop like that.

"How are you feeling?" she asks, her eyes meeting mine in a concerned way. "I was scared, Dacre, really scared. I thought you were *dying*." She chokes on the last word, swiping tears from her eyes. When she says those words, something hits me, and I bet she's thinking about how Matilda died because of the complications with her diabetes. Something that could have happened to me.

"I'm all right—just needed some water." I stare at the empty bottle now on the bedside to prevent myself from getting too emotional.

"I'm about to leave with Pa and head back home," Sal finally says. "The van's been fixed, but I told him I wouldn't leave until I saw you were okay. I'd ask you to come with us, but I know your mom probably wants you to go with her."

"I'm here, aren't I?" I shift my gaze from her face to the ceiling, because I don't want to keep looking at her. This is my life, right when I thought everything was okay, it isn't. Everyone's here. Her pa had to leave the avocado farm to come get Sal. Mom is missing work. Lach and Ez are having their lives disrupted all because I couldn't monitor something right.

"Are you?" she says softly, approaching me like a quiet deer. "I think you need to rest for a bit."

"I've rested enough," I whisper. "Just go."

Sal takes a step back as if I've wounded her, but then she shakes her head and comes a bit closer to me. Not one to give up. "I know we haven't known each other for years, but the weeks we've worked together all day, almost every day, and then this delivery..." She doesn't finish whatever she wanted to say.

"What about it?" I say, a bit harsh.

"I thought... I don't know... I thought what happened in the jungle between us, was something."

"It was in the heat of the moment." I shrug. It was more than that to me, but it's the best I can do right now. Every family vacation, every time we go somewhere, all anyone ever says is *Dacre, are you okay?* It's a never-ending drumbeat of a question because no matter what, during the day, there are going to be times when I won't be okay. That's a fact.

"You think I don't know what you're doing?" Her eyes narrow at me. "I'm not an idiot. The robot side of me knows these things. It knows how to shut people out, like you're doing right now."

I want to keep my eyes trained on the ceiling, so I can continue to lie to her, but I can't. "Fine. I don't want this. Not because I don't want whatever this is between you and me, but I don't want you to grow to hate me, resent things. Because with this shitty disease, there's going to be a whole lot of ups and downs, not only for me, but for you, and everyone around. And ... I don't want you to look at me one day, hating me because of it."

If I can easily hate myself at times, it's much easier for others to do the same. Especially when my highs and lows have my mood swings out of control.

"Dacre..." She chews on her lip, and I can tell she's starting to feel sorry for me, more than she was before.

I don't want that.

"No, Sal. We're done. You've already had to lose people before."

"This has to do with Tía Matilda, too, doesn't it? That's like saying if someone in your family died from cancer and then I got it, that you would just give up?" Sal frowns at me, but doesn't move an inch, not even a millimeter. She continues to hold her ground. The silence is uncomfortable. Thankfully, her phone rings, bringing the quiet to an end. She glances down at it but doesn't answer, only presses the button to send the call to voicemail. "It's Pa. He doesn't want you to come in until next week because you need rest. But we do have to get back to the farm."

"Then go." I'm even more pissed now since Sal's pa is being overly concerned. That's why I didn't want people to know I had this disease. I'm fine. I feel fine. I could go plant a hundred trees right now, but instead everyone is treating me as if I'm dying.

"If you want, I can stay and tell Pa I'll ride with your family." She wants me to ask her to stay, but I just … I just can't.

"I said *go*." I grip the edge of the bed in frustration.

Slowly, she turns around but stops as she opens the door to glance over her shoulder. "The main plaza's church has *castillo* fireworks Friday night. If you want to meet me there at nine, I'll be waiting for you."

I shake my head and close my eyes after I hear the click of the door.

A minute ticks by as I let our conversation soak in. When I decide to leap from the bed and hurry after her, the door opens and a nurse with dark hair pulled into a ponytail enters, reminding me why it's better to stay.

The nurse checks my blood pressure and temperature. Both are perfect. As she's about to do my sugar, the door flies open and Mom rushes in.

"Dacre!" she cries as if I'd been gutted up by a sword. There are tears in her eyes—she doesn't have her usual makeup on, and I'm … hollow.

"Let me finish up his blood sugar, and then you two can chat," the nurse says. She pricks my finger as if I'm a newborn baby and presses my finger to the test strip. My sugar is running a little high, so she's going to come back with a shot.

After the nurse leaves, Mom hurries to my side and pulls me into a death hug.

"Dammit, Dacre." She jerks back and stares me in the eye. "Next time, you tell me exactly where you're going. I don't care if you're eighteen soon, even then, if you live under my house, that's it."

"You drive a hard bargain." I've never seen my mom this upset over something I've done.

"Why? What's going on?" She slides up the empty chair right beside my bed. "I know it's not just Francisco."

I don't know if it's all the years of things built up in me that I've kept inside, but it comes spewing out. "Mom, you've never put us first. It's always been move, move, move. I know it's too late now, but why couldn't you have given up your job for Dad? Why couldn't we have stayed in one place? Why couldn't you have asked us how we felt?" With my fingers gripping my hair so tight, it's starting to make my head hurt, so I release it.

Mom rubs at her forehead, releasing a defeated sigh. "We're not moving anymore. Do you think I liked moving all the time? I've done all this for you and your brothers.

For college, for your future." She pauses to catch her breath. "Your dad and I had problems that wouldn't have ever been solved—even if I'd stayed. You're seventeen. You don't know everything. I still don't know everything, but I know I love you." There's a lock of hair on my forehead that she swipes to the side.

I don't say anything.

"I know it's the diabetes. If I could take that disease from you and put it in my body ten-fold and know you'd be okay, I'd do it, because you—you mean everything to me." She lets out a hard sob, and my heart clenches.

"But Lach's your favorite."

"Dacre, I don't have a favorite. He just listens the most."

I want to roll my eyes because Lach definitely is the sneakiest, but I'm not going to rat him out just to be the favorite son.

"What do you want? What do you want me to do? Drop Francisco? Because I will."

As much as I want to say, yes find someone your own age, I don't.

"No, Francisco is fine," I lie. "As long as you're happy, that's what matters." After what happened with her and Dad, she does deserve it. Maybe Mom holds everything inside, the way I do.

"What matters is that you're happy." She grabs my hand and gives it a soft squeeze.

"I'll get there. I just want to get home. That's what would make me feel better." Staying in my bedroom and reading for a few days will be perfection. I need that escape and maybe take my moped to see some waves.

"The doctor has to release you, and then we'll be

going home, baby." She kisses my forehead. "I'm not going to ground you because of the circumstances."

That's the thing. It's another reason for special treatment, when I actually want to be grounded like any other teenager, but I don't argue this time.

"All right."

"Let me text Lach to let him and Ezra know we'll be leaving, hopefully soon." She points to across the room. "You can get cleaned up before we leave."

"I will." I should be running straight to a clean shower, but for a minute, I stare up at the ceiling once again. My new favorite spot, and wish I was someone else—anyone else.

On the drive home, I sit in the backseat with Lach and fall asleep. My sugar seems okay for now. It was close to two-hundred before we left, but at least it wasn't through the roof. The nurse gave me a shot, even though I do it every day of my life.

We don't stop for the night. Mom wants to get us straight home. Lach and Mom switch off on the driving, telling me I need to rest, and we stop at a gas station for food on the way.

Most of the time in the car as we pass by rows of trees and colorful buildings, I pretend to be asleep because I don't want to talk to anyone. Ez's soft snores radiate through the car, and I think I may be drifting to sleep when my phone beeps in my pocket. It was charged before we left, courtesy of Lach. I don't want to answer it. I'm not going to answer it, but then when it beeps again, I think for a second that maybe it's Sal. Although, I'm not going to reply, I check it anyway.

Lach: **Quit pretending you're asleep.**

Me: **Quit being a dickwad.**

Lach: **Aren't you glad we were already out there to help save the day.**

Me: **Sure.**

Lach: **A thank you would be nice.**

Me: **Thanks for making me continue to suffer.**

Lach: **You're too dramatic.**

Me: **Only when I want to be.**

I run my hand through my hair when Lach looks to the side, I give him a smirk, and I feel a bit better as he grins back.

"What are you two discussing?" Mom asks, looking at us for a second before focusing back on the dark road where the night has already fallen. "You know, the two of you can just talk in the car instead of texting back and forth for no reason … like normal people." She laughs.

"Sorry, Mom, you're not part of the classified group," Lach sings.

"I have my ways of finding out things," she sings back.

Like knowing I went on a job delivery because Lach can't keep his mouth shut. I smile to myself.

Somehow, I finally fall asleep. Lach gives me a hard nudge when we pull into the driveway. The sky is still dark with bits and pieces of stars scattered about. I open the passenger side of the car and lift a still-sleeping Ezra up in my arms.

A loud creak sounds, and the front door swings open as soon as we hit the porch. Francisco is standing in front of us, shirtless and barefoot with worry lines across his forehead.

"Are you all right?" he asks me as I brush past him, so I can get Ez to bed.

"Yeah, I'm fine." I hate being put on the spot like this because I've ruined everyone's day, making it all about me.

I head up the stairs and place Ez gently in his bed and cover him up with the blanket. Then I go straight to my room. Not alone.

"Yeah?" I ask and turn to Francisco.

"Your mom was really worried."

"I know." I'm still wishing I had done things differently, but I hadn't.

He scans me over as if he's searching for wounds. "I was really worried."

"You barely even know me," I say but not feeling as annoyed as I used to.

His eyes meet mine, and he stays focused on them. "I love your mom, and I *want* to get to know you."

"Love?" I knew there was lust that I don't want to think about, but I didn't know he loved her.

"Yes."

I blink several times, realizing what a douche I've been to him. This guy who I don't even really know, besides him wanting to cook all the time—food which I've eaten and wanted to shove down his throat at the same time—waited up all night to make sure my mom got home safely. I may not be all for what's going on here, but I don't have to stand in anybody's way.

"What do you listen to?" I ask.

"Maná."

"Well, how about I show you some real music tomorrow." I shrug.

Francisco arches a brow and shrugs back with a tilt of the lips. "Okay. We'll see then if it's as good as you think." He backs up to the door. "Glad you're safe, Dacre."

With a final nod, I turn around and unload my backpack. A hard clatter of footsteps enters my room, and it doesn't take a rocket scientist to know it's Lach.

"So, I heard the conversation between you and Cisco. Or whatever *that* was."

I spin around to face my brother and lift a brow. "Spying?"

"But of course." Lach plops down on the bed and smooths out a wrinkle in the blanket.

Sitting down beside him, I set my diabetes kit on my thigh. "I don't know. He said he loved her. It's still weird, but whatever."

When I unzip the pouch, Lach wrinkles his nose. "What is that?"

I look down to see him staring at the gift I saved. "An avocado seed."

"Are you planning to grow something?" He takes it out and inspects it as if it'll turn into a beanstalk right there for him to climb like Jack did.

I swipe it back from Lach and tuck it back in the pouch. "No. It means something else."

"Would this have to do with a certain girl in a bandana whose papa we both work for?" Lach scoots closer.

"Seriously, you worked at the farm for like two days." I shove him away.

"Nope. I'm officially an employee after day one. I was waiting to surprise you with the news. *Surprise!*" He throws up jazz hands in the air.

And I throw them in the air right back. "Go to bed."

He wraps his arms around me, almost crunching my bones. It takes him a second to start breathing again. "I thought something had happened to you. This was worse than the night at the club, because what if something had happened to you in that jungle? What if you had disappeared and no one had ever found you? Then I would have spent my entire life wondering if you had been eaten, or if you were out there living like Tarzan. I just… I just…" Lach buries his head in my shoulder as he starts to cry, his breathing ragged. Small beads of liquid form in my eyes. I blink a few times, withholding the tears in my lashes so they don't fall.

"Hey, I'm right here." I hug him back. "All right? No matter how shitty of a mood I may get in, I'm here, surviving. You have my word."

He scoots back and runs a hand across his nose, shifting his septum ring as he sniffles. "Tomorrow, we'll both show Francisco the good music."

"Okay, baby brother."

"My favorite words in the world." He smiles. "And I wouldn't give up on Sal, you know? I overacted about Juan breaking up with me. With Sal, I can see how she really does care about you, whereas Juan didn't about me. Risks are what makes the world go round and love is disease blind, dear brother."

I ignore his words, because no matter what, he just doesn't understand. "I'm right next door if you need anything, Lach."

He nods and heads for the door. "Also, Polo, Polo, Polo. Those are the last words I'm going to leave you with."

Before I can say anything, he closes the door. I should have known he'd already have the cook from the avocado farm on his mind.

I'm left in my room, fishing out the avocado seed. Sitting on the bed, I stare at it as if searching for answers to the universe. Sal is something I didn't know I could find. She's beautiful and perfectly odd.

I push the seed aside because it's something that should be buried, the same as whatever I feel for Sal needs to be. She's fine without me. After seeing how upset my family and even Francisco was, it's for the better. She can do much better.

Sal

Home.

I'm finally home.

And I'm *so* bored.

I mean, Pa and I drove the van nonstop from Palenque all the way home for *ten* excruciating hours, arriving in the wee hours of the night. On the trip back, I told him about what happened when we dropped off the avocados to the "drug dealers." He slammed on the brakes and went off about why I didn't tell him right away when I had called him. The rest of the ride, he gripped the steering wheel tight and threatened that I wouldn't be doing long deliveries ever again. I agreed with him only to calm him down for now.

This morning, when I was getting ready to work on my avocados, Pa decided to intercept me and ask for me to take a break. "After all you went through," he said in a soothing voice, "I thought I'd lost you."

And that's when I realized he worried way more than he'd let on. "I'm here, Pa."

He nodded. "I shouldn't have sent you on that delivery. I could've contracted a professional driver to—"

"A driver who couldn't be trusted," I interrupted. "You said it yourself. Don't worry, Pa, you had no other choice."

"I…" He shook his head. "We needed the money, but no money is worth what you endured."

"Hey, I'm here." I patted his arm. "*Te quiero muchísimo,* Pa."

"I love you very much, too, Mija."

Now, I'm feeling fine, really, but, well, when Pa gets an idea in his head, it's difficult to change his mind. And I guess I need to rest? So here I am, alone in my bedroom, staring at the paper doll Dacre got for me at the magic carnival. It survived being left alone in the van—the jungle would have been a different story.

I turn it around to face the other direction so it's not looking at me, making me think about the mess Dacre and I got into during the trip. It's like my head turned into a piñata filled with thoughts, waiting for the stick to strike and release them. But what makes me crazy is *him*. What the *hell* happened between him and me? I mean, I understand his position, but I'm frustrated that he doesn't understand mine. Dammit, Dacre. Can't he see that I like him for who he is? And that includes his illness.

I can't stay in my room for the rest of the day—I've been away from the trees long enough.

But your father said—

Shut up, robot. Actually, from now on, I won't pay

attention to it.

Sneaking out of the house, I shuffle to the farm and admire the rows of avocado trees. As I study them, images of mahogany and cedar ones surrounded by luscious vegetation pop in my mind. I close my eyes for a second and shake my head. I'm back home.

I'm safe.

Letting dry air enter my lungs, I inhale deeply then slowly exhale. I pad to where the shack used to be. Pa hired people to haul away the wood on the Saturday I left, so the area is now ready for new trees. I smile at the empty spot which once held the old house that had brought him so much sorrow. And somehow, I know Tía Matilda is smiling down at me, too, telling me that it was the right thing to do.

New memories and new trees can now sprout here, bringing in new life and honoring what Tía Matilda would have wanted—expanding the farm.

Pa's right—I'm still confused by the whole ordeal. I walk back to my room and spend the rest of the day listening to music and binge-watching an old nature show.

The days slowly pass by as I wait for Friday, and when it *finally* arrives, I can only focus on one person.

Dacre.

I may see him tonight. Maybe. And if he doesn't show up, I'll make myself be okay with it. It's not as though it can be love yet. I'm not even sure how that really feels. The only thing I know is that I like being around him.

When evening comes, I take a relaxing shower then put on a dress I got last Christmas, a colorful *China Poblana* one with a white blouse and a skirt embroidered with colorful sequins and beads. I rarely wear it, but this is a special occasion.

After leaving my room, I find Pa, who's sitting on the couch in the living area, watching TV.

"*Hola*, Pa," I say, and when he turns his attention to me, I lift my long skirt and turn around, modeling my dress.

"You look beautiful, *mija*." He motions at me. "What's the occasion?"

I shrug. "I'm watching the *castillo* fireworks."

He narrows his eyes. "Since when are you interested in them?"

Since the last time I saw Dacre. I shrug, as if this weren't a big deal. The church at the main plaza seems like a good place to meet—safe and nice. Tons of people, too, so Dacre won't have to talk too much if he doesn't feel up to it.

"Why are you going there, dressed like this?" He fixes his gaze with mine.

"Just because," I say and after a second of silence, I let out a sigh. "Okay. I'm meeting somebody."

Pa nods. "Dacre is a good kid." My *papá* knows me so well.

"Yeah." I rub my forehead.

"What's wrong, *mija*?"

"It's just…" I look at my leather sandals. "I feel weird. He thinks it's best for us not to see each other anymore."

"Is he your boyfriend?" Pa asks, concerned.

I shake my head. "I don't know what we are." The night at the ruin flashes through my head. Us, together, playing a not-so-innocent game, then kissing and his skin against mine. "He wants to stop seeing me because he thinks his diabetes will cause me to suffer or something."

I grip my hands into fists. No. I take a deep breath. "So, I asked him to meet me at the church, and if he doesn't show up, that's the end of it."

Pa crosses his arms and smiles.

"What?" I ask after a long moment.

"He hasn't quit the farm."

"Because you gave him the rest of the week off," I say. "Who knows what's going to happen Monday."

"Sal," Pa says, his smile dropping. "Something like that happened between your *mamá* and me." His chest heaves with a sigh. "When we found out about her illness, she went through a similar phase. Sh-she wanted to set me free." He blinks. "Can you believe that?"

I nod. "That's kind of what Dacre said to me."

Pa grabs me by the shoulders. "If you really care for each other, don't let him push you away."

"That's what I'm trying to do." I smile. "Can I go now?"

He kisses my forehead. "Good luck, *mija*."

"*Gracias*." I step away.

"Sal?" Pa asks as I twist the doorknob.

"Yeah?" I glance back.

"I love you."

If my heart could smile at his words, it would. If I didn't have my pa, I'd feel completely lost. I push those thoughts away because he's here, maybe not forever, but he's here now. "I love you, too."

Once outside, fresh night air welcomes me, and I stroll for a few blocks before entering the cobblestone street leading downtown. Lots of people are heading in the same direction I'm going, and moments later, the main plaza comes into view—wooden food stands, a hexagonal gazebo with a red roof in the middle, and the stone church with its two towers in the back.

Crossing the cobblestone street, I enter the crowded plaza. The aroma of homemade potato chips, Mexican funnel cakes, and *tacos al pastor* fill the air, which usually makes me hungry. But not now, because there's this thing pulling at the pit of my stomach.

I search for a tall guy with brown hair in the multitude of people—men with *sombreros*, women wearing dresses like mine, and lots of kids. I can't find Dacre, but I just got here. *Cool it, Sal.*

"Sal!" A girl with long red hair wearing a short fuchsia dress waves at me in the distance.

"Flor," I say, when she joins me.

"I heard what happened!" She nudges my shoulder. "So… How did it feel to be alone with Dacre for days and days?"

"Not bad." I play it down.

"Liar," she says in a playful voice. "Did you find my gift and note I left?"

I roll my eyes.

"Okay," Flor says. "Tell me everything, including *every* single detail."

"Well," I start, "it was … good." As much as I want to tell her about my adventures with Dacre, I can't—not now. "Actually … I'm waiting for him."

"Are you guys dating now? I bet you are. Otherwise, why would you be dressed like this?" She smiles and rubs her hands in anticipation.

"No." I don't know what's going on between us, or if there's anything at all.

Her smile crumbles into a frown. "No? Why?"

Can she stop asking questions? I don't want to talk about him anymore. "I'll tell you later—I have to move."

Flor's frown deepens. "This is not the end of our conversation, Sal."

"Later." I leave her to go off and meet her boyfriend or whatever she's doing.

As I zigzag through people of all shapes and sizes, I take a look at the *castillo* firework set. Its large wooden frame rises about twenty meters high. This one has wheel-like structures made of reed and paper, which hold the actual fireworks. Right now, it appears dull, but it'll turn into something awesome when it lights up. Dacre hasn't seen it—I think he'll like it. If he shows up, that is. If not, it's his loss.

Sitting on a metal bench, I grip my knees and concentrate on the fireworks display. Seconds tick by, adding up to minutes, and he doesn't show up. When a frail man with a hat grabs the long string—the fuse, I think this is it. Dacre won't come. I'd hoped he would have shown up because I thought we were friends.

The man starts the fuse and lets it go, which slowly makes its way to the top of the frame. I look up at the big wheel as it lights up in an explosion of colors and starts moving slowly, then faster and faster, brighter and brighter.

And as pretty as this is, my heart constricts and shrinks, but I'll survive. Dacre decided not to come, and it is what it is. Taking a long, deep breath, I concentrate on the fireworks and the noise—everything around me.

"Eh, I guess they're okay," a guy says behind me.

"Dacre." My voice comes out hoarse, and I'm almost afraid to turn around.

He slides down beside me and bumps his shoulder with mine. "Hey."

Although I want to jump closer and hug him, I play it cool. "You made it."

Fireworks crack and whistle as they shoot in all directions, filling up the sky, creating a deafening sound. Sparks fly everywhere, illuminating the crowd.

"Wow," Dacre shouts over the noise, looking up with his mouth open.

My heart speeds up as I see him like this—euphoric. But at the same time, there's this seed of doubt in my head.

He rests his hand above my knee. "Look!"

The whole *castillo* ignites, and all its wheels spin, lighting everything and filling the plaza with sounds.

Bang, bang, bang. Buzz. Boom. Boom. Hiss.

I've never seen Dacre smile this way—his ear-to-ear grin makes him look like a kid as he watches in awe. I can't take my eyes off him. Bright-yellow sparks float down, like rain made of gold. Up ahead, a group of small kids chase each other, running with their arms stretched to the sky.

I've seen this show plenty of times in the past, but not lately, and never with a guy. Even though a bit of me is curious about whether Dacre came to tell me we're just co-workers now or something more, I stay quiet.

Moments later, the wheels stop spinning, and the show draws to an end with an ovation from the crowd. Looking around, I notice everyone standing, except us. I poke Dacre in the shoulder to get up. As I'm clapping, a strange, anxious feeling takes form inside me.

"So," he says, chewing on his lower lip.

"So," I reply.

He smiles. "I made it, Sal."

"Did you have a good trip?" What kind of question is that?

"Can't complain."

Why are you here? I think. "Nice."

"Do you want to take a walk?" he asks in a soft voice, almost hesitant.

"Okay." I'm not sure why he wants to do this, but I guess he wants to go somewhere quiet, so we can talk.

We stroll out the plaza in silence and cross the street after waiting for several cars to pass. Then he leads me to a one-story, old house with a sign reading, *Mini Bar.*

"This is new," I say. "Have you been here before?"

He nods and pushes the door open, uncovering a big patio with people seated around tables and a bar at the end with a wall of beer bottles.

"Follow me." He steps ahead and turns onto a set of stairs.

This bar seems shady, and I'm not eighteen years old yet, so I freeze for a second, deciding what to do. With a sigh, I climb up and reach the bar's rooftop, which is totally empty—no tables, no chairs, no people. Just a square black roof with waist-high walls all around. Farther out, I spot the main plaza and the orange lights illuminating the town.

"How did you find out about this place?" I ask.

He shrugs. "Francisco told me—Mom's boyfriend."

"This is cool." I guess Dacre's feeling better about his mom's situation, but I can ask him about that later. I can't wait anymore—no more small talk. "Are you here to say goodbye? Because if you are—"

Dacre holds out a hand, then fishes something out of his pocket and holds it between us. Under the streetlights, I make out an oval-shaped object. "What is it?" I ask. Did he bring me all the way up here just to show me this?

"It's the gift you gave me—I kept it with me," he murmurs.

"What? I never gave you a seed." I squint at it until recognition sets in and my lips part. "You kept the pit from the avocado I gave you? The one we shared at the hotel?"

"Yeah. It's probably stupid. Never mind." He drops his hand in a defeated way.

I grab his wrist before he can put the pit away. "Does this mean…?" I can't finish the question.

"It means whatever you want it to mean. I'm willing to let you put up with my bullshit. For once, Lach had a few wise words that really made me think about things. It made me realize that I'd be miserable not knowing what could have been because of me choosing to be a coward." He smiles and takes my hands, places the seed in between, and closes them with his large palms still holding mine. It's as if we're growing something together. "I feel like you're willing to see me, past Dacre and his diabetes—the way I'm able to see you, past Sal and her avocados. Even though they are both a part of who we are. You're just too special to let go and you've never been a coward once since I've known you."

My cheeks warm up at his touch. "If you're willing to put up with me and my trees, and possibly me sometimes sinking into my avocado shell."

"We'll have more deliveries to break you out again."

"So, we are…?"

In reply, he wraps his arms around me and presses his lips on mine. It's not wild or anything—a soft kiss, his lips gently caressing mine in a way that gives me the answer I was looking for. I rest my head on his chest, and we hold each other for a long time.

"I have a secret to tell you," Dacre whispers.

"Oh, yeah?" I mumble into his shirt.

"It was me who accidentally stepped on that avocado the day I met you." He chuckles.

I pull my head back to poke him hard in the chest. "You—"

Quickly, he tugs me close to him, and I give in and hold him just as tight.

Even with the mess of the avocado delivery trip, there was good from it too, like the magic carnival and our last night in the jungle. Sometimes a friendship starts from a seed and right now, ours is still sprouting.

I can't predict the future, but my present—*our* present—tells me this is a good day to start. No one in this world is ever a hundred percent okay.

But I'll make sure we stay close. We'll just have to follow the stars and try to make our own path because all we can ever do in this one life is hope for the best.

Did you enjoy Avocado Bliss? Authors always appreciate reviews, whether long or short.

Want another fun YA Contemporary Romance? Then try Bacon Pie!

Lia Abbie has the easy life—kicking it back with old school video games, hanging out with her best friend Barnabas, and alternating her living schedule between the apartments of her two dads and her mom.

Kiev Jimenez is a theater geek who loves him some Shakespeare and taking care of his pet armadillo. He has one set goal in life: obtaining the role of Horatio for the Hamlet school play.

When a showdown between Lia and Kiev lands them in the principal's office, they're forced into volunteer work at the cringe-worthy Piggy Palooza Festival, or risk being suspended. Lia and Kiev aren't thrilled about the situation, especially when it interferes with Lia's relaxed life and Kiev's theater role. But by working together, they may find more than just bacon— possibly a little love in the air.

ACKNOWLEDGEMENTS

We'd like to thank all the readers who decided to pick up our contemporary story which is a bit of fun, a bit serious, and a bit on the avocado side.

To our families who have been awesome on our writing journeys! And especially to Amber H. Donna, Alexa, and Sharon for beta reading our book and helping the process. You guys are fabulous!

For those who suffer from diabetes, especially Type 1, just know that you're not alone, be it if you're the one who has disease or your families who help you through it. The world is complicated, so we all just take it day by day. Thank you again for reading our book, and it means the world to us!

ABOUT THE AUTHORS

Candace Robinson spends her days consumed by words and hoping to one day find her own DeLorean time machine. Her life consists of avoiding migraines, admiring Bonsai trees, watching classic movies, and living with her husband and daughter in Texas—where it can be forty degrees one day and eighty the next.

Originally from San Francisco and raised in Mexico, former DJ, currently software architect by day and wordsmith whenever-is-possible, Gerardo Delgadillo writes about teens venturing into México or living in México. He has lived the life he writes about in his YA contemporary novels and loves to show México from an insider's perspective—the rich culture, mercados, tacos callejeros, futbol, and a lot more, intertwining as much Español as his editors allow him to.

www.ingramcontent.com/pod-product-compliance
Lightning Source LLC
Chambersburg PA
CBHW020741310726
48969CB00002B/361